THE STARSPUN WEB

ALSO BY SINÉAD O'HART

The Eye of the North

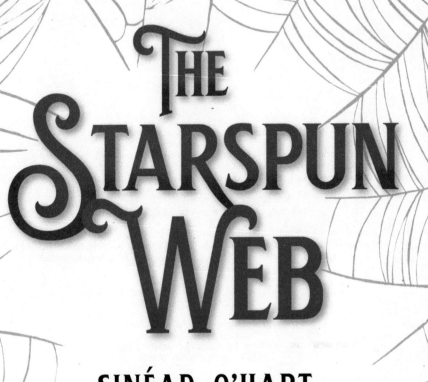

THE STARSPUN WEB

SINÉAD O'HART

ALFRED A. KNOPF
NEW YORK

THIS IS A BORZOI BOOK PUBLISHED BY ALFRED A. KNOPF

All rights reserved. Published in the United States by Alfred A. Knopf, an imprint of Random House Children's Books, a division of Penguin Random House LLC, New York. Originally published in the United Kingdom by Stripes Publishing in February 2019.

Knopf, Borzoi Books, and the colophon are registered trademarks of Penguin Random House LLC.

Visit us on the Web! rhcbooks.com

Educators and librarians, for a variety of teaching tools, visit us at RHTeachersLibrarians.com

Library of Congress Cataloging-in-Publication Data is available upon request.
ISBN 978-1-101-93507-1 (trade) — ISBN 978-1-101-93508-8 (lib. bdg.) —
ISBN 978-1-101-93509-5 (ebook)

The text of this book is set in 10.5-point Village.
Interior design by Ken Crossland

Printed in the United States of America
November 2019
10 9 8 7 6 5 4 3 2

First American Edition

FOR MY MOTHER AND FATHER,

AND THE PEOPLE

OF THE NORTH STRAND

PROLOGUE

THROUGH THE HOLLOW DARKNESS OF A WINTER'S NIGHT, A MAN was running.

"It's all right, darling," he murmured to the tiny baby bundled in his arms. "Not much further now." Snow fell all around them, making dizzying patterns in the air; the going underfoot was slushy and the man's feet were cold. His mind flashed with quick, sharp thoughts, made painful by anxiety. What had they done with his wife? How long did he have before they came looking for him? Would he have time to get the baby to safety? One thought was so urgent that it drowned out all the others: *She'll only be two worlds away—will it be enough?*

His thoughts were shattered as a sudden cry split the air,

loud and shrill—a call of triumph. It came from behind the running man, from the far end of the street. He stopped, peering over his shoulder through the lacework made by the snow. *Lights*. Indistinct figures moved against the night, muffled tightly in scarves and hats, and another voice shouted. A face, pale in the darkness, turned in his direction.

The man spun round and began to run once more. The tram wires overhead seemed to hum despite the lateness of the hour and he hopped across the tracks as he made a desperate dash across the road, landing heavily on the pavement at the far side. He paused long enough to catch his breath, feeling his heart hammering in his chest, and then he was off again.

Through it all the baby—his daughter—slept, as though she were tucked safely in the nursery he and his wife had prepared for her, when things were different.

Seconds later he came to a slithering halt outside a tall, narrow building on a street corner that faced a wide bridge over a streetlight-speckled river. It loomed into the night sky like a pale cathedral, its roof lost in the darkness. He gazed up, hoping he had the right place. Quickly he settled his child into the crook of one arm while he pulled an object smaller than his palm from a pocket with his other hand. He adjusted its face, listening for the *click*, and then rubbed his thumb across the object's surface. A void opened at its center, the barest *whir* giving away the complex mechanism that powered it. He raised the object to his eye, peering through the void, and looked at the building again.

He saw the differences straightaway—shutters closed where they had been open, a flowering window box where there shouldn't be one—and his throat tightened. He glanced up, reading the words above the doorway. In this world, at this time, the building was an insurance company headquarters, but he had to hope that what he'd seen was true and that somewhere else it bore a different name. *A place where she'll be safe,* he thought. *A home.*

He knelt, the snow trickling through his thin trousers, and laid his daughter down as gently as he could in the alcove of the building's front door. He checked one last time that the envelope thick with banknotes was securely tucked into her blankets, and he placed the object beside it, making sure it was hidden from view. Then he kissed the baby's warm forehead. He sobbed, the pain of losing her so soon after his wife almost too much to bear, before gritting his teeth and getting to his feet. He turned his back on his baby and stepped out into the haze of the streetlights, snow pattering on his suddenly empty arms.

"I'm here!" he roared, his tears hot. "Come on then! What are you waiting for?" The man strode into the middle of the road as the snow flowed around him, glancing down at the shadows of the street he'd just come from, where dark-clothed figures lurked. They were closing on him, not bothering to hurry now. They had no need.

The man faced them down, his chest heaving, his throat aching and sore. Slowly they circled him, as though mocking everything he had lost.

Finally he clenched his fists and ran straight for them. The sound of their truncheons raining down on his head and back made the baby's eyes pop open in shock. She opened her tiny mouth to cry, but between taking in a breath and letting it out again, she vanished without a trace.

THURSDAY, MAY 1, 1941

IN THE BASEMENT OF ACKERBEE'S HOME FOR LOST AND FOUND-lings, two young girls were at work. One had a pair of glasses perched on her nose and her pet tarantula, Violet, perched on her head. In each hand she held a piece of thin wire that she was gradually—and very carefully—bringing closer together. The other was watching, breath held, and trying not to get in the way.

"Steady," said the first girl, her dark eyes fixed on the gap between the wires. "Almost there . . ."

Unfortunately her friend—lost in admiration for the science taking place before her very eyes—chose just that moment to nudge some glassware with an unwary elbow and a round-bottomed beaker crashed to the floor.

There was a sudden spark as the wires the first girl had been holding met unexpectedly quickly, followed by a babble of apology from the other, who was already dropping to her knees to collect the shards of broken glass.

"Sorry!" she said for the tenth time in as many seconds. "I really am! I didn't mean to, Tess, I swear."

Tess sighed before joining her friend on the floor. "I know, Wilf. Your timing is perfect, though. As usual." She picked up the larger pieces of beaker with the skill that comes from long practice; Wilf averaged two breakages a week.

Wilf—who had discarded her given name, Wilhelmina, as soon as she was old enough to say it and long before she was old enough to know how to spell it—reddened. "I'm never going to be a scientist if I can't stop destroying my equipment," she muttered.

Tess looked at her friend. "Don't be silly, you goose," she replied. "You're *already* a scientist. Just think of it as a study of gravity. Or," she continued, holding up a shard and peering through it, "an examination of the smashiness of glass."

"That's not a word," Wilf scoffed, though her green eyes shone with amusement in her pale face.

"I just *said* it, didn't I?" Tess retorted, placing the shard carefully in her palm. As she reached for the next piece, her tarantula stirred on her head. "What's up, girl?" she murmured, glancing upward.

"Is something wrong?" asked Wilf, but before Tess had a chance to answer, the door to their "lab" was opened. Tess felt Violet relax, settling back into the tangle of Tess's hair.

"Girls?" came a voice they both knew.

"Miss Whipstead," Wilf said, getting to her feet. "We're down here."

"Ah. Wilhelmina. Another breakage?" their teacher said with a fond smile.

"Just a small one," Wilf replied, blushing again.

"Never mind, eh?" Miss Whipstead said, throwing her a wink. "Now, Tess? Miss Ackerbee needs you upstairs."

Tess clambered to her feet. Violet began to thrum a bit, sensing her worry. "Miss Ackerbee needs to see *me*?"

"As I said. Can you come now, please? It's a bit of an emergency. Leave that clearing up to Wilf—I'll come and give her a hand in a minute."

"An emergency?" Tess echoed. She took off her lab coat (really an old raincoat that she liked to imagine was white and that was equipped with many very useful pockets) and threw it over a nearby chair. Then she closed her experiments notebook, which had been sitting open on her workbench (really a spare classroom desk used mainly for detention), and folded it in two before sliding it into one of those very useful pockets. Violet skittered about a bit on top of her head. "Shush, girl. It's all right," Tess muttered to her, reaching up a finger for the spider to cling to. She met Wilf's worried gaze and tried to give her a reassuring smile.

"Is there anything I can do to help?" Wilf asked. Miss Whipstead glanced at her and shook her head.

"Miss Ackerbee just needs Tess for now, Wilf. Don't worry," she lied in a too-bright voice.

"See you later," Tess said, giving Wilf's arm a quick squeeze as she passed. Wilf nodded, frowning.

"It's nothing to worry about, girls," said Miss Whipstead, holding the door open as Tess and Violet ducked under her arm. She glanced back at Wilf as they left the room. "You'll be back to your experiments in no time, I'm sure." Wilf sighed, turning back to the clear-up as her teacher closed the door.

"Do you know we're *this* close to doing it?" said Tess, turning to Miss Whipstead wide-eyed. The teacher smiled, even as she shooed Tess up the corridor. "Actually making a faradic spark—real *electricity*—from seaweed!"

"If anyone can do it, it's you pair," said Miss Whipstead. "I have no doubt."

"What does Miss Ackerbee need me for?" Tess racked her brain quickly, trying to see if there was anything she'd done recently that she hadn't yet owned up to.

"I'm sure it's nothing," Miss Whipstead reassured her. "You're not in trouble is all I know. Though goodness knows

8

you *ought* to be." Tess glanced up at her, but the teacher's eyes twinkled.

They climbed the basement stairs into the house's large kitchen and Miss Whipstead paused for a minute to evaluate Tess's appearance. After telling her to clean her glasses, wipe her breakfast off her face and pull up that one sock that insisted on slipping down, Miss Whipstead deemed Tess fit to appear in the parlor. "Remember," whispered Miss Whipstead as she knocked on Miss Ackerbee's door. "You're not in trouble."

"Thanks," Tess replied, smiling up at her. Then she stepped through into Miss Ackerbee's domain, feeling knock-kneed. There wasn't often cause to stand in this room, and Tess found it was rarely a good thing for anyone to be summoned before the housemistress.

"Tess," said Miss Ackerbee, turning from a tall filing cabinet in the corner. "Why don't you take a seat."

Tess did as she was asked, feeling somehow untethered, like she could just float right up into the corner of this tall room. She glanced out of the window, hoping that would help to keep her steady.

"Now." Miss Ackerbee sat behind her desk. A short stack of paperwork topped with a blanket was within her reach. She folded her thin brown hands and took in a deep breath. "I suppose I'd best begin in the most obvious place. A man came for you today, Tess. A man who has laid claim to you and wants to take you away from here."

Tess swayed in her chair. She grasped its arms, fearing she might fall headlong onto the carpet otherwise.

"My—my father?" she croaked.

Miss Ackerbee shook her head, closing her eyes momentarily. "No. I don't believe so. In fact, I don't believe he is any relation to you, despite his assertions to the contrary." Tess listened, hauling breaths in and out, hoping she wouldn't be sick. Violet reached down a forelimb to stroke her forehead and she began to calm.

"So—who was he?"

"Before we get to that, Tess, let's have a chat. Have I ever told you properly about the night you arrived here?"

"Well, you said I was found in a blanket, on the doorstep . . ." Tess's words trailed away as her eyes found the blanket on Miss Ackerbee's desk again. "*That* blanket?" She looked up at the housemistress.

"This blanket," Miss Ackerbee replied. "And it contained more than just you, though you were gift enough by yourself." She smiled at Tess, who was too overwhelmed to return the smile. "There was an envelope full of money, which was useless as it was in a currency nobody had ever seen. And there was this."

Miss Ackerbee's hand slipped between the folds of the blanket. When it reemerged, it was clutching an object small enough to nestle in the hollow of her palm. The object was made of metal but Tess couldn't have said what sort—it looked dark, like brass. It was a short cylindrical thing like you might keep buttons in, though it was far too elegant for that, and the swirling weblike pattern that swept across it made it look like something that had been grown, not made. There were markings around its upper circumference, a bit like those on a clock face to denote the hours, or a compass to indicate direction, except there were eight of them. Each was a different color and one seemed to be discolored or tarnished somehow. It looked out of place.

"Is it—is it for false eyeballs?" said Tess, her gaze fixed on the small metal box.

Miss Ackerbee froze. "I beg your pardon?" she said.

"It's just something I read once. A man kept his false eyeball in a tin exactly like that one."

Miss Ackerbee's lips twitched. "I have no idea what this object is, Tess, but as far as I'm aware, it has nothing to do with eyeballs of any sort." She paused to place it on the table in front of her. "And remind me to monitor your reading material a bit more closely," she murmured, sliding the box toward Tess.

"So—what is it?" said Tess, who hadn't moved from her chair.

"I made a thorough examination of it when you arrived here," said Miss Ackerbee. "In case there was a clue to your identity or your family. But when I discovered I had no idea what I was looking at, I put it away and it's been in that filing cabinet for the past twelve years."

"And why are you giving it to me now?"

"I had intended to give it to you when you reached eighteen, or as soon as you decided to move away from this house to forge your own life," said Miss Ackerbee. "Along with every last note of the money we found with you, in the hope you could make use of it somewhere. But that's just the problem." Miss Ackerbee sighed, taking off her spectacles to rub at her eyes.

"What—what is?" said Tess after a minute.

"My dear, I don't quite know how to put this." Miss Ackerbee kept her eyes shut as she paused to think. Eventually she opened them again to gaze at Tess. "It is my considered opinion that neither you, nor the money you arrived with, nor indeed this object, comes from anywhere on this earth," she finally said, settling her spectacles back on her nose and fixing Tess with a look that was, given the circumstances, surprisingly calm.

Tess gaped at the object on Miss Ackerbee's desk as Violet trembled in the midst of her hair. She wanted nothing more than to get up, walk out of the room, run up the two flights of stairs to her own snug dormitory and pull her blankets over her head.

"I don't . . . ," she finally managed to say, "I don't know what you mean."

"My girl, I hardly know what I mean myself," said Miss Ackerbee with a sigh. "All I know is this object is somehow inextricably tied with you, and that you are an extraordinary girl. A most extraordinary girl indeed."

"Am I?" Tess was dazed. She'd never imagined she was extraordinary, and wondered how extraordinary people were supposed to act. Probably, she thought, they weren't supposed to go about with one sock down and their glasses smudged, and she wondered if Miss Ackerbee mightn't be mixing her up with one of the older girls.

Then Miss Ackerbee began to speak again and Tess did her best to focus.

"When you were very little, Tess, you used to disappear. Just—*vanish*, like that, out of the blue. You'd only be gone for five or maybe ten seconds at a time, but it was enough to make my heart skip." Miss Ackerbee gazed at her with steady brown eyes.

Tess blinked at her. "Um. Miss Ackerbee, I don't think that's—"

"Possible?" Miss Ackerbee finished Tess's sentence. "I didn't think so either. Not until I met you, at least."

"But where did I go?"

Miss Ackerbee licked her lips and took a deep breath. She stared at her desk and it looked to Tess like she was trying to find a pattern in the swirl of knots in the wood. Finally she looked up. Her kind face was earnest, as though she hoped Tess would believe what she was about to tell her.

"The night you came to us, I was here. In this parlor. Drinking a cup of cocoa. The entire house was asleep and I was standing by my window, gazing out at the river and indulging in a bit of thought." She smiled at the memory.

"And then, out of the blue, a shimmering circle appeared in midair—just for a second, you understand. Had I blinked at the wrong moment, I would have missed it. It hung right in front of the door before winking out of existence again. But it was there long enough for me to see."

"See what?" Tess asked.

"A man. Young and thin, and frightened. He looked up at the door of Ackerbee's. Snow was falling all around him. And then he was gone. The next thing I knew, there was a wail. I put my cup down on the windowsill and ran to the door—and there you were in the porch, wrapped in this blanket."

"And where was the man?"

Miss Ackerbee smiled, but there was sadness beneath it. "He wasn't there, Tess. And all around you was snow, tiny flakes in your blanket and even one on your baby eyelash, which I wiped away." Miss Ackerbee rubbed her forefinger with her thumb, as though reliving the moment. "Except it wasn't snowing that night. Not in this world, at least."

Tess fought to understand. "You said that before—'this world.' What does that mean?"

"I think," Miss Ackerbee began, speaking carefully, "that you have the ability to move between our world and other worlds, Tess. I'm not sure how, but that's my theory."

"Other—other *worlds*?" Tess scrunched up her face. "Like—different planets?"

"No, I don't think so. Other versions of this planet is what I mean. *Different realities* might be a better way of putting it, perhaps."

Miss Ackerbee lifted the blanket off the pile of paperwork, opened the topmost folder and began to flip through some documents until she came to a collection of letters, speaking to Tess all the while. "When you were very small and your extraordinary abilities began to appear, I made some discreet inquiries of a scientific nature. Over the course of making those inquiries, I made a friend who, until a few years ago, was a professor of physics in a university in Ostravica."

She glanced at Tess and smiled. "Several years ago he wrote to me about an idea he was working on, something he was calling the many-worlds theory, which basically means, as far as I understand, that all possible versions of our world might exist simultaneously. They don't interact because they can't—or at least that was his thinking at the time."

Miss Ackerbee sifted through the letters until she found the one she was looking for. "Here we go. *Could it be true, then, to say that everything which could exist, does exist somewhere? That every choice made creates a 'branch,' in effect, where both outcomes can come to independent fruition, entirely unknown to the other? It would mean an almost unimaginable abundance of universes, but who is to say such things cannot be true?*" She looked back at Tess. "Such things can be true, Tess. You are the proof."

"I—I don't know what to say." Tess's mind was a whirl. *Many worlds?* It was too much to think about all at once, so she seized on the one thing Miss Ackerbee had said that she could fully understand. "Why can't I do it anymore? The vanishing thing?"

Miss Ackerbee placed the bundle of letters down. "It stopped happening when you were about four, I think. Up to that point you might flicker in and out ten or twenty times a day. Only myself and Rebecca—Miss Whipstead, I suppose I ought to say—were aware of it, because we made sure one of us was with you all the time. We kept a log." She glanced at the pile of paperwork again. "Date, time, length of absence. Just in case."

"Just in case what?"

"You didn't come back," said Miss Ackerbee simply, meeting Tess's eye. "But you always did. And then you stopped." She looked up, her gaze settling on Violet, who sat still as a stone on Tess's head. "Which, incidentally, coincided with Violet's arrival here at Ackerbee's."

"So now Violet is from some other planet too?" Tess said, her voice wavering. "I really don't—"

"Violet is simply a spider," interrupted Miss Ackerbee. "But she has one extraordinary quality—she was loved. By you. From the moment you saw her. And that was enough to keep you here."

The girl cradled the spider close against her chest, thinking about the day they'd first met. She remembered the magician who'd come to Ackerbee's to entertain the girls one rainy afternoon. How he had pulled cards out of sleeves, handkerchiefs out of hats, and made shilling pieces appear from behind Miss Ackerbee's ear. Most of all, Tess had been transfixed by the spider living on his lapel like a colorful brooch. That spider had been Violet's mother, whose clutch of babies hadn't long hatched. The tiny tarantulas had been like walking jewels and Tess had fallen in love with Violet as soon as she laid eyes on her.

"Here you are then," the magician had said, holding Violet out on the end of one finger, like a tiny black berry. "I'll give her to you. Seems like you're made for one another." Tess remembered looking at Miss Ackerbee for permission, her dark eyes meeting the housemistress's darker ones, and how Miss Ackerbee had nodded, smiling in bemusement at her odd little charge. Violet had crawled onto Tess's shoulder that day and she'd never left.

Tess brought herself back to the present, lifting Violet until she could look into her shining cluster of eyes. They were as familiar to her as her own.

"And Violet was an anchor," Miss Ackerbee continued.

"A tether to this world that kept you from slipping out of it. Rebecca and I worried what would happen to you if anything happened to Violet, but we were lucky. She's robust and you take excellent care of her."

Tess blinked hard, trying not to embarrass herself by letting the tears behind her lids leak onto her face. "It's a lot to deal with, I know," Miss Ackerbee said, removing a handkerchief from her sleeve and sliding it across the desk. "And we don't have a lot of time. The man—his name is Mr. Norton F. Cleat—will be returning in a few hours and he wants to take you with him."

"Who is he?" said Tess, wiping her nose with Miss Ackerbee's handkerchief before scrunching it up and handing it back to her.

"Why don't you keep that one, dear. I have plenty," Miss Ackerbee replied, waving the handkerchief away. Tess stuffed it into her pocket. "And as for our friend Mr. Cleat, well, I simply don't know who he is. But I know his claim to you has to be a weak one, no matter what legal papers he can conjure up. Proving it, however, will take time—time that we don't have at the moment."

"But what does he want with me?"

"Nothing good, I fear," said Miss Ackerbee, gazing at Tess with concern. "Which means we need to think about what to do with you."

"Can I ask one more thing?" said Tess.

"Of course, dear," Miss Ackerbee replied, her smile suggesting she already knew what the question would be.

"The man. The other one, I mean—the one in the circle in the air. Who was he?"

"It's only my theory, Tess," Miss Ackerbee replied, her voice measured and careful. "But I think—in fact, I'm fairly certain, because it could hardly be anyone else—I think that man was your father."

Just then a sharp knock sounded on Miss Ackerbee's door, making Tess jump.

"Come in, Rebecca," Miss Ackerbee called.

"Tess's things are ready," said Rebecca, coming in and closing the door behind her. "Wilf gave me a hand with the lab bits and pieces."

"And you told her Tess has to go into quarantine?"

"Hang on a minute," Tess said before Rebecca had a chance to answer. "Quarantine?"

"It's what we're going to tell the other girls when they ask where you've gone," Miss Ackerbee replied. She raised an eyebrow. "I'm sure not all of them will believe that you've been stricken with an infectious disease, but we'll have to hope for the best."

Tess sank into her chair, feeling like her chest was folding in on top of itself. She stared at the blanket on Miss Ackerbee's desk, wondering how on earth she'd gone from conducting experiments on seaweed to being told she was some sort of *monster*, all in one morning. She felt like a stranger in her own skin, but in another way she felt as though she finally had some of the answers she'd needed all her life.

"You can have it, Tess, if you want it," said Miss Ackerbee in a soft voice. Tess glanced up at her. "The blanket. It's yours, after all."

Tess lifted it into her arms as though it still contained her baby self, and a fold of it fell open to reveal a name tag stitched carefully against a seam.

"Teresita Mariana de Sousa," she read, her eyes filling with tears again. "My name."

"It's how we knew what to call you," said Miss Ackerbee, her own voice thickening. "I wondered if your mother made it for you. It looks as though she might have."

"In another world?" whispered Tess, looking up at her housemistress. Two fat tears finally spilled out, pooling a little in her glasses before trickling to her chin.

"That's my belief, yes," said Miss Ackerbee, straightening her shoulders and sniffing, just once. Her eyes were shining.

"It's almost one o'clock, Miss Ackerbee," said Rebecca, behind Tess. "If we're to get her going . . ." Her words trailed off as a cloud fell over Miss Ackerbee's face. The house-mistress nodded and got to her feet.

"Tess," she said, bending over her desk and leaning heavily on the flat of her palms. "You've got to leave the house now, I'm afraid. Just for a short time, we hope—until this Cleat person can be satisfied with going away empty-handed. But as soon as we can, we'll come to fetch you home."

"Hang on—what? Where am I going?" Tess clutched the blanket tightly to herself.

"To my sister's house, in the country," said Rebecca, coming to stand beside Tess's chair. She knelt, folding her hands in her lap, and looked up at Tess sympathetically. "Nobody knows about its connection to this house. So you should be safe there for a while. And I'll stay with you all the time."

"But—wait." Tess closed her eyes. She put the blanket carefully in her lap and took her glasses off, rubbing her damp eyes with the heel of one hand. "Just wait a minute."

"Tess, time is really against us . . . ," Miss Ackerbee began, her voice low and anxious.

"Miss Ackerbee—please. *Why* is this man—Mr. Cleat?—why is he coming for me? Why does he want *me* in particular?" She licked her lips, put her glasses back on and stared at Miss Ackerbee.

"What difference does it make?" said Rebecca. Tess turned to look at her. "He's not having you, and that's that."

Tess turned back to the housemistress. "But there has to be a reason. How does he even know about me? If what you're saying is true. If—if I'm not—if I'm not supposed to be here?" Tess struggled to find the words, but Miss Ackerbee knew what she meant.

"I can't explain that, Tess. I truly don't know. But as soon as I saw your name on his documents, I knew we had to keep you safe. We *have* to get you away from here."

"But—" Tess began.

Miss Ackerbee leaned forward, her words urgent. She fixed Tess with a stare. "Your father left you here to *save* you from something. He must have had a good reason! If he brought you here, somehow, from another reality, hoping you'd find a loving home far away from the world you were born into, how can I possibly betray that by giving you up now?"

"But—just listen!" Tess scrunched her hands into fists, and Miss Ackerbee leaned back a little. "Mr. Cleat might be looking for me because he knows something about me—like, maybe, about these things I can do, the things you've been telling me about?"

"Well, yes. Of course. I can't think of any other rea-son," said the housemistress, sinking back into her chair. She frowned slightly as she looked at Tess. "He claimed he was related to you, but I don't see how that's possible. Plus," she continued, her face hardening, "he didn't seem like the type of person I'd trust to care for a dog, let alone a child."

"But don't you see? If he knows something about me," Tess persisted, "I have to go with him, not run away."

"What?" Rebecca got to her feet in a hurry. "Go *with* him? What sort of scheme is that?"

"But if he knows something about me, Miss Ackerbee, maybe he can tell me who I am? Where I came from?" Tess swallowed a lump in her throat. "Where my parents are?"

"There has to be another way, Tess," Miss Ackerbee said, her eyes dull with sorrow.

"But there isn't, is there?" Tess replied. "It's been twelve years and this is the first time there's been any hint that anyone outside of this house has ever even heard of me. This might be my only chance."

A long moment of silence passed. "It's a risky strategy," said Miss Ackerbee finally, her steady gaze on Tess's face. "I don't like the idea of you being all alone, trying to figure things out by yourself while this man holds all the cards."

"He doesn't hold all the cards." Tess sank her fingers into the blanket. "You've told me as much about me as you can. He doesn't *know* I know. That gives me a card or two, doesn't it?"

Miss Ackerbee smiled. "I'd say it gives you a royal flush," she said.

"So—am I hearing right?" said Rebecca, putting her hands on her hips and striding away from Tess across the room. "Are you proposing we send one of our charges into goodness knows what sort of danger? This isn't right, Aurelia." She cut a glance at Tess and cleared her throat. "I mean, Miss Ackerbee."

Miss Ackerbee leaned across her desk and took a sheet of notepaper in her hand. Quickly, in her neat writing, she printed a telephone number. "Take this," she told Tess, handing her the paper, "and keep it somewhere about yourself, always. It's the number for this house. If you need me, you get to a telephone and ask the operator to connect you here. Simply say the word *quicksilver* and I will know you need help. Do you understand?"

"Quicksilver," Tess repeated. "Atomic number eighty. Atomic symbol Hg." She blinked, looking up at Miss Ackerbee. "I won't forget."

"I know," Miss Ackerbee said, capping her fountain pen. She got to her feet. "Right. Why don't you go and finish packing, Tess, and we'll wait here for Mr. Cleat. You can meet him yourself, and if your instinct tells you not to go with him, I will fight with everything I have to keep you here. If, however, you wish to leave, you may go with my blessing and I will be waiting here for you until you return."

"This is lunacy," Rebecca muttered. She turned away from Tess to face the corner of the room. "Utter madness."

"I'm sorry, my dear," Miss Ackerbee said, her words soft. "I hate to go against you like this, but I have to admit that I agree with Tess. This is her chance to find the answers neither you nor I can give her—answers she's entitled to. Anyway, she can always come home once"—she paused, swallowing hard—"once it's all over. We'll find a way."

Tess saw Rebecca shaking her head, but she didn't say anything else.

"Thank you, Miss Ackerbee," said Tess, getting to her feet. The hair on top of her head sat up and Tess glanced at her own forehead. "Violet says thanks too."

"The best way to thank me is to come home safe—both of you," Miss Ackerbee replied. "And you're to write to me every single week, without fail. I shall miss you terribly." She turned away quickly, as if to busy herself with putting away some documents, and Tess felt Rebecca's hand on her shoulder. She allowed herself to be led out of the room, feeling like her ears were stuffed with cotton and her heart was a banging gong.

Tess sat on her half-made bed, her mind in a muddle. Rebecca had already packed away most of her clothes and books but she'd left Tess's nightie, her toothbrush and her treasures box untouched. These things now sat around Tess like a fallen army, forgotten, as she stared at the blanket in her hands.

Then the door banged open. Two of her dorm-mates, Priscilla and Proserpina—who weren't sisters but really should have been—walked in, gabbling away to one another about hockey, as usual. They stopped short and fell silent when they saw Tess, taking in the scene.

"Are you getting *adopted*?" Prissy came to sit on Tess's bed, dropping so heavily onto it that Tess bounced a little.

"You simply *must* tell us all about it," said Prossy, sitting on the next bed, her face alight with excitement.

"Are they marvelous? Do they have a summer house?" Prissy, who read a lot of books about orphans coming into riches, clutched her chest and closed her eyes. "Do they *sail?*"

"I—um. Actually, I'm going into quarantine," Tess said. Prissy immediately clapped one hand over her mouth and nose, rather overdramatically, while Prossy recoiled a bit, looking disgusted.

"What do you *have?*" she asked, her face screwing up even further.

Tess drew a blank. *Miss Ackerbee forgot to tell me what my fake disease is,* she thought. *Typical.* "I—um. I don't think it's *too* contagious."

"Still," said Prissy, her words muffled by her fingers. "If they're sending you away, it must be fairly serious."

Tess sighed. "If you were going to catch it, you'd have caught it by now."

Prissy looked suspicious, but she dropped her hand. "Where are you going?" she asked. "Is it far away?" Tess wondered if there was a hopeful note in her voice.

"No idea," she answered truthfully. "I hope he'll tell me when he gets here."

"Who?" Prossy said, frowning at Tess.

"Mr. Cleat," Tess said, wishing she could bite the words back as soon as they left her mouth. "I mean—I think that's his name."

"Is he a doctor?" Prissy asked.

"I hope not," Tess said fervently.

"Is he some ancient warty beast?" asked Prossy with a shudder.

"Ooh! Maybe he'll keep you locked in a tower," said Prissy, getting lost in the drama of the moment. "And you'll have to fashion tiny paper birds with things like *Help me!* written on them in your best calligraphy, and send them out the window, hoping some handsome passing prince will find them and come to rescue you."

"You do talk such nonsense, Priss," said Prossy. "Where would she get paper, locked in a tower?" Prissy scowled at her.

"Nobody is getting locked anywhere," said Tess, hoping she was right about that part. "And if I *do* get locked in a tower, I'll find my own way out, thank you very much."

"You're no fun, either of you," grumbled Prissy.

"Anyway," Prossy said, rolling her eyes. "How long will you be away for?"

"I'm not sure," Tess replied, settling the blanket on her lap. The object was buried within it, and Tess made sure it wasn't visible. She liked Prissy and Prossy, but not *that* much.

Prissy wrinkled her nose as she stared at Violet. "And is he letting you bring *that*?" she said.

"Yes," Tess answered in an incredulous tone. "At least, I'm bringing her, no matter what he says."

"Mm," said Prossy, tossing her thick plait over one shoulder. She crossed her legs, rotating one foot impatiently. "What about all your tubes and bottles and springs and things?"

"My *equipment*," Tess answered, "is also coming. I'm this close to a breakthrough." Prissy simply raised her eyebrows at that.

All three of them jumped as the door to the dorm burst open again and a third-floor girl stuck her head into the room. "There's a *man* outside!" she called breathlessly. "And you should *see* his car!"

Tess felt like someone had doused her in a bucket of icy water. *He's here.*

Prossy went to the nearest window and peered out through it; Prissy joined her a heartbeat later. They looked out at Mr. Cleat and then they looked at one another.

"I think this calls for our best dresses," Prissy said, and Prossy nodded. They pulled themselves away from the window and began to rummage through their wardrobes. Tess ignored them and walked slowly to the window herself, unsure even as she looked out whether she wanted to see.

A man stood beside a long, sleek black car. He held his

hat in his hands as he squinted up at the façade of Ackerbee's Home for Lost and Foundlings. He had a thin mustache, hair slicked back with pomade and a smart suit. He was younger than Tess had expected. As she watched, he approached the house, eventually vanishing from sight.

"Smarmy, isn't he?" came a voice at her shoulder. Tess didn't need to turn to know it was Wilf.

"Like a crocodile wearing a human," Tess agreed.

"You're not actually going to go, are you?"

Tess looked at her friend. She didn't even have to ask; of course Rebecca would have told her the truth. Wilf was as reliable as a rock and she never broke her word. "I have to," she replied, and Wilf's only answer was to frown.

Tess threw a glance at Prissy and Prossy; they were knee-deep in hand-me-down lemon-yellow organza, the dresses dotted with the stitches of their many previous owners, and were paying her and Wilf no heed. Then Tess looked at Wilf. "Come here," she whispered, walking back to her bed. She flipped up the blanket to reveal the object, and Wilf stood staring at it for a long moment.

"What is it?" Wilf asked.

Tess shrugged. "I don't know yet," she said. "But I know it might help me find out who I am. Where I came from."

"But you know who you are," Wilf protested. "And who cares where you came from?"

Tess deflated. "It's all right for you," she said. "You *know* all that stuff. I don't. I never have and it leaves a hole, you know? It makes me feel like I don't belong anywhere."

"Of *course* you belong. It's idiotic to think that you don't," Wilf scoffed.

Tess took a deep breath, an ache settling inside her chest. "You don't understand," she said, folding the blanket back over the small round object.

"What do you mean?" Wilf's voice was as miserable as her expression. "How can you say I don't understand?"

Tess bit her lip, flooded with remorse. "Forget I said it," she replied.

"No, it's all right," Wilf said, wrapping her hurt up inside herself. "Don't worry about it. You just go off and have a jolly old time with your new dad. We'll be fine here without you."

"Wilf, *please*," Tess began, throwing her hands in the air, but the other girl turned on her heel and strode out of the room. Prissy and Prossy watched her go, their eyes round.

"Trouble in paradise?" Prissy asked.

"Oh, give it a rest," Tess muttered, turning back to her suitcase. She shoved everything on her bed into it haphazardly and then had second thoughts. She upturned the suitcase, retrieved the object and put it in her pocket, then repacked the suitcase, all through a haze of angry tears.

"Tess?" came a quiet voice. She turned, a fresh apology to Wilf on her lips, but saw Rebecca in the doorway instead. The teacher's pale face was like a curl of dough, and she looked as though she'd received a lifetime's worth of bad news all at once. "Could you come down to Miss Ackerbee's parlor, please. Quick as you can."

Tess picked up her case and took a step or two into the middle of the floor, while Prissy and Prossy stood awkwardly beside their beds, wearing their best and second-best dresses, respectively. Rebecca glanced at them, which turned into a full-on glare, and the girls immediately began to pull off the fancy taffeta and silk, looking embarrassed.

"He's here?" Tess said, and Rebecca looked at her.

"Ahead of schedule, yes," she answered, holding out a hand. "And he's not in the mood to wait." Tess walked to Rebecca and took her hand, gripping her suitcase tightly with the other.

"We'll miss you, you odd little creature," Prossy said in her making-the-best-of-it voice.

Tess looked at her and tried to smile. "Hope you get a nice new dorm-mate."

"One without livestock would be my preference," Prissy muttered. "Not that there's anything *wrong* with living with a tarantula as such," she added as Violet gave her a reproachful stare from her perch atop Tess's head.

Rebecca squeezed Tess's hand. "Come on now," she urged gently. Prissy and Prossy stood at the end of their beds, looking like they didn't know what to do with their hands. Tess sucked hard on her lower lip, blinking up at them.

"See you later," she said, and then she was gone.

MR. CLEAT GOT TO HIS FEET AS TESS ENTERED THE ROOM. HE wore a dove-gray three-piece suit, very shiny shoes and a grin that seemed rather too pleased with itself for Tess's liking. His eyes were very blue, and even from all the way across the room, they seemed sharp and piercing, like daggers ready to be thrown.

"So here she is," he said. "It's a pleasure, Tess."

"Tess, I'd like you to meet Mr. Cleat," Miss Ackerbee said, rising from her own chair and walking around her desk. Tess stood in the middle of the floor, clutching her suitcase to her front.

"Say hello, Tess," Rebecca muttered, and the sound of her voice snapped Tess out of her daydream.

"Oh, that's all right!" Mr. Cleat said, laughing too loudly. "It's all a bit much, I expect, learning you're not alone in the world anymore. That you have family. I can only imagine how it feels."

"Tess has always had a family," Miss Ackerbee responded to nobody in particular, her voice crisp.

Mr. Cleat turned to her and inclined his head politely. "Quite so. No offense intended, Miss Ackerbee. I trust, however, that you appreciate the distinction I'm trying to make."

Miss Ackerbee gave no reply and didn't so much as glance in Mr. Cleat's direction. "Tess, I told you earlier today that the choice to leave was yours." She kept her steady gaze on Tess's panicked one. "You will always have a home here. But neither I nor Miss Whipstead"—Tess glanced at Rebecca, who was bristling a bit at the use of her proper name—"has ever stood in the way of any girl who wished to leave us, for any reason. I will not stand in yours, either."

Miss Ackerbee paused, blinking hard. "You've been with us practically since the day you were born, Tess. I love all my charges equally, but you—well. Rebecca and I have raised you like our own daughter. Nonetheless, your wishes for your future will be respected." She cut a glare at Mr. Cleat. "By all the adults present, I trust."

Tess's mouth fell open as she struggled to find the words to reply.

"I might remind everyone that I have legal papers here, to bolster my claim to Tess," Mr. Cleat interjected. He gestured to a slim folder sitting on Miss Ackerbee's desk. "It's not a case of allowing the child to make her own choices so much as ensuring she lives in the correct and most appropriate place for her. Which is, I'm sure we'll all agree, with a family member."

"The most appropriate place for Tess is *here*," Rebecca muttered.

Tess looked at Mr. Cleat. His hair shone in the daylight coming through Miss Ackerbee's tall windows, and she could hear the faint sounds of the city rolling past outside. The view from those windows was all that Tess had ever known: the wide River Plura flowing past Ackerbee's front door, spanned by the mighty Carlisle Bridge, which led straight to the heart of the city of Hurdleford, and the busy quays along the riverside that buzzed with trade and crowds and familiar sights and sounds. She couldn't imagine looking out of a window and seeing something else, a totally different world with unfamiliar things and people in it.

"I want to stay," she said, her heart thudding in her chest at the thought of what that decision meant and everything she was losing as a result. It didn't feel good but it felt *right*, and Tess tried to quieten her conscience. Miss Ackerbee's face relaxed into a smile, the lines around her dark eyes softening as she gazed at Tess steadily through the lenses of her gold-rimmed spectacles.

"Well, that's that. We'll make the appropriate arrangements and I'm sure Mr. Cleat—"

"Mr. Cleat is going nowhere," the stranger in the room retorted. "Not without the child, at least."

"Sir, you heard Tess's wishes," Miss Ackerbee replied in a voice like flint.

"And, madam, you have seen the contents of this folder." He tapped it with one long finger. "Tess is the heir of my great-great-uncle-in-law, late of Hurdleford. I am her only living relative, albeit a distant one, and I am the executor of the deceased gentleman's estate. My claim"—he leaned across the desk—"outweighs yours."

"I have never *claimed* a child in my life," Miss Ackerbee said, her arms clasped at her waist like a barrier. "Children are not parcels, Mr. Cleat, nor objects to be traded. For me, their wishes about their own lives are paramount."

Mr. Cleat's mouth twisted. "Lucky for those of us who set our stock in the law, then, that people like you are not in charge of things."

"Enough of this," Rebecca snapped. "Tess has made her feelings clear and that's the end of the matter. If you want to discuss a plan for future visits, Mr. Cleat, I'm sure we can accommodate you, but if not, I'm going to have to ask you to leave."

Mr. Cleat's nostrils flared as he turned to the folder on Miss Ackerbee's table. He began to flip through it. "My great-great-uncle's will," he declared, pointing to a document, "which clearly sets out his relationship to Tess, and which creates, in law, a cast-iron connection between my family and hers. And *any* family connection invalidates her right to stay here." He looked around, an air of faint disgust on his face as he took in the slightly shabby room. "As fine an establishment as it is, Tess's presence here robs a deserving orphan of her place beneath your roof. It's hardly fair, is it?"

"Can't you at least wait until my own lawyers can look over your paperwork?" Miss Ackerbee said. "A week at most. That's all I ask."

Mr. Cleat slapped the folder shut. "I'm afraid not, Miss Ackerbee," he said. "The nature of my business is such that I can't predict when I'm going to be out of the country or called away from the city. So it's best if I bring Tess home now, and we can discuss any loose ends at a later date."

Tess's heart began to race. "But I *am* home," she said, squeezing hard on the handle of her suitcase.

Mr. Cleat walked toward Tess and then got down on one knee so that his face was almost level with hers. He pressed his thin lips together into a short-lived smile. "I promise you, you'll be happy in this new life I'm offering. This in-heritance makes you rather a well-off girl—or at least it *will*, when you're older. Until then, I'm to be your guardian. You can come and visit your friends here whenever you want." He paused, studying Tess carefully with his sharp blue eyes. "Give me a chance."

Violet chose her moment to shift position on top of Tess's head and Mr. Cleat leaned back quickly, his eyes widening. "Settle down, girl," Tess whispered, reaching up to her.

"Whatever's *that*?" Mr. Cleat said, staring at Violet.

"Violet comes with me. Wherever I go, she comes too," Tess said.

Mr. Cleat forced himself to smile. "Well then. I welcome both of you."

"Tess," Miss Ackerbee said, her voice low. "There's no need—"

"Ah, but there's one more thing in here I haven't yet shown you," Mr. Cleat interrupted, getting to his feet. He picked up the folder again and flicked to a different document. "A court order, Miss Ackerbee. One declaring me Tess's legal guardian and your status over her null and void. After all," he con-tinued triumphantly, "you can't prove the circumstances of Tess's arrival here. I wonder if a thorough investigation into all your charges is in order? Just to be on the safe side, of course." Tess saw Miss Ackerbee's face crumple.

"What does that mean?" Tess asked, willing her house-mistress to make things right.

"It means," Miss Ackerbee replied, her eyes shiny with fresh tears, "that we have to let you go or risk losing all our girls while a baseless examination of our methods takes place."

Tess swallowed hard. Violet, settled in the nest she habitually made in Tess's hair, thrumming as gently as a plucked string, but not even that could make Tess feel better.

"There has to be something we can do," Rebecca said, stepping forward to put her hands on Tess's shoulders.

"Have your people draw up a legal challenge," Mr. Cleat said, his voice cool. He closed the folder of documents and slipped it under his arm. "But in the meantime, Tess is coming with me."

Miss Ackerbee met Tess's eye. Her stricken expression made Tess feel like she was shattering into pieces right here in the room in which she'd learned, only a couple of hours before, that everything she'd ever thought about herself had been wrong.

As bad as that had been, this was infinitely worse.

THE GIRLS OF ACKERBEE'S LINED THE HALLWAY AS TESS WALKED
toward the open front door. They hung through the banis-
ters, calling their goodbyes; they spilled out of the door and
onto the street, causing curious passersby to stop and stare.
Tess tried to hold as many hands and catch as many blown
kisses as she could, and she told herself that no matter what,
she would not cry.

She almost managed it.

Just as she was setting foot outside the door, on the
threshold of the world she'd always known and a world she
couldn't imagine, someone shouted her name. She turned
just in time for Wilf to barrel into her.

"What will I do without you?" Wilf whispered into her ear.

"I'll be back, goosie," Tess told her. "I promise."

"You can't promise that," Wilf said.

"I just did."

"But you might forget me, what with your new life and all." Wilf flicked away a tear.

"I could never forget you, Wilf," Tess said. "You're too annoying," she added after a beat.

They released one another and Wilf laughed, rubbing her runny nose with the back of her hand. Then her laughter faded. "I'll miss you. And Vi. You'll write, won't you?"

"Every day, and twice on Sundays," Tess replied. "Promise."

"You'd better," Wilf whispered.

"If we're quite ready," came Mr. Cleat's voice, like a jab in the ribs.

The girls let go of one another's hands, and both of them wiped their cheeks. Tess took off her glasses to scrub at her eyes properly, and when she replaced them, Wilf had stepped back to join the others. Beside her was Eunice McMullen, a girl from the next dorm, who put a comforting hand on Wilf's arm. Prissy and Prossy stood by the stairs, waving, and Tess tried to press them all into her memory, taking their images and putting them in a book inside her head.

Then Miss Ackerbee was on her knees in front of her, pulling her close. "This is your home," she whispered into Tess's ear. "Never forget how much we love you." Her voice faltered and Tess nodded, her tears soaking into her house-mistress's hair. Miss Ackerbee kissed her on both cheeks and stood up, letting Rebecca take her place.

"And don't let that *beastly* man upset you," she muttered, squeezing Tess tightly. Finally Rebecca got to her feet and stood arm in arm with Miss Ackerbee, both of them grim-faced, and Mr. Cleat placed his hand between Tess's shoulder blades, pushing her forward.

"Time to go," he told her, and Tess found herself walking to the sleek black car. Mr. Cleat urged her inside, and she twisted in her seat as soon as she sat down, trying to see out of the back window.

The slam of the car door closing made her jerk around, surprised. Mr. Cleat settled into his seat, which faced hers across a short expanse of meticulously clean carpet. Behind a glass screen sat the driver, the same person who'd opened the car door for Tess, and with a sharp rap of his knuckles, Mr. Cleat gave the order to leave.

Tess turned again, watching Ackerbee's in the rear window until it vanished from her sight.

When she eventually faced forward in her seat, Mr. Cleat was looking at her quizzically, as though wondering what on earth to do with her. She clutched her small suitcase to herself and tried to ignore him, looking out of the window beside her instead. They were heading straight for the center of the city, swooping left and right seemingly at random down narrow, winding streets, and very quickly Tess lost any sense of direction.

Mr. Cleat cracked open a newspaper and buried himself behind it. Tess noticed the large ring on the smallest finger of his left hand as he held the paper; it was engraved with something but Tess couldn't quite make out what. It looked like two letters, intertwined—was that an *H*? She leaned forward, squinting at the ring, but Mr. Cleat tucked his finger behind the paper, hiding it from further inspection.

Thwarted, Tess studied the newspaper instead. She could read the date, May 1, 1941, and the leading story: *KING GEORGE AND PRINCESSES CONTINUE THEIR ROYAL TOUR OF THE BRITERNIAN ISLES; SOJOURN IN HIBERNIA A SUCCESS.* She rolled her eyes and looked away, continuing to watch the world pass by outside, trying unsuccessfully to get a handle on where they were going.

Finally they turned to drive through a tall wrought-iron gate. The car's interior fell into shadow as they passed beneath some overhanging trees, and Mr. Cleat was forced to put his newspaper to one side with a sigh.

Up ahead, on the far side of the road, she caught a glimpse of large squat buildings, which seemed totally at odds with the landscape around them; something like a ship's propeller made of sheets of metal riveted together stuck out from the front of one of them, but Tess couldn't figure out what it was.

She turned to Mr. Cleat, the question on the tip of her tongue.

"My work involves developing large machinery," he told her before she had the chance to ask. "But don't trouble yourself about it. It's terribly boring."

"So we're nearly there?"

"Not far now," Mr. Cleat said.

Then the car turned again and Tess caught sight of an extraordinary house. She gaped up at it as the car approached. The house was made of gray stone and had four turret towers. The main roof, high and steeply angled and covered in greenish-tinged copper, rose almost as high as the towers; into it were set many small square windows. Ivy grew up one wall, its glossy leaves like a companion to the green roof. The front door was thrown open, a beautiful fanlight stretching above it, and a bellpull with a red tassel hung by its side. People in uniform lined the steps leading up to it and Tess began to feel distinctly awkward.

"Time to introduce you to the staff," Mr. Cleat said as the car came to a stop.

The driver opened the door and helped Tess out as Mr. Cleat stood, settling his jacket. None of the people on the steps, Tess couldn't help but notice, looked entirely welcoming.

There was an older lady who Tess assumed was the cook; alongside her were four young ladies in uniform, probably maids. The youngest looked barely older than Tess herself. On the other side of the steps stood a weather-beaten man whose age was impossible to guess, and Tess had him pegged as the gardener. Beside him, facing the car with her hands clasped in front of her, was a tall woman in a black dress. She had a thin-lipped smile on her chalk-pale face, and her eyes looked like two black beetles fixed in place with pins.

The driver made his way to the steps, where he took his place beside the gardener. Then Mr. Cleat extended his hand to Tess, ushering her forward, and they began to walk toward the house.

"Pauline," Mr. Cleat said as they drew near, and the beetle-eyed woman stood straighter, her face radiating helpfulness. "Will you take Tess under your wing? I've got something I need to attend to." He turned to Tess. "I'll see you for dinner," he told her. "Pay attention to Mrs. Thistleton, won't you? She knows the run of things." And with a nod at everyone, he was gone.

"So you'll be Tess," said Mrs. Thistleton. "Welcome to Roedeer Lodge."

"Th-thank—" Tess began.

"Now," Mrs. Thistleton continued, "I'll just tell you who's who and then we can get on with the rules of the house."

Rules? Tess was so preoccupied that she forgot everybody's name the second Mrs. Thistleton introduced them—except for the youngest maid, who was called Millicent.

"Millie will do, miss," the girl said shyly as she bobbed a curtsy to Tess.

"Please," Tess said. "Call me Tess."

"Come," Mrs. Thistleton said, her tone crisp. "Millicent will show you to your room."

"Is it just this, miss?" Millicent—*Millie*—asked, holding out a hand to take Tess's suitcase. Tess handed it over without thinking, immediately feeling awkward but not knowing how to ask for it back, but Millie simply smiled and led her through the huge door and into the house.

"You'll be up here, miss, on the second floor," Millie said as Tess followed her across a black-and-white-tiled lobby and up a set of wide, thickly carpeted stairs. At the first turn in the staircase, Tess began to feel odd, and by the time they'd reached the second floor, she was distinctly queasy. "And your room is this one— Miss?" Mille turned, looking concerned, and she took Tess's elbow in a firm, reassuring hold.

"I—I think I'm going to be sick," Tess managed to say, and Millie helped her the last few steps to her room, leading her to a chair in the corner. Then quickly she placed Tess's suitcase on the floor, pulled a chamber pot out from beneath the bed and held it to Tess's face just in time for her to throw up into it.

"There you are now," she said soothingly, rubbing Tess's back. "All up, and you'll feel much better."

"I'm so sorry," Tess began as she started to tremble. She felt wrong inside, like something had gone missing. An ice shard was lodged in her chest and her head was buzzing, like something inside it had been struck. Millie took away the large ceramic pot, covering it with a cloth and placing it on the table beside the bed. Just as she turned back around, Violet crawled slowly out from Tess's hair to settle above her heart. The gentle movement made Tess take a deep comforting breath, but she looked up when she heard the young maid give a tiny squeak of surprise.

"Millie!" Tess said. "Don't be frightened. This is Violet. She's perfectly harmless."

"I'll—I'll just leave you to get settled, miss," Millie said, picking up the chamber pot. She bobbed a slow careful curtsy, keeping her eyes on the pot, and then hurried out of the room.

Tess slumped in her chair, looking around. The room was large and clean, with three tall windows. Gauzy curtains billowed in the breeze. The bed looked comfortable, the wash stand gleamed, the carpet was neat. It was the first room Tess had ever had entirely to herself.

But she knew she'd give it all up in a heartbeat to have her old dorm at Ackerbee's back, Prissy and Prossy and all.

"RIGHT," SAID MR. CLEAT TO TESS AFTER DINNER THAT EVENING as the dessert things were being cleared away, "I didn't mention the most important thing yet. I've prepared you a welcoming gift. Shall we go and take a look at it?"

Tess glanced up at him. Her mostly uneaten pudding still sat on her dish and she put down her spoon. She'd hardly had any dinner but—unlike at Ackerbee's—nobody had seemed to notice, or care. "Thank you," she replied, unsure of what else to say. Violet stirred in her hair so slowly it almost felt like she'd been sleeping and had woken at the sound of Tess's voice.

Mrs. Thistleton cleared her throat. "Isn't it a bit late for that?" she asked in a mild tone. Mr. Cleat looked at her, the start of a smile on his face.

"Beg pardon?" he said, though Mrs. Thistleton had spoken clearly.

"Tess has had rather a day of it, don't you think? We don't want too much excitement before bed." She gazed coolly at Mr. Cleat. "It leads to dyspepsia. Disturbed sleep. That sort of thing."

Mr. Cleat looked amused. "Finish your biscuit, Pauline, and leave the guardianship of my charge up to me, thank you," he said, and Mrs. Thistleton turned bright red. Instead of pudding, Mrs. Thistleton had made a point of allowing herself only a cup of weak-looking tea and a single plain biscuit, most of which still sat on her saucer. She glared at it as though hoping her stare could set it on fire.

"Of course, Mr. Cleat," she said, pulling her lips tight once the words had slipped through.

"Good. No further complaints?" Mr. Cleat said, looking brightly from Tess to Mrs. Thistleton and back again. Neither of them said anything. "Come along then," he said to Tess. He threw his napkin down beside his scraped-clean pudding dish and got to his feet. Tess followed suit and soon they were walking down a long corridor lined with tall windows. Every few feet there was a piece of sculpture, or a potted plant on a spindly table, or a stiffly upright chair with ornate legs. She wondered why everything seemed so strange—like she'd seen it all before but every bit of it had been different.

The sick feeling rose up her throat again but she forced it down.

"Here we go," said Mr. Cleat. His voice broke into Tess's thoughts, making her jump. "I hope it meets your requirements."

He pushed open the door of a room halfway along the corridor and flicked on a light switch. The bulbs pocked and flickered before finally coming on and Tess caught her breath as she looked around. There were her glassware and her old gas burner—and there, on a desktop, her experiments notebook, its blue-and-yellow cover unmistakable. Across the back of a chair lay her lab coat, and her heart lurched painfully at the thought of Ackerbee's, where she'd last seen it, and of Wilf, who must have been the one to pack it away. Violet sat up, as though she recognized it too.

"My—my lab!" she said. "But these aren't my things," she added after a few seconds.

A proper full-sized rack filled with gleaming test tubes and beakers stood on one desk and laid out beside it were a pair of tongs, a selection of spatulas and a box that looked to be filled with glass rods. A heavy pestle and mortar made of white marble stood on another desk beside a wall-mounted magnifier, its lens as large as Tess's face. It had a handsome band of brass around it, which shone like it was freshly polished, and gearwheels down the side to adjust focus and clarity—it was something she'd never dreamed she'd own. She looked at Mr. Cleat. "I hope there hasn't been a mistake. I don't have any of this equipment—maybe there was a mix-up somewhere?"

"I told you this was a gift, didn't I? A present, from me to you."

Tess's mouth fell open as she took in the lab. "Thank you," she said. "I don't know what to say."

"What you've already said is plenty," Mr. Cleat assured her. "Now, does this room suit your needs?" He let the question hang as Tess looked around, her head slowly shaking from side to side.

"My last lab was in the basement classroom," she told him with a shrug. "It was mostly used for detention."

A warm laugh burst from Mr. Cleat. "I should think this is an improvement then."

"You could say so," Tess agreed, still looking around. She walked to the magnifier and ran her hands over its brass fittings and flywheels, almost afraid to properly touch it. "This is *really* for me?"

Mr. Cleat came to stand beside her. "The person in the shop said it was the top-range model. Will it do?"

Tess held her breath and let it out slowly. This equipment cost more than she could bear to think about. "It must have been very expensive," she said.

"Not too bad," Mr. Cleat said, unconcerned. "And if you find it useful, then it will be worth the price."

"It will be *brilliant*," Tess said. "Imagine the drawings I'm going to be able to make with this! I'll be able to see cell features, and crystal structures, and I'll be able to do a close-up study of—" Tess stopped short, almost clamping her hand over her mouth. She'd been about to say *a close-up study of the object Miss Ackerbee gave me.*

"A close-up study of what?" said Mr. Cleat, looking at Tess curiously.

"Of Violet," Tess said, thinking fast. "But I didn't want you to think I was cruel."

Mr. Cleat's face twisted in distaste. "What on earth for? Don't you see enough of her?"

"But I'd be able to do detailed anatomy sketches," said Tess, improvising. "I could do a study of her eyes, maybe, and I've always wanted to take a closer look at her leg joints—"

"Yes, yes!" Mr. Cleat said quickly, drowning out Tess's words. "That all sounds wonderful. And it'll keep you busy, at least. Too busy to be sad, I hope."

Violet shrank back against Tess's scalp as Tess looked up at Mr. Cleat. "I'm still going to miss my home," she said after a moment or two. "No fancy equipment is going to fix that."

"But this is your home, Tess," Mr. Cleat replied. There was a strange light in his eyes. "You won't be returning to

Ackerbee's. So I did my best to bring some of Ackerbee's to you."

"And I said thank you," Tess retorted, suddenly lacking the courage to raise her voice.

"The best thanks is seeing you in here, content and productive," he said. "Why not pick up on that experiment you were working on a few months ago, trying to make a flame burn with several different colors at the same time? That looked promising."

Tess stared at him. "How do you know about that?" A thought clicked into place and her gaze fell on her experiments notebook for a moment before returning to Mr. Cleat's face. "Have you been looking through my notes?"

"Only the last few entries," Mr. Cleat said, unfazed. "I wanted to get a sense of what sort of thing you were interested in." He gave Tess a sidelong glance. "Just making sure I hadn't wasted my money equipping you with the lab of your dreams."

Tess thrummed with rage. Her notes were private; he'd had no business looking at them. "No, of course not," she found herself saying. "Thank you. But please don't look in my notebook again."

"If you insist," Mr. Cleat said with a sigh. "Though I *am* interested in your work, you know. You have talent. And you have what every scientist needs—attention to detail, methodical thinking and seemingly endless patience." He raised an eyebrow. "With objects, at least. Not so much with people, I see."

Tess felt her cheeks grow hot. "I didn't mean—"

"It doesn't matter," Mr. Cleat said, backing toward the door. "It's getting late, so I'll bid you good night. I'm looking forward to seeing what sort of work you produce in here— and of course if there's anything you need, just let me know. I'm happy to be a patron of scientific inquiry." He raised the corner of his mouth in a half grin.

"I'm not really *that* good. I just sort of make things up as I go along and see where I end up." Tess put one hand on the fabric of her old lab coat, hoping it would help her to feel less light-headed and more solid.

"But that's how most of these world-changing discoveries were made, my dear," Mr. Cleat replied as he opened the door. "Completely by accident or while searching for something else."

"Really?"

"Of course. Remind me, once you're happily settled here, to tell you about some of the stuff I like to tinker with. Who knows, maybe you'll be able to take my work to new heights. Now *that* would be worthy repayment for this gift."

"All right," Tess replied, because she couldn't think of anything better to say.

"Until tomorrow, then," Mr. Cleat said. "Sleep well. I hope the demons of indigestion don't keep you awake all night as Old Thistlebum—" He stopped himself, drawing his lips tight as he tried to hold back his mirth, and raising his eyebrows at Tess. "I mean, Mrs. Thistleton, of course, had feared," he continued after a beat.

Tess, despite everything, managed a watery grin. "I'll try my best," she told him.

"Good enough for me." He gave her one final nod, then slipped out of the room, leaving the door standing open.

Tess turned back to face her new lab. She reached out to touch her coat again, the sad pressure in her head beginning to build once more, and then—

"Before I forget," came Mr. Cleat's voice from behind her. Tess jumped and let out a yelp as she turned to see him standing in the doorway. "Oh! I'm so sorry," he said, stepping into the lab again. He held out a hand; clutched between two fingers was a small key. "I just wanted to give you this—the key to the room. So you have the security of leaving your experiments running, knowing they won't be disturbed." He paused, shrugging. "Or of storing things here if you wanted to." His voice was light, the words an afterthought.

Tess took it from him with a nod and slipped it into her cardigan pocket. It touched the object hidden there with a tiny *clink* of metal against metal, but Tess glanced up at Mr. Cleat; he gave no sign of having heard it. "Thanks," she said finally. Her heart was still thudding fast.

"And now I'll say a proper good night," he said. "One where I'll actually go away rather than frighten you silly just before bed." He gave her an apologetic look and ducked out of the door before she had a chance to reply.

Tess waited a few minutes, then gathered up her experiments notebook and her lab coat. She slid the notebook into one of the coat's pockets before putting it on, burying her nose in its frayed collar and feeling for its loose button, third from the top, which had always hung by a thread. Violet began her slow, careful trek from the top of her head to the space just above her collarbone. Tess kissed her finger and tapped Violet gently with it and the spider curled up, content.

Then Tess turned off the lights and closed the door. As she turned away, ready to make her way to her too-big, too-empty room upstairs, she saw Millie approaching from the far end of the corridor, her arms full of folded laundry. Tess stood back to let her pass.

"Good night, miss," Millie whispered as she went by. Then she paused to look at Tess's collar with bright, interested eyes. "And good night to you too, Miss Violet," she added, glancing up at Tess and giving her a warm grin.

Then Millie was gone, but Tess clung fast to her smile—the only bright thing to have happened on an otherwise terrible day—for long into the night.

Dear Tess,

It's sixteen days now since you left here and there's still no letter from you so I suppose you forgot to write? I know you said you'd write every day, but maybe once a week would be easier. Let me know when you reply, then, what day you're going to write from now on so that I can stop watching the letter box. I think Miss Whipstead thinks there's something wrong with me, because I've been sitting in the porch every morning waiting for the post to fall on the mat, and those tiles are cold. Especially when I'm still in my nightie!

Maybe there is something wrong with me.

Anyway. So. Things without you are awful. Eunice

has gone right off her food. Even Prissy and Prossy aren't
themselves (which isn't completely bad as they've been a bit
less annoying than normal) and I think it's safe to say that
everyone misses you.

Miss Ackerbee looks like she's covered in dust. She's gray
and sad and slow and she's started to forget things. And
Miss Whipstead is even whippier than usual, but Angela
Goody reckons she saw her wiping tears off her face last
Wednesday, and Miss Whipstead got really snitty with
Angela when she asked her what was wrong—

The paper Wilf was writing on suddenly vanished from underneath her pen, leaving a streak of ink across the page.

"Wilhelmina Siddons," came Rebecca's voice. "Have you been paying attention?"

Wilf looked up. Rebecca—or Miss Whipstead, as she was from the hours of 8 a.m. to 1 p.m., Monday to Friday—stood over her, the letter Wilf had been writing held between two fingers.

"Miss," Wilf said. "I was just—just making some notes."

Rebecca gave a slow blink. "The current capital of the Briternian Isles, please, Wilhelmina," she said.

"Er," Wilf replied, trying to think. She cast her gaze around in desperation and caught the eye of Eunice, who mouthed the answer. "Er, Cardiff, miss?" she said, looking

61

back at Rebecca and wondering if Eunice had just dropped her in it.

"Good guess," Rebecca replied coolly.

A wave of yawns whispered round the room and Rebecca struggled not to join in. The day was warm and the sun was out and nobody wanted to learn about which corner of the Briternian Isles was most famous for its dairy farming.

"All right," said Rebecca, folding up Wilf's letter and tucking it into her pocket. She turned away from Wilf's desk and strode toward the top of the room. "We'll finish early for the day." An excited clamor immediately began. "Miss Siddons! You'll stay behind, please."

The children began to file out, Rebecca issuing gentle reprimands here and there as she spotted untied shoelaces or dirty faces, and finally the only two people left were her and Wilf.

"So," Rebecca began, taking a seat at the desk beside Wilf's. "You miss her."

"Miss who?" Wilf chewed on the inside of her lip, pulling at a long splinter peeling away from her desk.

"Leave that alone, please," said Rebecca, nodding at the desk with her eyebrows raised. Wilf pulled her hand away and folded her arms. "And you know who," Rebecca continued.

"Not even a letter," Wilf said, still not looking at Rebecca.

"So she doesn't miss *me,* that's for sure. Off scoffing ice cream every hour of the day, no doubt. Or too busy taking piano lessons, or horse riding, or something."

"Wilf," chided Rebecca gently. "You know that's rubbish."

"Is it?" Wilf finally turned to face her teacher. Her eyes were heavy.

"Of course! There could be a hundred reasons why Tess hasn't written." *None of them good,* Rebecca continued, but she kept that part to herself. "She's adjusting to an entirely new life. It's hard."

"It's hard, all right," said Wilf, looking away again.

"We miss her too, you know," said Rebecca. "Miss Ackerbee and me. Being without Tess . . ." Her voice trailed off because she didn't trust it to continue.

"I just wanted to let her know I hadn't forgotten her," Wilf began, her voice so low Rebecca had to strain to hear it. "I don't forget my friends."

Rebecca reached into her pocket and fished out Wilf's letter. "Sorry for making your pen slip," she told her. "But here you are. You can finish it while we're waiting to see Dr. Biggs."

Wilf looked up at Rebecca, her face horror-struck. "That's not today, is it?"

"Had you forgotten? Again?"

"Well, *obviously,*" Wilf muttered, rolling her eyes.

"Come on," said Rebecca, getting to her feet. "We have to be there by two."

Fifteen minutes later, Rebecca and Wilf convened in the front porch of Ackerbee's Home for Lost and Foundlings and Rebecca couldn't resist straightening Wilf's hat and smoothing out the collar of her coat before she put her hand on the front-door bolt. "Ready?" she asked her charge, and as Wilf nodded, she pulled open the door.

Just as she was about to step through, Wilf spoke. "Miss Whipstead, you are trying to get Tess back. Aren't you?"

Rebecca stopped in her tracks, squinting at Wilf—the day outside was bright—and considered her answer carefully.

"Yes. Of course we are. We're doing everything we can. Why do you ask?" She kept her voice low.

"Because something's wrong," Wilf said, looking up at her teacher with anxious eyes. "You know it too."

Rebecca met Wilf's gaze, and the girl swallowed hard. "Do you even know where she is?"

"We have a post office box number," Rebecca replied after a moment. "No address but she's got to be somewhere in the city." She cleared her throat and straightened a little, giving Wilf a sympathetic look. "Miss Ackerbee and I are constrained by the law, Wilf, but we're doing our best, despite appearances. Can you trust us?" She paused. "Please?"

Wilf considered this for a moment and nodded.

"Let's be off then," Rebecca said. "And try not to worry."

But as the steam car clanked its way out into the suburbs of Hurdleford, Wilf leaned her head against the cool glass of the window and thought—about Tess, about Violet and about ways to bring them home.

"I bet Wilf's forgotten her doctor's appointment again," Tess said with a fond grin. "She always does."

"Nothing serious, I hope?" Millie replied. She was dusting in the library—or pretending to. Tess stood at a nearby bookshelf, running her fingers along the spines.

"She's got something to do with sugar in the blood," Tess answered as Violet crawled onto her fingers. "She has to have tests every week or two, just to see how things are."

Millie pursed her lips sympathetically. "That sounds like an inconvenience. But I'm sure she bears up as well as can be expected."

Tess chuckled, thinking of Wilf's irritated face. "She does her best."

"Do you like reading, miss?" Millie said, turning to Tess. "It's just you spend a lot of time in here, despite having that fancy experiment room all to yourself."

"I like it in here because there are fewer interruptions,"

Tess said. "Mr. Cleat is *forever* coming into the lab with something or other to tell me. I like having space to think and he doesn't let me do very much of it." As she spoke, her eyes fell on a book with a gold-plated title on the spine. *The Secret Garden,* she read. She blinked and frowned at it, then reached up to pull it out.

Millie began to wipe the nonexistent dust off the next shelf down. "I suppose he must be interested in you, miss. Trying his best, I mean."

Tess sighed, running her hands over the front cover of her book as she spoke. "Perhaps. It feels more like he's trying to catch me out, though doing what I can't imagine. And I've asked you a hundred times, Millie. Call me Tess. Please?"

"I'll try, miss," Millie replied with a wink.

Tess took a seat at a nearby table, settled Violet on her head and pulled her experiments notebook out of her pocket. She laid *The Secret Garden* flat on the table and flipped to the back of her notebook, where she'd done some drawings of the object she'd brought with her from Ackerbee's. She'd been studying the pattern on its body through her magnifier in the lab, but with Mr. Cleat's tendency to burst in at unexpected moments, she'd never had time to properly sit and look at her sketches. There had to be a pattern but so far it had evaded her.

She tried to focus but her eyes kept drifting toward the book she'd chosen from the shelf. Beneath its title there was a picture of a girl kneeling on the ground, holding what looked like a flower. Tess picked up the book and angled it, letting the light flash off the gilding.

"What's that, miss?" Millie asked.

"*The Secret Garden,*" Tess replied. "Have you read it, Millie? I've never heard of it."

Millie gave a quiet snort. "I don't read, miss. I never get time. I hardly have time to—"

Her words were cut off by sudden, quick footsteps outside the library door. Tess sat up, her spine stiffening as she shoved her notes away. Millie stood to attention and then Mrs. Thistleton entered the room with the speed of a pouncing cat.

"Millicent, I thought I told you to mop the lobby floor this morning." Mrs. Thistleton's voice was like ice.

"Yes, ma'am, I was just—"

"I don't want to hear it. Just get to work, please." Millie stood frozen for a moment, glancing at her half-polished shelves. "Now, if you don't mind!"

"Yes, Mrs. Thistleton," Millie said, gathering up her polishing things. She nodded at Tess, who waved sadly as she disappeared through the door.

"Good day to you," Mrs. Thistleton muttered, fixing Tess with a glare as she left the room. Tess didn't have time to reply.

She let out a breath as Mrs. Thistleton's footsteps vanished into silence. "Somehow," she whispered to Violet, "I get the feeling that woman *really* doesn't like me."

With a sigh, Tess picked up *The Secret Garden* and stroked its cover again. Then, not quite knowing why, she stood up and walked to the nearest window seat, where she tucked herself up and started to read.

9

Tess sat in her lab at Roedeer Lodge, her magnifier propped at the perfect angle. She focused on losing herself in the swirls of the metal object on her desk, thinking of Ackerbee's all the while. She'd been gone for almost three weeks now, and the object felt like her last link to home. She'd been neglecting her study of it since she'd taken *The Secret Garden* from Mr. Cleat's library. Somehow, despite not liking the story very much, Tess could hardly leave the book out of her hand.

She pulled off her glasses, rubbed hard at her eyes and then opened them wide. The metal object sat on the desk and Tess couldn't help but feel it was displeased with her. *I'm not here to read books about spoiled rich girls,* she told herself. *I'm here to find out what this is. Don't forget.* Mr. Cleat was supposed to have an early meeting at his office this morning and Tess knew this was her chance to get some work done without any unwelcome interruptions.

"All right. Come on then," she whispered to the object, placing it in the hollow of her palm. It sat there, dark brown against her light brown skin, as though it had been made for it, warming to her touch like something alive. *Whatever this is, it came with me,* Tess told herself. *Which means—if Miss Ackerbee's not completely off her rocker—that it must have come from another world too.* She shuddered, sudden fear gripping her—and not just fear of Mr. Cleat and what he might want by bringing her here, but fear of *herself,* of the thing she held in her hand. *I've been really stupid,* she thought, trembling a little. *I should have run with Rebecca while I had the chance.*

"Too late for that now," she whispered to herself—and to Violet, who crawled onto the back of her free hand, gazing up at her with quiet concern. Tess closed her eyes, remembering her last day at home and what she'd learned about herself. *If I could pop in and out of this world when I was little, I wonder if I can still do it.* She squeezed her eyes more tightly shut, as if that would help her to think. *Perhaps all I have to do is remember how.*

Several minutes passed. The only result of Tess's efforts was a painful cramp in her face. Then a knock sounded on the door, sudden enough to make her jump; instinctively, she shoved the object into her pocket.

"Are you in?" said Mr. Cleat, opening the door and sticking his head into the room without being asked to. "I wondered if you'd had breakfast," he continued.

Tess swallowed, closing her experiments notebook; her throat was suddenly dry. *Not again! Can't you leave me in peace, just once?*

"I—yes, thanks," she replied a little croakily. "I had some porridge earlier."

"Piffle," said Mr. Cleat, waving a hand. "Come on. I've got Cook to make us some syrup cakes. For a treat. You need to try one."

"I should really—"

"I'm not taking no for an answer," Mr. Cleat continued before Tess could finish. "These cakes are just too tasty." He gave her a pleading look. "Don't make me eat them all myself."

Tess did her best to smile. "All right," she said, slipping down from her stool. On the pretext of taking off her lab coat, she shoved her notebook into her cardigan pocket, where it sat beside the metal object, as concealed as it could be. She tried to look as casual as possible, then worried that made her look guilty instead.

She draped the lab coat over the back of her chair and Mr. Cleat turned his nose up at it while holding the door open for her. "That reminds me, I really must get you a new lab coat. A proper white one. One that's clean and not threadbare." He paused. "This reminds me of that scruffy place you came from," he finished in a careless tone.

Tess felt her throat tighten and her teeth clench for a moment. "Thanks, but I like this one," she replied, ducking out under his arm. "And Ackerbee's is *not* scruffy," she added in an undertone, though part of her knew that wasn't true.

"If you say so," Mr. Cleat replied.

They left the room and Tess locked it behind them, keeping one eye on Mr. Cleat. He gave her a bright smile when she turned to him and Tess returned it before it had occurred to her not to. She pocketed her key and stood there feeling awkward.

"Now, ready for the off?" he asked, extending his arm politely. Tess took it gingerly. "I hope you've brought your appetite."

"Can I ask you something?" said Tess as they walked.

"You may. But only if it's not something spelling-related," he told her. "I'm terrible with that sort of nonsense."

"No, nothing like that," Tess said, looking away. "I'm just wondering—well, I'm wondering whether you've heard from Miss Ackerbee yet?"

Mr. Cleat frowned, looking concerned. "What do you mean?"

"It's just she hasn't written." She looked back at him. "She said she would."

"Oh yes. Of course. No, my dear. Not yet," Mr. Cleat said. "I expect she will, though. Never fear. Parents—or the next-best thing—never forget their children. Isn't that right?"

"I suppose so," Tess said, a ball of surprised disappointment rolling down into her tummy. "I wouldn't really know."

Mr. Cleat gave her an odd look, a mix of apologetic and something else, something not so nice. "I forgot, Tess. Forgive me. I've long been without my parents too, but somehow I don't always remember that younger people carry the same burden."

Tess glanced at him. "I'm sorry—I didn't know. About your family."

"Ancient history now," Mr. Cleat said with a jaunty-seeming shrug, though there was a brittleness in his tone that Tess couldn't miss. "Think no more of it."

"I just wish I knew something about them," Tess said. "My parents, I mean. When they were born, where they got married, if they did. It doesn't make sense. If there are records of *me*, why not of them?"

"You're just registered as 'foundling,' my dear," Mr. Cleat said, looking at her sympathetically. "Parents unknown. Your good Miss Ackerbee simply had your name."

"But you told me you had my birth certificate," said Tess, frowning. "How can you have one of those if my parents didn't register me?"

"It's a mystery all right," Mr. Cleat replied lightly. "I suppose things work differently when you're a lady like Miss Ackerbee, well known for taking in strays. Rules get bent, so on and so forth." His tone seemed to suggest he'd said all he was going to say on the subject for now and Tess squashed back her frustration as he continued. "Now it's my turn to ask a question. Aren't you happy here, Tess?"

"I—um. Well, it's very nice," Tess said, her voice small.

"That's good," Mr. Cleat replied. "Is everyone being kind to you? Mrs. Thistleton? Her staff?"

Tess glanced at him, but his eyes seemed interested, even kind. "Yes," she answered, not quite truthfully. Mrs. Thistleton, Tess had often thought, was a very well named woman. Everything about her was thistly, even her hair.

"I'm pleased," he said with a sigh. "I wish I could say the same. Mrs. Thistleton doesn't seem to like me at *all*."

"What do you mean?" Tess asked. From what she had seen, the opposite seemed to be true.

"Oh, you know—I'm always late for this, or late for that, or not eating a proper dinner and filling up on pudding, or working too hard, or not working enough. I simply feel like I can't win." He gave another heavy sigh.

Before she knew it, Tess found herself grinning. "Well, you *do* eat a lot of pudding," she said, just as they reached the dining room.

"There's no such thing as too much pudding," he declared, pushing open the door. "Now, speaking of which. Are you ready to tuck in?"

Tess followed him into the room, feeling awkward. "Can I ask one more thing?"

"Hm?" Mr. Cleat turned, his eyebrows raised.

"When can I go home? I mean, to Ackerbee's. For a visit," she asked. His mouth fell open and he frowned as she continued. "You promised I could. You said I could go whenever I wanted."

"Ah." He scratched at his chin and Tess got a look at his ring again. The letters engraved on it, she now saw, were *I* and *H,* intertwined; she wondered, briefly, what they stood for. "I did, didn't I?"

"I just miss my friends," Tess said, realizing as she said it how true it was.

Mr. Cleat's frown smoothed out. "Friends come and go, Tess. I think you need to draw a line underneath that part of your life. Your future lies elsewhere now."

Tess stared at him. "What? But—"

"You've been through a lot lately, don't forget," he interjected, and something in his tone made Tess's skin prickle. He walked to the head of the table, pulled out his chair and settled himself into it. "You've had a lot of upheaval, all at once. It would be best to avoid even more of it, wouldn't you agree?"

Tess pulled out her own chair. The lightheartedness of

a few moments before had gone, like a candle snuffed out, and she began to wonder whether it had ever existed at all. *Everything keeps shifting,* she thought. *I wish things would just be, without changing—but nothing seems real here.*

"Perhaps we can think about it in a month or two," said Mr. Cleat as Tess sat down. "Let's get you settled in first and then we can see. It may be that Miss Ackerbee is too busy to write and she wouldn't welcome a visit. Perhaps she's trying to help you, Tess, by giving you the freedom to move on. I'll bet that's what it is."

Tess simply stared at the empty plate in front of her.

Mr. Cleat forked a syrup cake onto her dish. "Let's hear no more about it for now," he said, licking some treacly ooze from his thumb. "Get stuck in. They're better when they're warm."

Tess poked at her cake while Mr. Cleat polished his off and helped himself to a second, and she wondered if he was right: her mind had felt out of focus since she'd arrived at Roedeer Lodge, and it was spinning now. She was in a strange new place. Perhaps it was only to be expected that she'd be confused and unsettled—and anyway, going back to Ackerbee's wouldn't change the fact that she'd have to return here in the end.

"May I leave the table?" Tess asked after a few minutes.

"You have free run of the house, Tess," Mr. Cleat replied,

wiping his mouth with a napkin. He gave her a smile that was warm but short-lived. "You don't need permission."

She pushed back her chair. "Thanks," she muttered. "For the cake." Mr. Cleat nodded, spearing the last cake with his fork. He waved her goodbye with it.

Tess left the room and wandered toward the black-and-white tiles of the front lobby. It felt like a hundred years had passed since she'd first seen them. She checked her pocket for the note with the phone number of Ackerbee's on it, and that was enough to bolster her spirits. *I will get back,* she told herself. *I will. Despite what he says, I know where my home is. I know what's real.*

Just then the sudden *clang-clang* of the front doorbell shattered the silence of the house. Tess yanked her hand out of her pocket and ran.

10

Tess HURTLED ACROSS THE FLOOR TOWARD THE FRONT DOOR OF
Roedeer Lodge as the bell jangled a second time. *Finally! I'm
going to get to the post before Mrs. Thistleton!* But as she reached
the inner doors leading to the vestibule, the housekeeper appeared from behind a large potted plant, armed with a damp
cloth and a vicious expression. Tess leaped back as though
she'd been stung.

"Miss de Sousa," the housekeeper said, running the cloth
over one of the plant's wide, glossy leaves.

"You even dust the *plants*?" Tess gasped in disbelief.

Mrs. Thistleton simply sniffed in reply, tucking the cloth
under one arm as she reached out to unlock the front door.
The postman stood on the step, a bundle of letters in his

hands. It was tied with string and all Tess could see were the backs of the envelopes, which gave no clue as to what address these letters bore—nothing to add to Tess's meager knowledge of where she was.

"Just this?" Mrs. Thistleton said, and the postman nodded.

"No parcels today, missis," he confirmed.

"Very good." Mrs. Thistleton began to close the door again.

"Wait!" Tess shouted, trying to push past Mrs. Thistleton. "Is there anything for me? From Miss Ackerbee? Of Ackerbee's Home for Lost and Foundlings?"

The postman looked away from Tess and glanced toward Mrs. Thistleton. He looked back at Tess again with guilty eyes.

"I—er. I don't believe so, miss. No." He cleared his throat and pulled his cap down low before turning away, his steps crunching over the gravel.

"Wait!" Tess called. *"Please!"* But the man was already through the gate and locking it behind him. He gave Tess one last look and then climbed into the cab of his van. It trundled down the road and out of sight, its steam engine hissing.

"I'll thank you to get out of my way," Mrs. Thistleton said, bumping against Tess, keeping the bundle of letters tight to her chest.

"It's been almost three weeks!" Tess said, barely aware she'd spoken out loud. "Why hasn't anyone written?"

Mrs. Thistleton stood at a table in the vestibule, deftly flicking through the post. "Children are fickle, I suppose," she said in a light tone. "They forget. Perhaps you thought you were more important to them than in fact you were."

Tess turned to face her. "Wilf would *never* forget me."

Mrs. Thistleton looked up and gave a thin-lipped, short-lived smile. "If you'll excuse me, I need to go through this correspondence and sort Mr. Cleat's from mine. I'm sure you have plenty to do to keep yourself entertained in your . . . *laboratory.*"

"So there is nothing for me?"

"Nothing, I'm afraid," Mrs. Thistleton said with a slight sigh.

"Please can I just look? For myself?"

"No, you may not," Mrs. Thistleton said, turning her nose up. "And close the door, please. You're letting in a draft." She turned away and began to cross the lobby, her shoes *click-clack*ing on the tiled floor.

"Did you even *send* my letters?" Tess called after her, but there was no response. "Of course you didn't," she said to herself as she banged the door shut. She closed her eyes and put her hot forehead against the cold metal of the lock, then pulled the door open again. She strode out of the house, pulling her cardigan tight around her body. Violet, nestled above Tess's collarbone and almost hidden by a swath of her long dark hair, stirred as if in protest at the sudden change in temperature.

Tess crunched her way across the gravel driveway and looked back at the house. The windows of its upper floors flashed as they reflected the sunlight, and ivy rustled in the slight breeze. All was still and Tess knew she couldn't bear to go back inside. She'd never had more space to call her own than she had here, but she had never felt so trapped.

Then an idea popped into her head. "It's about time we went on an expedition. Right, girl?" she whispered to Violet, who perked up, curling a leg out of Tess's collar as though testing the air. Tess turned and made for the garden. It was bounded by a neatly clipped hedge, and at its far end there was another gate, which gave way to the scrubbier, more overgrown property beyond. Tess made straight for it.

She kept an eye on the house as she picked her way around the perimeter of the garden. The gate was padlocked shut, the iron bars themselves rusted with age and neglect, but beyond it Tess could see rolling greenness and a distant tree line. Mrs. Thistleton had told her she was never to go beyond this locked gate but it was too tempting to resist.

"Ready, Violet?" she whispered, and then, pulling her skirt up over her knees, Tess began to climb. She placed a foot on a curl of ironwork at the bottom of the gate and hauled herself up, using an overhanging branch to get high enough to sling one leg over the top. Quickly she dropped to the ground on the far side of the gate, where she caught her breath, wiped her hands on her cardigan and looked around.

She found herself in a field, the grass almost to her knees and heavy with moisture. Before long she had reached the trees, their branches so old and thick with leaves that they almost touched the ground. She turned and saw that she had almost lost sight of Roedeer Lodge—just the tops of the turrets and the bristle of chimneys at either end of the roof were visible beyond the high hedge around the garden, and the gate Tess had climbed was hidden among the shadows. Facing forward again, she stepped through the crackling un-dergrowth to see a sheltered path, long unused, which led away through the forest. She took the deepest breath she'd taken since she left Ackerbee's.

Suddenly she felt Violet stand to attention.

"What's up, girl?" she said, keeping her voice low. Violet simply thrummed in response, like a plucked string. Tess kept walking, and ten steps later, she finally saw what the spider had spotted.

A turn in the path led toward an old ivy-choked building buried amid the trees like something that had fallen from the pocket of a passing giant. Its roof was domed, with a segment missing from it almost like a cake with a slice cut out. The building was octagonal, with a tall pointed window on each face and a door that had been beaten open a little, either by bandits, or the weather, or both. Tess was cautious as she approached.

She paused to pick up a fallen branch as she drew close to the door and she hefted it in her right hand as she used her left to push the door all the way open. Tess tumbled through into the interior of—of *what* exactly?

Four long wooden benches sat on either side of a narrow aisle, facing a raised platform of bare stone with a window stretching above it. Once, the window had probably been filled with color and light; now it was dirty and broken, branches poking through the smashed pane. A rickety worm-eaten lectern sat at one side of the platform, most of its boards missing.

Tess looked around. Each of the windows on the eight faces of the building was made up of small, intricate colored panes, though they were dull in the shadow of the overgrown trees. The whole place was filled with windblown leaves and dotted with rancid pools of rainwater, and some of the ceiling boards near the back had fallen through, giving an unnerving glimpse into darkness overhead. Tess had the sensation of space and silence up there, and the softness of decay. She put her branch on the floor as gently as possible, finally understanding where she was.

It's an old chapel, or something similar, she thought, a smile breaking over her face for the first time in what felt like days. *It doesn't look as though anyone even knows it's here anymore.* "And it's perfect," she whispered into the silence.

In A Bower Seat In An Otherwise Empty Garden, Tess Was sitting cross-legged. In her lap was her borrowed copy of *The Secret Garden* and she looked to be reading it. Her eyes were tracing the lines and her hand occasionally turned a page, but she hadn't taken anything in for the last chapter or two.

It was strange; when she was supposed to be thinking about the object, the book proved a huge distraction, but whenever she tried to read the book, all she could think about was the object. She'd spent hours in the old chapel the previous day examining the small metal object in as much detail as she could manage in the dim light, but she'd discovered nothing. She'd been sure that finding the space to think freely would lead immediately to a breakthrough, but it seemed things weren't going to be as easy as that.

She sighed. *Dear Wilf,* she wrote, in her mind. *Today was just as boring as yesterday, and that was every bit as boring as the day before. I wish I'd never come here. I wish I'd never left you. I wish—*

"Nice day for it," came Mr. Cleat's voice, intruding on her thoughts.

Tess scrambled to undo her folded legs and sit more properly, dropping her book in the process, and Mr. Cleat laughed. He bent to pick it up, wiping a little loose soil from its cover.

"Ah. *The Secret Garden,*" he said, handing it back to her. "One of my favorites too. This was mine, as a boy."

"Yes," said Tess, who could hardly admit to being halfway through it with no knowledge at all of what it was about. "It's, um . . . very good." She settled herself on the seat and Mr. Cleat nudged in beside her.

"Can I ask what drew you to it?" He turned to her with a strange look in his eye, like he wanted to laugh but didn't want to offend her and was doing his best to hide it.

Tess shrugged. "No real reason. I liked the picture of the girl on the cover and I like gardens . . ." Her voice trailed off and she couldn't help but feel silly.

"Don't go digging up my flower beds looking for buried keys now," he said with a note of good-natured teasing in his voice. Tess smiled but looked away as quickly as she could. Her gaze fell on Mr. Cleat's hand, outstretched on his knee. His ring with its mysterious engraved initials glinted up at her from his smallest finger.

"I've seen you observing this before," Mr. Cleat said, lifting his hand. "Sadly it doesn't come off anymore, or I'd let you take a closer look."

"Oh, that's all right," Tess replied, feeling her face grow hot. She and Mr. Cleat hadn't really spoken since he'd told her she couldn't visit Ackerbee's and something inside her was still bruised from that encounter. She hoped he'd be going soon.

"Can you make out the letters?" he asked, holding his hand toward her. He nudged the ring with his thumb, from behind. "They're a capital *I* and *H,* linked together."

"Yes, I see," said Tess, glancing politely. "Someone's initials?"

"A lost love?" Mr. Cleat said with a chuckle. "Nothing so poetic, I'm afraid. They are the initials of a club of which I'm a member. I was a founding member, in fact."

"Oh?" Tess said, hoping she sounded interested.

"It stands for the Interdimensional Harmonics Society," Mr. Cleat continued, despite Tess not having asked him to. "Have you heard of it?"

Something uncomfortable prickled behind Tess's ear and it took her a moment to realize it was just Violet. "Um," she began. "No, I'm afraid not." She allowed Violet to crawl onto her hand before depositing the spider on top of her head.

"It's a science, I suppose," Mr. Cleat said, pausing only briefly as he watched Violet's movements, as though unsure whether she was going to fling herself at him, fangs bared, or not. Once it seemed clear the only thing Violet was hunting was a comfortable place to nap, he relaxed. "A type of experimental research," he continued. "Into alternate realities."

Tess felt like someone had sucked all the air out of the garden. Her ears began to ring, faintly at first but rapidly growing louder. "I—I beg your pardon?" she managed to say. Her heart started a rapid *thunk-thunk-thunk* as she tried to stay calm.

"I know it seems nonsensical," Mr. Cleat said with a chuckle. "Alternate realities? Who could possibly have any interest in such a dusty theory? Yet it seems there's life in the old dog yet. Our membership numbers hold steady, year on year. We're hoping 1941 will be our best year to date." He waggled his ring-bearing finger in front of his eye, as though trying to make the letters dance. "But why am I boring you with all this?" He placed his palms flat on his thighs, getting ready to push himself into a standing position. "I should leave you to your reading." He nodded at the book and gave Tess a quick smile.

"No—wait!" Tess said as Mr. Cleat began to rise. He turned

back to her, looking surprised. "I am interested. What does it mean, alternate realities?" She blinked and tried to look simply curious, instead of bristling and on her guard.

"Well," Mr. Cleat began, sinking back into the bower seat. "It's a bit complicated." He looked down at his own hands, locking his fingers tightly together as he spoke. "I suppose you could say there are lots of theories around the idea of alternate realities—some people think there are universes wrapped up together like balls of string, and some scientists postulate that universes fit together something like a jigsaw puzzle, only in dimensions we can't even conceive of. Many people feel the realities work like a spider's web: a disturbance at one point leads to tremors being felt in many other places, just as a spider knows when a fly gets stuck in its trap."

He paused, as if thinking. "But the theory we prefer in the Society is the one that imagines the layers of reality like a stack of paper, each sheet with a tiny cushion of air between the page above it and below it, so that the sheets are all close by one another, but none are actually touching. Does that make sense?" He glanced at her and she tried to cover her fear with her growing interest.

Mr. Cleat continued, seemingly oblivious. "And each sheet, potentially stretching to infinity in all directions, is a reality. A world, if you like. Just as this one is." He released one hand and waved it around, taking in the house and garden. "Each sheet—or each reality—might be as different from one another as you and I are, or they might be almost exact copies of one another save for one tiny but crucial detail. Nobody really knows for certain."

"But where did they all come from?" Tess asked. "The theories, I mean."

"Idle curiosity mostly," Mr. Cleat said with a half grin. "But interest in the concept of multiple realities began in earnest about thirty-three years ago, or thereabouts. Around 1908. I'm not old enough to remember the early days"—he cleared his throat—"but when I was about twelve, I took a more personal interest in it. My father—well, it was his interest really, and then it became mine."

Tess frowned at him. "I don't think I understand."

Mr. Cleat began to explain, observing Tess closely as he spoke. "In 1908, in a distant part of the Rus Empire, a gigantic explosion occurred one quiet day completely out of the blue. It left no crater and thankfully claimed no lives because of the location's remoteness. At first, nobody could explain it. Theories sprang up about what caused it almost straightaway, of course, each more outlandish than the last, but one—the one I believe to be true—was that the event was an echo of something that took place in another reality. Something so significant that it left ripples, or impressions, in the realities surrounding it."

"Like a pencil nib leaving a mark on the page beneath it, if you lean too heavily," Tess said before she could help herself. Mr. Cleat's face brightened.

"Exactly so. *Exactly* so. I couldn't have put it better myself," he told her.

"And that was enough to make people think that there was more than one reality?" Tess sounded dubious.

"I think the idea had been floated before," Mr. Cleat said. "But it became fashionable, I suppose, after that time." He cleared his throat and looked at his hands again.

"So the different sheets of paper—the different realities," Tess said, enthusiasm getting the better of her caution, "that's the interdimensional bit." She gave him a questioning look.

"Bingo," replied Mr. Cleat, looking pleased. "That's the interdimensional part—the different realities lying in layers, one on top of the other. We don't know for certain how far they extend, how many there are or"—Mr. Cleat blinked and focused intently on Tess—"how to get from one to the other, or if that's even something that can be done."

Tess shrugged, looking away. "Seems like it's impossible to know things like that," she said.

"And that's where the harmonics bit comes in," Mr. Cleat said, his tone casual and bright again. "The Society I belong to believes that radiophone technology can be used to send messages between realities—that in essence we can 'hear' between worlds, if we listen carefully enough." He paused, sitting back a little. "We came up with the name *harmonics* because we work with sound waves, and we're experimenting all the time with frequencies, trying to find one that can cross the void between worlds. We're certain it can be done." He paused to clear his throat again. "Or we believe it can."

Tess swallowed, her own throat suddenly sore, as though there were something in it that wanted to get out. "Do you mean there are people who don't believe it?"

Mr. Cleat laughed but it was cold and humorless. "You could say so," he said. "Most people think we're crackpots, sitting around tables in silence, holding hands, listening. But we know we're onto something."

"I'm sure you are," said Tess, hoping she sounded like she shared that opinion.

"At any rate," Mr. Cleat said, color rising to his cheeks, "I really had better get going now. I'm off to a Society meeting, actually. We're hoping to welcome our new members." He got to his feet, settling his jacket as he found his feet. "I'll be late home, so please let Old Nettleworth—whoops! I mean, Mrs. Thistleton, of course—know not to keep any dinner for me. I'll eat at the club." He gave Tess a conspiratorial wink.

"All—all right," Tess responded, not sure what else to say.

"Do enjoy the book. I'd be very happy for you to keep it if you'd like to." He gave her, and *The Secret Garden*, a strange sad smile. "My father gave it to me for my twelfth birthday.

He died later that year, so it means rather a lot to me, you see," he said, and then he was gone.

Tess watched him walk toward the house. As soon as he'd gone through the kitchen door and it had been closed behind him, she leaned her head against the bower and took several long shaky breaths. Violet clambered down to her comfort place, folding herself into the hollow of Tess's throat, and Tess felt her pulse start to slow.

He knew. Or he suspected, at least. Tess still didn't know what had led him to her, or how he'd known where to look for her, but she'd have to figure it out—and as quickly as she could. There was no way any of the discussion they'd just shared had been an innocent coincidence. Mr. Cleat had been sounding her out, trying to find a way in. Tess was almost glad she knew so little.

She kept her eyes on the house as she slipped her hand into her pocket. The object was there, along with Miss Ackerbee's folded note, and her experiments notebook was stuck in too for good measure. She gripped the cool metal, and as soon as she was certain the coast was clear, she darted out of the bower seat and made a run for the gate.

She was already halfway across the field before she remembered she'd left Mr. Cleat's book behind and she cursed herself. She hoped Mrs. Thistleton wouldn't come looking for her in the garden, find the book in the bower seat and figure out that Tess was somewhere close by. She wouldn't have put it past the woman to sit there, waiting, the book on her knee, for Tess to come back—and she could hardly explain what she was doing clambering back over the gate.

But since there was nothing she could do about it, Tess strode on, and soon she was through the trees and gone.

12

TESS WAS SLIGHTLY OUT OF BREATH BY THE TIME SHE REACHED THE chapel door. She paused to collect herself and to look around but everything seemed the same as it had been the last time she'd seen it. The place was completely deserted, quiet but for some birdsong seeping through a broken window. Somehow the peace helped her to slow her thoughts. The conversation with Mr. Cleat was sharp-edged, urgent; her mind whirled around it, trying to take it in. *I need to figure this thing out, and fast,* she told herself. *It's time to try again.*

She walked to the center of the chapel, her footsteps sounding loud in the silence, and looked up. What remained of the ceiling boards radiated from the point directly over her head to all eight walls of the small building; they dovetailed in the middle, fitting together perfectly. Once, the ceiling had been painted blue—some of it still remained—and in several other places dots or speckles of gold could be seen on the peeling boards. *Strange,* she thought. *It's domed on the outside, but flat in here. I wonder what's up there.* She pushed away her inner voice and tried to focus.

She looked down, focusing on the floor in front of her, and made her way to the furthest corner of the top pew. The wooden seat felt unpleasantly damp beneath her, and something nearby smelled terrible, but at least from here she had a clear view of the door and could take cover if someone happened to walk through it. She hoped that wouldn't happen: part of the benefit of finding this place was knowing that she wouldn't be disturbed.

Tess pulled her gaze away from the world outside the chapel and drew the object from her pocket. Placing it gently on the pew beside her, she fished out her notebook. She peered at the pencil drawings she'd made the day before, comparing them to the real thing. She'd managed to capture the lacy latticework of the metal, woven over and under like a braid, but it was the markings around the object's circumference that interested her now. There were eight of them, set into the device like the hour markings of a clock. They were all the same teardrop shape, but made of different materials. *What are you for?* Tess asked, frowning at them.

She reached up into her hair and pulled her pencil free.

Violet, as though curious, crawled slowly to the crown of her head and settled there, looking down on Tess's work as she quickly sketched the colors and textures of each marker. Some seemed to be rock, others metal, and two were shards of gemstone that glittered in the light. Experimentally, she tried pressing on each in turn—and sighed. She'd been hoping something would happen but the object remained quiet.

She put the object down again, took off her glasses to clean them on her dress and put them back on. She peered at the object, her eyes narrowing. Instinctively she held it with the tarnished marker uppermost; she couldn't have explained why.

And then she saw it.

An eight-pointed star, formed by the whirling whorls of metal. An eight-pointed star, right at the heart of the object in her hand. An eight-pointed star like the ceiling above her head.

Tess felt her pulse quicken. She flipped the object over to examine its underside, which gave her nothing new to go on; the pattern simply continued, as finely worked as the top. Then she turned it over again. Her eye was drawn once more to the center of the pattern, the point where it seemed to begin and end, and she ran the pad of her thumb across it. The metal shone beneath her touch as though many other fingers had stroked it in just the same way.

Tess lifted her thumb away from the metal and brought it

back to the center of the pattern. It hovered in the air above the object for a second or two and then she placed it down.

Immediately there was a gentle *whir* from the object and Tess pulled her thumb away. She watched openmouthed as the pattern—or what she'd taken for a pattern—revealed itself to be a tightly woven mechanism made of strands of metal, some as fine as a single hair. They began to move and spin, unraveling with purpose, their speed increasing until finally the whirring ceased. The machinery came to rest and a perfectly circular void with a shimmering veil flowing through it like running water was revealed at its heart.

Once this was done, the object seemed to fall still, as though it had done everything it wanted to do. The sparkling void remained, shining brightly in the gloom. Tess held her breath. Violet shrank against her scalp, trembling with anticipation.

Tess blinked and shoved her glasses up her nose. Then, because she couldn't think of anything better to do, she lifted the object to her left eye and looked through the void.

All she could see was—nothing. She could make out the patterned tiles on the chapel floor, and as she moved her head (keeping the object in front of her eye the whole time), she saw the pew beside her and a pile of hymnals, which—

Tess paused. *A pile of hymnals?* She dropped the object from her eye and stared at the pew beside her. There were no hymnals there. She tried to think logically. In a chapel as unused as this one, hymnbooks would rot and swell with damp, but the books she'd just seen through the star were straight-backed, neatly stacked, with gold lettering on their spines.

The window. Tess put the object back in front of her eye and turned to look at the nearest one. Instead of the broken, dirty thing she was expecting to see, she discovered a set of stained-glass panes half covered over with a shutter. Sunlight streamed through the uncovered half. It all looked odd, of course, through the flickering light of the void, but still. It was the same, but different.

She got to her feet, carefully keeping the void before her eye. She scanned the whole chapel, noting the lack of stray branches and leaves on the floor and the fact that the door was unbroken—though it was closed and bolted. On impulse, she glanced up at the ceiling; it was whole, with a steep, narrow wooden staircase leading from the back of the chapel up to a square trapdoor set into the ceiling boards. Tess couldn't see beyond the point where the stairs vanished into the shadows. There was also a beautiful pattern painted on the ceiling, a large eight-pointed star at the center and a constellation of smaller stars around it. It was hard to tell through the device, but Tess took a guess that they were painted in gold.

She drew a deep, shaky breath, feeling suddenly afraid, and forced herself to look back at the pew she'd been sitting on.

Through the shimmering haze, she saw a boy. He was sitting almost exactly where Tess had been and he had a book across his knees. On his shoulder was a handsome mouse, whose dark eyes sparkled at Tess. The boy was looking right at her, wide-eyed, and Tess gaped at him for the space of three or four breaths. Then he threw her a quick grin and raised his hand in a wave. Tess shrieked and dropped the object on the floor.

She stood for two or three seconds, aghast, staring at it, before falling to her knees and fumbling to pick it up.

"Don't be broken, don't be broken, please don't be broken," she whispered. It had landed near a pool of rainwater, but a quick examination of its surface seemed to show no real damage. With trembling fingers, she raised it to her eye again.

The boy was still there.

He held up one finger and Tess held her breath. Then he flipped to the back of the book he'd had across his lap and wrote something on the blank endpapers with a stub of pencil. When he was finished, he displayed it for Tess to see.

IT'S ALL RIGHT, Tess read.

She stared at him, hardly daring to think. Through the void, the boy grinned. His mouse scampered from his shoulder to sit on top of his head, where he kept lookout, his nose twitching constantly. Tess felt Violet in just the same place. The boy turned back to the book and continued writing.

DID SOMEONE SEND YOU? said the new message, and Tess could see the yearning in the boy's eyes. She felt guilty when she had to shake her head.

"No," she mouthed. The boy's face fell. "Sorry," she said aloud, hoping the boy would be able to understand. He gave her a quick, sad smile, so she hoped he had.

"What's your name?" he said, slowly enough for Tess to follow.

"Tess," she replied, spelling it out when his confused frown told her that he hadn't understood.

"Thomas," he answered, placing his hand on his own chest.

He looks just like me, Tess thought, her heart thudding as she looked at the boy's dark brown eyes, the black hair curling neatly around his ears, his olive skin and the thick-framed glasses he wore.

He bent over his book and began to write again, holding it up when he was done. *YOU LOOK SO FAMILIAR!* Tess read, and laughed.

Then she watched as he bent over the book again, trying to find space to write. Eventually he held up the message. Tess frowned at it and read it again, just in case, but there it was.

WHO'S WINNING THE WAR ON YOUR END?

"What?" she mouthed through the lens, meeting Thomas's eye. "What war?"

Thomas looked incredulous for a second, then bent to write again. *HITLER, AND ALL THAT? THE ALLIES VERSUS THE AXIS?*

Tess gaped. Her expression was enough reply for Thomas.

NEVER MIND, he wrote. Then he began to write something else, but as Tess watched, the light in the void began to fade, and she pulled it away from her face. Confused, she watched as the circle started to close, the metal threads spinning themselves back into position, and just before the light went out, she caught a final glimpse of Thomas.

"Don't go!" he seemed to shout, and then Tess lost sight of him.

13

Thomas blinked. On his shoulder his mouse dug his tiny claws in, making Thomas feel like he was being poked by needles, and he finally closed his mouth.

"Moose," he whispered. "Did you *see* that?" The mouse offered no reply except to scamper to the top of the boy's head. Gently but impatiently, Thomas lifted the mouse down and looked him in the eye. "Moose. Unless I've contracted some sort of food poisoning from that last batch of canned peaches and I'm already hallucinating, that was a *person*. A person talking to me from a circle in midair. Don't you see?"

Thomas stared into Moose's shining black eyes, like two tiny berries in his small furry face. "Mum and Dad were *right*! They must have been. No matter what Mackintosh or anyone else says about them being a pair of loonies, this *has* to prove that they were on the right path." He paused, considering, and then gave a shrug. "I don't know if that's what they would've *expected,* but we've got to take what we can get."

He stood up, popping Moose onto his shoulder. "Let's go and record our findings, my friend," he said. Thomas closed his book and tossed it on the pew before hurrying down the aisle. He clambered up the stairs to his father's workroom. Storm lanterns were dotted about, throwing a gentle glow onto the dark wooden cupboards and desks. His father had built everything in here except for the telescope.

Now that his dad was gone, this was Thomas's place.

He made for a nearby desk with two radio sets on it— or at least what appeared to be radio sets. One was normal enough: a short, squat thing made of wood, which Thomas always had tuned to the BBC Overseas Service. The other machine was the interesting one. It had a large round face with a single delicate hand, long and tapered. The hand bobbed back and forth, measuring what sounded like tiny variations in the sea of static that poured from the machine's speaker. It was always on too, but it had never picked up a single radio broadcast and it never would. His parents had always called it an Oscillometer and so Thomas did too.

On this occasion Thomas ignored both machines, instead

pulling out the top drawer of his desk and taking out his log-book. Thin and hardbacked and bound in black leather, this book contained every detail of Thomas's life. What he ate, who he saw, whether he had any contact with Mackintosh, how often he took a bath—and most importantly whether there was ever any change in the signal put forth by the Oscillometer. Monitoring its output was the only interesting thing he ever wrote about in his logbook—at least until today.

He opened the logbook and flipped to the correct page, which had been prepared with boxes drawn carefully with a ruler and his precious, rationed ink.

May 20, 1941, he wrote in the box marked *Date* before checking his wristwatch. *10:04 a.m. approx.,* he recorded in the next box, marked *Time.* Then it came to filling in the largest box: *Event.* He tapped his pencil on his chin for a moment or two, trying to gather his thoughts. Finally he began to write.

Spent the morning (08:40 onward) reading downstairs. With no warning at 10:00 approx. a circle appeared in midair, about the size of a shaving mirror. In it, a girl—11/12? Dark hair, curly; spectacles; dark eyes; overall complexion dark; name: Tess (?). Visual contact only. No sound. Communication via written notes, miming. Had not heard of War. Had no connection (as far as can be discovered) with M and D.

Thomas paused for a moment, tightening his lips and swallowing hard. He had never stopped looking for his mum and dad, and he knew he never would. There *had* to be something out there that could tell him where they were—and perhaps this girl was it. He clenched his fist and continued. *Girl (Tess) did not seem to know what was happening and seemed to have no control over contact.* Thomas grimaced at his own words, the tiny flare of hope that had been lit inside his chest already fading.

"Thomas!" came a shout, loud and guttural, from outside. "*Thomas!* I know you're in there, you pest!" *Mackintosh,* Thomas thought, his stomach churning. He slid the logbook away and closed the drawer silently. Then he lowered himself to the floor and folded up tight, his knees against his chest, and waited.

"I'm not calling you again, lad! I've made breakfast. You can come in and eat with me, or you can do what you normally do and sneak in like a thief once my back's turned." Thomas, listening upstairs, grinned to nobody but himself.

"Have it your way," the man outside continued, sounding weary. "But why you want to eat terrible food *cold* is beyond me."

"Because it's better than eating with you," Thomas whispered.

After a few minutes of silence, he guessed Mackintosh had started making his way back to the house—but still Thomas moved carefully. He reached his provisions cupboard and took out a small silver-wrapped square—the last of his chocolate. He undid the foil and broke off a single piece, letting it melt on his tongue, but not before snapping off a corner of it to give to Moose. Together the boy and the mouse enjoyed their bounty and wondered whether their luck was about to turn.

Tess sat rooted to the spot on the chapel pew.

"What on earth was *that*, Violet?" she asked the spider, but all she got in return was a long look from Violet's shining eternal eyes. "Yes, of course," Tess said, as though Violet had answered. "You're right. It was *another reality*. I looked through and it was another reality. One with a war in it, apparently." She blinked. "Excuse me for a minute."

She bent forward and kept her head low, having once read that it helped you not to faint. Violet made her way along Tess's leg to sit, confused, on her owner's knee.

"I'm all right, girl," Tess whispered, her eyes shut tight. "Or at least I will be. I hope."

Tess's heart finally calmed and she sat up. Slowly she settled back into the pew. Then she picked up her experiments notebook and pulled her pencil out of her hair.

It was like a circle of fast-moving water with light shining through it, she wrote, the words tumbling out in such a rush that her handwriting became like a shorthand only she could read. *It was like looking through a waterfall only without getting wet. It was silent. It didn't smell of anything and it didn't give off heat or cold, at least that I could feel. The place I could see when I looked through seemed almost exactly the same as here, but the differences were: chapel looked newer and instead of me there was a boy. And a mouse. The boy (Thomas) didn't seem afraid or upset, even though I must have looked like someone peering through a circle in the air . . .* Tess's pencil stilled on the page. Her mouth fell open and her heart began to race again.

"It's what Miss Ackerbee was talking about," she said. "The circle in the air!" She put the pencil and paper down and picked up the object again. Her fingers were shaking. "That was what she saw, the night my dad—" She stopped, not quite able to finish her sentence out loud. *The night my dad left me,* she continued, inside her mind. *She saw him looking through this thing, just like I was doing. Miss Ackerbee even said the circle shimmered. It has to be the same.*

"So she wasn't being poetic, or dramatic, or making it up," Tess said, and Violet gave her a look. Tess pulled a face. "I know, I know, Miss Ackerbee wouldn't do that and I should have trusted her from the start—all right, Vi. Stop going on about it, won't you?" She heaved a sigh. "And as for my dad . . . ," she continued, stroking the device and running her fingertips along each marker, "he touched this, same as I'm doing now." She smiled, but it was a sad and fleeting thing. "So this is almost like holding his hand." *But why did he leave it with me?* Tess shuddered, thinking about the power of the device she'd just wielded. It could see between worlds—and now it was hers without even a note to explain why, or how it worked.

"Well, one thing's for sure—it has to stay away from Mr. Cleat," Tess whispered to herself, tightening her grip on it. "Whatever my dad was trying to do, he must have meant this for me alone. And if he wanted me to be safe"—she paused, sucking hard on her top lip—"if he wanted me to be safe, he wanted *this* to be safe too."

Eventually she came back to herself with a shiver. She'd forgotten her watch and so had no idea of the time; it felt like a millennium had passed.

"We'd better be heading back, girl. They'll be wondering where we are," she said to Violet, gently settling her onto her head-top perch. Then Tess got to her feet, slid the object back into her cardigan pocket and hurried down the aisle. The area around the chapel was deserted and Tess was soon safely on the garden's gravel path. She glanced at the bower seat as she straightened her clothes—there was no sign of Mrs. Thistleton and she was glad to see Mr. Cleat's book was still there. With luck, nobody had even noticed she'd been gone.

She picked up the book as she passed and tucked it be-neath her arm as she hurried toward the house trying to look like nothing was amiss—but the device in her pocket had never felt more conspicuous than it did now. She felt like she was carrying around a hive of sleeping bees, or a ticking bomb. Sooner or later it was going to explode and she had no idea what would happen once it did.

14

TESS SAT ON HER BED, HER NIGHTIE-CLAD KNEES A SNOWY PEAK in miniature. In her hands she held the device. She'd barely put it down in the hours since she'd gone to bed and she'd thought so hard—about Mr. Cleat and his Society, about what she'd seen that day, about Thomas and her father and how it could possibly all fit together—that she knew she'd never be able to sleep. Violet sat on top of Tess's thick nighttime braid, but could offer no advice on what to do next. She thrummed gently, patiently, waiting for Tess to decide.

"It's like a jewelry box, isn't it?" Tess whispered to Violet. "Only there's something in it better than jewels. It looked like *starlight*, didn't it, girl? Starlight, captured somehow." Tess chewed her lip as she thought. She slid her experiments notebook off the table that stood beside her bed and flipped to a fresh page, and then she thought for a moment, tapping the end of her pencil against her chin.

Solid starlight, she wrote. *Does it exist?* It had felt like the void at the heart of the viewer had been filled with *something,* not just light, when she'd managed to open it earlier that day. Tess had the sense that she couldn't have stuck a finger through the void, for instance; there would be a barrier in the way. *So the light has to be solid, somehow.* She frowned. *Like glass. But how is that possible?* She thought for so long that she found herself doodling stars on the page, but nothing useful occurred to her. Violet grew so bored she began to crawl down Tess's arm and away, determined to explore the crocheted jungle of the blanket.

Tess shook herself out of her thoughts, skipped a few lines on her page and began again under a new heading: *Markings.* She underlined the word three times, a sure sign she was about to draw some conclusions.

Equally spaced, she noted, *and equal in size. They look precisely measured and cut.* She picked up the viewer again and held it to the light, angling it so that the markers were illuminated one by one. *Three metal,* she continued, holding the viewer in one hand and writing awkwardly with the other. *Three stone. And two precious stone—sparkling, faceted. One red-tinged, one green.*

Tess nodded, satisfied with her progress. She placed the

viewer back in her lap again. It was a warm weight, like something alive.

One has a tarnish—not quite like rust. More like dirt? She'd tried scrubbing the discolored marker with a wet handkerchief, rubbing it with a licked fingertip and scratching at it with her thumbnail, but none of these had made the slightest difference. *Perhaps not significant. Might be a property of the metal?* It didn't look like anything Tess had ever seen, but she had to remind herself that this device wasn't like anything she'd ever held in her hand before. *For all I know,* she thought, *that metal might have come from another world.*

The realization hit her in the gut like a swallowed-down mouthful of cold porridge. "But that's exactly it," she whispered to herself. Violet, busily attacking a rose made of knotted yarn, paused to look up at her. "They come from a different world." She picked up her pencil again and began to write, faster and faster with every word.

Not just one different world—many? Perhaps a different world for every marker? They might be like . . . Her pencil hovered over the page as she tried to find the right word. *Keys?* She continued. *Each marker is a setting*—she underlined the word so hard her pencil nib almost snapped—*that can bring the person using it to the particular world the marker comes from.*

She sat back and stared at the words she'd just written. They made no sense whatsoever and yet Tess knew—*felt*—that they were right. Violet began the slow journey up the bed and Tess picked her up as she drew near. "But feelings are no good," she whispered to the spider. "I need to do some experiments, don't I? I've got to test this theory. Facts are what I need, not feelings." Violet kept her thoughts to herself, but her gentle thrum was enough to let Tess know that, as always, she and her beloved friend were in agreement.

Taking in a deep breath, Tess ran her thumb over the surface of the device; did she dare to open the void here, in a house where there was nobody she could trust? *Well,* she thought with a shrug, *there's Millie. But nobody else.* She dug her teeth into her lower lip, and before she quite realized what she was doing, she'd raised her thumb, ready to place it over the metallic whorls—

The floorboards creaked outside her bedroom door and there was a gentle but insistent rap. Tess jumped, scrambling to shove the viewer underneath her pillow. "Miss de Sousa," came Mrs. Thistleton's voice from outside the door. "It's almost eleven o'clock and long past your bedtime. I'll thank you to douse your light now, please, and get some rest."

Tess didn't trust her voice to reply. She simply leaped for the lamp and switched it off with quivering fingers. Luckily for her, it seemed the housekeeper was content to assume Tess would do as she was told.

"My thanks," Mrs. Thistleton replied. "Pleasant dreams," she added in a tone that suggested she felt disgusted by the very notion.

Tess lay back against her pillows and tried to catch her breath. She had to continue her experiments; that much was clear. *But I can't do them here,* she told herself. Her thoughts turned to the chapel. *It's just what I need,* she thought mournfully, *but how am I going to get there?*

Just then a gust of night air puffed her curtain out into the room. Behind the billowing curtain, there was an open window.

Thomas yawned. He lay on his sleeping mat on the workroom floor, reading a newspaper by torchlight. The news was almost two weeks old, but Thomas had to rely on what he could swipe from under his guardian's nose and Mackintosh usually kept the papers in his bedroom for days after he'd finished reading them.

"My *parents*' bedroom, I mean. Not *his,*" Thomas muttered to Moose, who gave him a sympathetic look.

Thomas flipped the paper closed. Its headline screamed about the still-ongoing Liverpool Blitz, and the photo beneath it was chilling. Dublin felt safer than anywhere in Britain, but only just. Thomas hoped the enemy wouldn't think of dropping bombs here, too.

"But I suppose it might be exciting, eh?" he said to Moose, who perched on his hand to take a better look at the picture of the destroyed city across the narrow sea, his nose twitching all the time. "The whine and the waiting, then the *boom*." Thomas tried to grin, but fear quickly suffocated his enthusiasm. The radio broadcasts and the newspaper reports made it *sound* like the war was a great adventure, but Thomas knew better than that. He knew how death felt, up close.

He threw the paper on top of the pile he'd scavenged. There were a lot of uses for newspaper, Thomas had discovered, particularly when you were trying to sleep in an abandoned observatory in the middle of winter. He guarded them like they were treasure.

Finally he flicked off his torch—and blinked, confused.

"Do you see that, Moosie?" he asked the mouse. Moose's nose quivered and he scampered to Thomas's shoulder. There was a bluish light coming from downstairs, shining up through the trapdoor.

Carefully, but as quickly as he could, he peered down through the trapdoor. At the bottom of the ladder, he could see an eerie but welcome sight and he couldn't help but laugh. It was the girl he'd seen earlier, floating in her shining circle, peering at him across the gap between worlds.

"You're *back!*" he said, clattering down the ladder. He could see his own wide smile reflected on her face and she gave him a wave. Moose ran up onto his head and the girl laughed. It made no sound.

She held up a finger as if to ask him to wait and the next second she lifted her hand again—and there was a spider as big as her palm.

"Aargh!" Thomas said, recoiling a little, but the girl raised her eyebrows at him. She brought the spider closer to the surface and Thomas and Moose leaned in. The spider's eyes shone with a friendly light and Thomas found himself smiling at her.

"She's very lovely," he said, speaking slowly so that his words were clear. The girl—Tess, Thomas suddenly remembered—grinned widely and nodded.

Then the girl was speaking. Thomas watched her lips, frowning in concentration. "Where are you?" she said.

"Dublin," he replied. "Ireland." He spelled out the words, but the girl's confusion remained. "Where are *you*?" he asked, and she turned away to scribble a note. When she held it up, all Thomas could do was blink.

"Hurdleford?" he said, frowning. "In the Briternian Isles? I've never heard of it." He looked at her and noticed she was chewing on her lip, just as he did when he was thinking hard.

Tess turned away to scribble another note. This time it read: *I want to go where you are. No idea how! Help me?*

Thomas barely had time to say "Yes!" before the light in the void faded and Tess once again vanished from view.

15

TESS WOKE IN THE COLD, EMPTY CHAPEL AND PULLED HERSELF UP
into a sitting position, looking at the viewer. She'd tried to
open it again after speaking to Thomas but it hadn't worked
and she must have fallen asleep out here all alone.

Checking her wristwatch, she saw that it was almost
five o'clock in the morning—which meant she didn't have
long before the staff back in the house would be awake and
beginning their day. She'd have to hurry. As much as she
hated the thought of climbing back up the ivy she'd used
to make her escape the previous night, she knew she had
little choice.

Tess made her way out of the chapel and across the
dew-sodden field as quickly as she could. Within minutes

her nightgown was sticking to her wet legs, and when she reached the gate, her fingers were so numb she could barely climb it. She stumbled past the bower seat, crunched across the gravel past the kitchen door and was making for the front of the house when, suddenly enough to make her gasp, the kitchen door opened.

Inside stood Millie, who gaped out at Tess. In the dim light of morning, in her sodden nightclothes, Tess could only imagine what she looked like.

"Miss? What on earth are you doing out here?" said Millie. "Get in before you catch your death!"

"I—I w-was just out for a w-walk," Tess began, her teeth chattering so hard the words came out in pieces. "D-d-didn't mean to wake you."

"You didn't wake me, you silly thing," Millie said, reaching out to grab a handful of Tess's cardigan, ushering her into the warm kitchen. "I'm awake for ages. I heard you clattering about outside and presumed it was Johnny." She glanced at Tess, who looked blank. "The milkman, miss. He usually comes with the day's delivery around this time. Anyway, you get on upstairs and back into your bed. Go on! I'll bring you up something hot as soon as I can."

Tess gave her a grateful look and left the kitchen, cursing her numb-footed clumsiness on the stairs. Soon she was back in her bedroom. The window she'd left open the night before had made the whole room smell damp and earthy. She hurried to close it and the pane clattered home with a *thump*. She made grateful use of her chamber pot before undoing the buttons on her boots and kicking them off. Finally she pulled off her cardigan and then her wet-hemmed nightgown, leaving them all in a pile, and got into bed in just her underthings, shivering in the cold sheets.

When someone entered the room a few moments later, she turned, expecting to see Millie arriving with a mug of warm milk—but instead she met the eye of Mrs. Thistleton.

"I heard a noise," she said in a voice chillier than Tess's frozen toes. "I wanted to check whether you were all right?"

"Y-yes, Mrs. Thistleton. Thank you. I'm fine. I just had to—um. Well. I had to use the convenience." Tess felt her cheeks begin to burn.

Mrs. Thistleton raised a frosty eyebrow. "I'm sure it didn't necessitate you throwing the contents out of the window," she said. "Perhaps that was how things were done where you came from, but I can assure you it's not how we do things here."

Tess didn't know how to answer. As she struggled to find the words, she heard Millie's quiet voice in the corridor. "Begging your pardon, Mrs. Thistleton, but I have something for the young lady."

Mrs. Thistleton turned. "What on earth has you away from your duties at this hour, Millicent?"

"Miss Tess needed a cup of warm milk, ma'am. It was only a minute's work to prepare it and bring it up." Millie cringed outside the door, holding a tray with a single cup on it. She'd even thought to put a cube of chocolate beside the mug, as an extra treat. "I'll get back to laying the fires now."

Mrs. Thistleton reached out and snatched the tray from Millie's hands. "Yes, you most certainly will," she snapped at the young maid, and Millie threw Tess an apologetic glance as she hurried away.

Mrs. Thistleton turned back to Tess and crossed the room in three angry steps. She slapped the tray onto Tess's dressing table, hard enough to make the milk slosh over the lip of the cup. She glanced at the pile of soggy clothes on the floor, noting the presence of Tess's walking boots, which stood wet and muddied on the bedside rug, and walked slowly toward them.

For a horrible moment Tess thought she might be about to touch her things, and an image of the viewer falling out of her cardigan pocket flashed across her mind's eye. *Careless idiot!* She began to sit up, the protest already on her lips—but Mrs. Thistleton just turned to stare at Tess, her dark beetle eyes glittering.

"Mr. Cleat might have taken you in as his particular pet," she said, her voice a vicious murmur as she took two slow menacing strides in Tess's direction. "But I can guarantee not even his special favor will excuse you from distracting the staff of this house, instructing them to do your will on a whim, or playing them for fools."

Tess sat up fully, not caring that she was half-dressed. "What? I never asked Millie—"

"I *beg* your pardon!" Mrs. Thistleton continued in a strangled hissing whisper. "You'll lower your voice and speak to me with respect. And how *dare* you present yourself to me in that condition." She glanced down at Tess, who quickly drew the bedclothes up to her shoulders.

"It's only a vest," she muttered, her cheeks reddening.

Mrs. Thistleton straightened up and refolded her arms. "Enjoy your warm milk," she said. "Don't let it spoil your appetite. You're expected for breakfast at seven sharp." Then, without another word, she turned and left the room.

Tess sighed and flopped back onto her pillow. Her head ached with tiredness, but she knew she'd never sleep now. Violet crawled onto her open palm, her eyes shiny and sad-looking. She gazed at her mistress with endless sympathy.

"What a mess, girl," Tess whispered to the spider. "Mrs. Thistleton hates me, Mr. Cleat has me here as some sort of experiment and my only friend—besides you and Millie, I suppose—is in another reality. Great, eh? Just peachy."

Violet, as was her usual way, made no reply, but exuded an air of gentle understanding nonetheless. Tess settled the spider on her head and dressed herself, carefully transferring Miss Ackerbee's note, the viewer and her experiments notebook into her new pockets.

Then, because she had nothing better to do, she sat back on the bed and picked up Mr. Cleat's book. She'd lost track of where she'd reached; there wasn't really anything memorable about the story so far, and once again she wondered why on earth she'd bothered taking it from his library. On the flyleaf, she spotted an inscription she'd missed before. It read, in slightly faded blue ink and the most beautiful handwriting Tess had ever seen:

To my dear son, Norton Francis Cleat, on the occasion of his twelfth birthday, September 27, 1918. From his loving papa.

Tess ran a finger gently over the words, and she wondered why Mr. Cleat had allowed her to keep a book like this, a book with such precious memories attached to it. Perhaps other people were so used to having gifts from their fathers that they thought nothing of it . . . but then her anger faded and she slid off the bed, placing the book on her bedside table, knowing there was no point in trying to read it now.

A quiet knock sounded at her door. Before Tess had a chance to turn round, the door had opened and Millie slipped into the room.

"Just here to collect your tray, miss," she said.

Tess nodded, flashing a quick smile. "I'm sorry if I got you in trouble," she said in a low voice.

Millie snorted. "Trouble? Breathing's enough to get you into trouble with that one. Don't give it another thought." She walked to the dressing table and picked up the tray, blinking at the undrunk milk and the ruined chocolate. Then she looked up at Tess. Her eyes were wide but not with fear. They shone with something like anger, a fury barely contained—but Tess knew it wasn't directed at her.

"They're not sending your letters," she said in a quiet, private voice. It wasn't a question.

Tess nodded. "And maybe keeping letters from me too. I don't know."

The maid gave a determined nod. "I'll see what I can do about that, miss. You leave it with me," she whispered, and before Tess could answer her, she was gone.

Wilf sat on a too-hard chair in Dr. Biggs's consulting room, kicking her heels a little harder than strictly necessary against its legs. She folded her arms and glared at the world in general as she listed off her woes, which were many. The worst of the lot, however, was that it had now been three whole weeks since Tess had left Ackerbee's and there was *still* no word from her.

Her gaze traveled idly around Dr. Biggs's office as she waited. On the desk in front of her sat a large red folder full of records dating back to when Wilf's condition had first been diagnosed. She had no interest in leafing through that, as she'd seen it all before. Beside the jotter was a selection of pens and a mostly empty inkwell and a pile of post for Dr. Biggs's attention. Along the wall behind the desk were bookshelves packed with medical dictionaries and folders full of other patients' records. Dr. Biggs's stethoscope hung on the arm of his chair and Wilf was considering trying it on for size when something she'd only half noticed drew her attention back to the top of the tower of correspondence.

A card edged in gold foil caught Wilf's eye, and she saw the word that had snagged her. That word was *Cleat*, written in an elegant hand, and Wilf licked her lips, trying to resist the temptation to have a peek. *It's not like you're opening a sealed letter, for goodness' sake,* she snapped at herself. *It's a card! It's right there!*

She threw a glance at the door; there was no sign of anyone returning, and Wilf knew this was her chance. Slowly and as carefully as she could, she nudged the envelope on top of the card slightly to one side, revealing more of the message underneath.

*As an esteemed member of
the Interdimensional Harmonics Society
I have pleasure in inviting you
and a guest of your choice
to an exhibition of Unparalleled Importance
on May 30, 1941, at 8 p.m. sharp
at Roedeer Lodge, Fairwater Park, Hurdleford*

None of that meant anything to Wilf—but a handwritten message beneath this invitation was what made her eyes widen. *Charles,* it read. *Looking forward to greeting you and Adeline at my little soiree. All best! N. F. Cleat.*

"Cleat," Wilf breathed. She snapped out of her surprise long enough to pull the envelope back over the card and sit back in her chair. Her mind thudded with thoughts of Tess and she tried to be certain that the name of the man who'd come for her had been Cleat.

If it was, Wilf knew, then what had started off as a terrible day could have turned into the best one she'd had since her dearest friend had been taken from Ackerbee's. A tight grin broke over her face and her eyes widened, shining with purpose and energy. *If that's the same Cleat, now we know where to find him,* she thought, her heart rising. *And if we can find him, Tess won't be far behind.*

16

"ANOTHER HELPING, TESS?" MR. CLEAT WAVED A SERVING SPOON filled with mashed potato in the vague direction of her plate and Tess nodded. "Good," he declared, plopping it down into the remnants of her gravy. She'd already eaten enough for her ribs to start creaking, but she felt sure she'd find space for the extra food. *Making up for this morning,* she told herself, digging her fork in.

"Hm-*hmm*," said Mrs. Thistleton from behind her napkin, throwing Tess a disapproving glance. Tess swallowed her potato unconcerned.

"What a relief it is, at least, to see something in your hair that *doesn't* have eight legs," Mrs. Thistleton continued, noticing the pencil stuck in Tess's topknot. The words were barely out of her mouth before Violet stuck a hairy forelimb out from underneath Tess's cardigan. Mrs. Thistleton jumped, almost sucking her thin lips completely into her mouth as she stifled her surprise. Tess risked a grin.

"Ruddy *imbecile,*" Mr. Cleat muttered suddenly, making Tess's grin vanish. She turned to look; his eyes were on the evening newspaper spread out beside his dinner plate.

"Something upsetting in the news, Mr. Cleat?" asked Mrs. Thistleton mildly.

"Nothing more than usual," he answered. "Henderson's up to the same antics. The man never stops."

"Has he declared your Society a menace to society again?" Mrs. Thistleton asked with a smirk.

"He'll see. I'll show them all," Mr. Cleat muttered. "There'll be none of his scaremongering when I—"

Mrs. Thistleton cleared her throat and Mr. Cleat stopped short.

Tess frowned at him. "When you what?"

"Beg pardon?" He raised his eyebrows at her.

"There'll be none of his scaremongering when you what?" Tess prompted.

He gave her a slow blink. "Never mind," he said, looking back at the paper.

"And who's Henderson?" Tess continued through a mouthful of food.

"I'm sure it has no relevance whatsoever to you," Mrs.

Thistleton replied, her nose wrinkling in distaste at Tess's table manners.

Tess shrugged. "I was just asking."

"And I," Mrs. Thistleton responded with great dignity, "merely answered you." She picked up her napkin and forcefully shook it out before settling it back on her lap.

Mr. Cleat observed this exchange with a patient, long-suffering look. "Mr. Cornelius Henderson, Tess, is a newspaper journalist. He pretends to be a correspondent on matters of science and industry, but in truth he is a creature with a vendetta against my every venture." He gave a tired sigh. "If he'd only give me a chance, he might see I'm not the greedy businessman he seems to think I am. Or, at least"—he paused to chuckle—"I'm not *just* a greedy businessman."

Tess couldn't think of a way to reply beyond giving Mr. Cleat a polite smile, which he didn't seem to notice and which faded as soon as she caught sight of the viperous look on Mrs. Thistleton's face. She took another forkful of potato before realizing her appetite had vanished, and the laden fork was put back on her plate uneaten. She sat in silence for a moment or two, watching Mr. Cleat reading and Mrs. Thistleton watching him, before clearing her throat and getting to her feet.

"Not so fast, young lady," came Mrs. Thistleton's voice as Tess stood. "Mr. Cleat and I need a word with you."

Tess looked up at her. "A word? What about?"

"We should probably discuss your schooling," Mr. Cleat said. "As in whether you're going to have any," he continued, folding the paper over and pushing it away.

"My schooling?" Tess stared at him in turn, her feet rooted to the floor. She hadn't expected that.

"Mm." Mrs. Thistleton looked up at her, not *quite* smugly, Tess thought, but not far off. "Mr. Cleat and I have been discussing the matter ever since he mentioned the problem to me a number of days ago. He hasn't yet decided whether to send you away as a boarder or to deal with the matter in-house, so to speak."

"In-house?" Tess frowned at Mrs. Thistleton.

"I used to be a governess of sorts in my youth," Mrs. Thistleton said lightly. "I am more than capable of instructing you, should the need arise. Latin, Greek and grammar are my particular points of expertise."

Tess hoped she wasn't pulling a face. "Right."

"In any case, it will have to be decided upon soon," Mrs. Thistleton said with a small sigh. "You're roaming around the place like a wraith, in and out of the garden doing goodness knows what." She gave Tess a cool look, which made the girl swallow hard. "The sooner you're occupied from morning till evening, the better. It'll keep you out of mischief."

"The things I do in my lab aren't 'mischief,'" Tess muttered.

"You'll have plenty of time to do your experiments after lessons, Tess," Mr. Cleat said. "Don't let that concern you."

"In any case I'm quite certain the world of science will wait," Mrs. Thistleton said. "It's not like you're inventing a perpetual motion machine, or anything of its ilk." She gave a derisive chuckle. "Or are you?" She shared a look with Mr. Cleat, who frowned at her and turned back to Tess. Mrs. Thistleton deflated a little.

"Your scientific work is important, Tess, of course. But you do need a wider education. History, geography, mathematics, things like that. It'll be good for you." He paused, pursing his lips thoughtfully. "So Mrs. Thistleton's offer to tutor you is an option I'm considering, along with that of sending you to boarding school."

"I know a good one," Tess muttered. "It's run by a very nice lady named Miss Ackerbee."

Mr. Cleat gave Tess an indulgent smile. "Very good, Tess. Most amusing. But get all thoughts of Ackerbee's out of your head." Tess bit her tongue at this. "Now," he continued, "if we *are* to send you away to school, there are a few things to be weighed up. Firstly, the cost. Secondly, the location. And thirdly, the question of what to do with your pet."

"What?" Tess felt like her stomach had turned over. She stepped closer to the table. "What does this have to do with Violet?"

"You can hardly expect a school to accept a *tarantula* on its premises," said Mr. Cleat, extending his hands as though appealing to Tess to be reasonable. "Don't be absurd. So if it is to be boarding school, I'm afraid Violet will have to be destroyed."

The floor seemed to drop away from beneath Tess's feet. "De-*destroyed*? You can't do that!"

"As your guardian," Mr. Cleat said, "you'll find I can do whatever I choose, if I feel it's in your best interest."

"But—no!" Tess took another step toward the table, her fists clenched. "I won't let you! She's *mine*!"

"I'm sorry, Tess," Mr. Cleat replied. "But you must appreciate my hands are tied here. I can't be expected to care for her, and neither can Mrs. Thistleton. Most of the staff can barely stand to be in the same room as the creature, so it's hardly fair to ask them."

"Then don't send me away. I'll stay here," Tess said, setting her jaw. "You can't have Violet. Nobody is taking her from me."

Mr. Cleat settled back in his chair with a smile and a strange self-satisfied look in his eye—almost like he'd heard exactly what he wanted to hear, or that Tess had given him the right answer to a question she didn't know he'd asked her. She felt a pang of unease. "That settles it then," he said. "You'll begin lessons tomorrow morning with Mrs. Thistleton in her office."

"Wonderful," Mrs. Thistleton said. "I'll look forward to stretching my old teaching muscles. Thank you for the opportunity, Mr. Cleat." She nodded at him, but he ignored her.

"Right. I'm glad that's settled," he said. "If only everything were so easy," he murmured, grabbing up his newspaper again and getting to his feet. "I'll retire for the evening then. I bid you both good night." He nodded at them.

"Good night, Mr. Cleat," Mrs. Thistleton replied, but he left the room without appearing to hear her. As soon as he was gone, she turned to Tess. "We'll begin straight after breakfast. I think we'll take Latin as our first lesson, so you'll address me in the following manner in the classroom: *Salve, magistra.* Do you have that?"

"Sal-*what*?" said Tess.

Mrs. Thistleton sighed. "I'm going to have a job with you, aren't I? You may as well go and enjoy your evening, child. Tomorrow, we work." Her eyes fell on Violet and her lip curled. "And I'd appreciate it if that thing could stay out of my way while I'm teaching. She is, to say the least, a distraction."

Tess's nostrils flared. "So I can go?"

"You *may* go," Mrs. Thistleton said, rolling her eyes.

Tess didn't need to be told twice.

From the observatory window, Thomas watched Mackintosh's car as it drove out of the gates. His trips to the city were infrequent now; fuel rationing meant it was often more trouble than it was worth to travel. When the car vanished from sight, Thomas knew it was time to make his move. He didn't know how long he'd have before Mackintosh returned.

"Come on, Moose," he said, helping the mouse into his top pocket. Together they hurried down into the vestry behind the disused altar in the old chapel. Thomas pulled open a low, squat-looking door in the corner of the room and dropped through it. As soon as he landed, he flicked on his torch. A tunnel yawned, its long dark throat like the twisting gullet of a snake, but Thomas wasn't frightened. He'd done this journey a hundred times.

A few minutes later, Thomas emerged at the tunnel's other end—into the scullery of the house he'd once shared with his parents. Mackintosh hadn't yet spotted the door to the tunnel, though Thomas dreaded the day he did—he'd surely block it off, and then Thomas would have to come up with an alternative plan for getting in and out. *But,* he told himself with grim determination, *I'll have evicted him by then anyway.*

He slipped his knapsack off and filled it with food—as much as he could carry and the sort that would keep—and steeled himself for the next part of his mission. "You're behind enemy lines," he whispered to himself. "Just you and Moose. You've got to be brave now."

Thomas opened a small wall cupboard to reveal several

keys and he slipped one off its hook. Then he sneaked out of the kitchen, his heart hammering. He quickly made his way up the corridor, reaching the door of what had been his parents' study. He hadn't been here since the day three years before when they'd had their accident, and when . . .

He pushed the thought away and unlocked the door with his pilfered key, and then he was inside. The tall bookshelves and the long, familiar desk he remembered from before—the one his parents would often sit at together, working late into the night—were still there. He blinked hard, telling himself the air was dusty, and made a dash for the nearest pile of books.

"*Quantum Mechanics,*" he muttered, running a finger down the spines. "Gobbledygook. None of it any use."

He turned to the bookshelves behind him and instantly saw a row of notebooks, each with his mother's handwriting on its narrow spine. He pulled one out. *Helena Molyneaux, Notes, 1934,* he read, and his heart gave a lurch. The shelf was full of his mother's work, and without thinking about it for a second longer, he upended the knapsack and shoved as many of the notebooks as possible into the space where his food had been. He was only sorry that he couldn't bring them all.

The remaining notebooks slumped to one side now that their shelf-mates were gone, and Thomas knew Mackintosh would spot the gap straightaway. He told himself he didn't care. *There's got to be something in here that can help Tess,* he told himself.

He looked back at the knapsack. "Not a lot of room left for grub, eh, Moose?" he muttered. With a sigh he crammed in as much food as he could and slung the heavy bag onto his back again. Then he bent to pick up the rest, more than filling his arms. As he struggled to lock the door behind him, a tin of something or other—condensed milk, he thought— fell and rolled away, losing itself in the shadows beneath the console table in the lobby. "Drat," Thomas muttered, but there was nothing to be done.

Slowly, awkwardly, he made his way with the booty back through the tunnel, hoping he wouldn't have long to wait before Tess came back—and this time, he promised himself, he'd have something useful to tell her.

17

TESS SAT IN THE DARK ON THE EDGE OF HER BED, FULLY DRESSED, and waited for the house to fall quiet. It was a big house and there were a lot of people in it, so you could never be completely sure. She wanted to see Thomas again and she hoped he'd be waiting. If she peered through and found him sleeping, it wasn't like she could just poke him until he woke up—but it was a chance she had to take.

I know I can get through, she told herself. *I* know *I can. I want to get to wherever he is, and I need his help.* She chewed her lip. *I know he knows something about all of this—I'm sure of it. I need to talk to him, and properly.*

Finally she worked up enough courage to move. She slid down off the bed and crossed the floor on silent feet, slipping the viewer into her pocket as she went. Her stomach churned at the thought of throwing herself out into the darkness with only ivy to cling to, but it was better than creeping through the house hoping someone had left a door unlocked. Readying herself for the descent, she began to pull on her boots.

I need to tell someone about these stupid lessons, too, she thought, her nose wrinkling. *Broadening my education, my eye! They want to keep me distracted in case I figure something out.* She tied her bootlaces with angry fervor. *And the very idea of spending all day every day in a room with Mrs. Thistleton! Of all the people—*

Her thoughts were disturbed by something unexpected—a yellow glow, faint but unmistakable, beneath her door. Tess froze in horror before dropping to her knees behind her bed. Her heart hammered so loudly she was certain it could be heard throughout the house and she regretted her decision to hide, realizing that if it was Mrs. Thistleton at the door and if she looked into her room, the first thing she'd see would be an empty bed—and an open window . . .

Then Tess heard a tiny *hiss* from the door. She risked looking up. A small white square lay on the floor of her bedroom and then the yellowish light began to fade away, accompanied by the lightest of footsteps. *Someone's just slipped a note beneath the door,* she realized. *Not Mrs. Thistleton for sure!*

Quickly Tess hurried to the door and stuck her head out

into the corridor. She saw a panicked face staring at her over the quivering light of a candle.

"Millie!" Tess whispered. "What are you doing?"

The maid blinked, taking a step in Tess's direction. "Miss, I thought—I wanted . . ." She shook her head and started again. "Why aren't you *asleep*?"

"Come in here," said Tess, grabbing Millie's hand and closing the door of her room behind them.

They huddled in a corner, Millie's candle illuminating both their faces. She seemed to be searching for Violet, and once she saw that the spider was sitting quietly on Tess's shoulder, she relaxed. Something about her fearful face made Tess notice, for the first time, how young she was.

"You're not much older than me, are you?" Tess finally said.

"Fourteen last birthday, miss," the maid replied, looking away from Violet and focusing on Tess. "Plenty old enough to be in service, my mam said."

"Do you like it here?" Tess settled herself more comfortably on the floor, the weight of the viewer in her pocket a reminder of how long she still had to wait before she could sleep tonight.

"It's all right," Millie replied nervously. "Same troubles as you'd have anywhere. Why are you asking?"

"Because I hate it," Tess replied, surprising herself a little.

"I can't *stand* Mrs. Thistleton. And now she wants to teach me *Latin!*"

Millie fought a grin. "She's a bit much, all right."

"What do you think of Mr. Cleat?"

Millie frowned. "He doesn't have a lot to do with the staff, miss. I'm sure he's fine." She cleared her throat nervously.

"I'm not going to *tell* on you," Tess said incredulously.

Millie leaned forward. "Listen, miss—I don't have much time. If I'm caught out of bed, there'll be hell to pay." She paused, glancing at the note on the floor. "I'm here because I wanted to tell you I might have a way to get a message home for you. Maybe not a letter, but I could get someone to let your Miss Ackerbee know you're all right."

Tess gaped at her, hardly believing her ears. "But that's wonderful, Millie," she said. "Thank you!"

"I have a cousin who works in Mr. Cleat's club," Millie explained. "I don't think he knows we're related. We haven't the same name, not that I'd say he even knows my name. Anyway, my cousin—she's called Rosaleen—well, in her boardinghouse, she shares a dorm with a girl called Kate. And Kate works near Ackerbee's. She says she can slip out on an errand, call on your Miss Ackerbee, no problem."

Tess blinked hard. "You'd really be able to get a message home that way?"

Millie nodded, her own eyes shining. "They shouldn't

be stopping your letters, miss. That's not right. And Mrs. Thistleton treats you terribly—worse than one of us. You haven't done anything to deserve that. All of us belowstairs think so."

Tess leaned forward suddenly to give Millie a hug, making the other girl almost drop the candle. Millie laughed quietly. "Hold your horses, miss," she whispered. "I haven't done anything yet!"

"I know just what I want to say in my message," said Tess, wiping her cheek. "Just one word—*quicksilver*. But I don't want you to send it straightaway."

"Why?" Millie frowned.

Tess licked her lips, thinking fast. "I can't tell you," she finally said. "There's something I have to do first."

Millie blinked at her. "Does it involve traipsing through the garden?"

Tess stayed very still. "Why do you ask?"

"Because you have a boot on," said Millie. "And your window's open."

Tess cursed herself. "Please don't tell anyone," she began. "I'll be back soon, I promise, and—"

"I couldn't care less what you're doing, miss—that's your business," Millie interrupted her. "But I can show you a better way out than trusting your life to the ivy."

"What?" Tess said, gaping in disbelief.

"Take that clodhopper of a boot off and come with me. Tread lightly, just where I do, and you'll be grand. We'll get you out the kitchen door, nobody the wiser."

"Except you." Tess grinned.

"Except me." Millie nodded. "Now, let's go. And pull that window closed, in case Mrs. Thistleton sees it. I'll give you the key to the kitchen door so you can let yourself back in."

On Millie's advice, Tess stuffed her bed with pillows to look like a sleeping body and picked the note up from the floor. Soon they were creeping carefully through the house, Tess carrying her boots in one hand and Violet perched, sentrylike, on top of her head. Millie's steps were like silk; she knew each creaky floorboard by heart. Before Tess could believe it, they'd reached the kitchen. It seemed so strange to see it empty, its stoves damped and quiet.

"You have to press your foot against the bottom of the door as you turn the handle," Millie whispered, demonstrating. "Otherwise it'll stick as you pull it." Tess nodded, watching carefully as Millie soundlessly opened the door. The older girl pressed the key into Tess's hand as she ushered her out into the dark. "Put that under the butter dish when you're finished with it; I'll make sure it's left there whenever you need it. Lock the door from the outside—and remember to pull it toward yourself when you're unlocking it, or you'll never get it open without waking someone."

"Thank you, Millie," Tess said.

"You're very welcome, Tess," Millie said, giving her a smile Tess was quick to return. "And go on now. Good luck." Then the door was closed without a sound. Tess locked it, pocketed the key and turned to face the garden.

She took one deep breath and made for the gate.

In a second-floor dorm in Ackerbee's Home for Lost and Foundlings, four girls were attempting to hold a midnight meeting. It had begun well, until Prissy and Prossy had allowed themselves to become sidetracked into a heated discussion about hockey.

Finally Wilf cleared her throat as loudly as she dared. They looked at her and fell silent, settling themselves properly on the bed and assuming an air of attentiveness.

"Sorry," Prossy said, straightening her nightgown.

"Sorry, Wilf. Do carry on," said Prissy grandly.

"Now," Wilf whispered. "Are we ready?"

"Ready," said Prossy firmly. Prissy simply nodded.

"I'm ready, Wilf," said Eunice, her dark eyes round and earnest.

Wilf settled herself more comfortably on the floor and looked at them all in turn. "Right. First things first. I wanted to tell you all that I found out where Tess is."

Prissy's mouth dropped open and she slid to the floor,

bumping knees with Wilf. "No! How on earth? And *where* is she?"

Wilf explained what she'd seen in Dr. Biggs's office and what she thought it meant. The others listened with rapt attention.

"Fairwater Park's just at the far end of the quays—not far from the old Kingsbridge train station," Prossy said once Wilf had finished. "The steam car runs fairly close."

"But it's huge," Prissy continued. "And even if we knew where to go once we're inside, simply getting through the gates might be a problem."

"Why?" asked Eunice, her dark brown skin glowing in the candlelight.

"It's out of bounds to the public, as far as I know," Prissy replied. "Locked, surrounded by high walls, guards, that sort of thing."

"Miss Ackerbee and Rebecca are trying to get Tess back with lawyers, but they're not having any luck. Telling them what we know won't speed things up; they'll just waste it trying to do things properly. So it's up to us," said Wilf in a determined tone. She paused and the others held their breath as they waited for her to continue. "And that means we might have to break the law. A bit."

Eunice drew her lips into a grim line. "Tess wouldn't leave any of us behind," she said. "If we were in trouble, Tess would help. I'm in, no matter what it takes."

"Oh, by all means, us too. We're as in as it's possible to get," said Prossy as she and Prissy shared a nod. "But we still need a plan. We have to have a reason to get through those gates."

"An invitation," Eunice said, looking at Wilf with eyebrows hopefully raised.

"But how are we supposed to get one of those?" Wilf replied. Her small victory was a deflating balloon and she felt her mood sinking with it.

Prossy frowned sympathetically. "We'll find a way. Without your eagle eyes, we'd still be none the wiser about where to start looking for our girl."

"Fat lot of good it does, though," Wilf muttered. "Tess might as well be on the surface of the moon. And knowing she's there doesn't exactly help us build the rocket."

"No, but it gives us something to aim for," said Prissy, her eyes glinting.

"That's enough whispering, you lot," a voice said outside the door. "Lights-out was almost two hours ago. Priscilla, Proserpina—back to your own dorm, please."

The four co-conspirators scattered, Eunice for her bed in the corner of the dorm and Wilf for hers on the far side. Prissy and Prossy slunk out to face the corridor warden, a top-floorer in her last months at Ackerbee's, who ushered them away.

"Night," whispered Eunice from the far side of the room as soon as the corridor warden closed the door.

"Sleep well," Wilf replied.

"Shut *up*," came an irritable voice from the bed next to Wilf's, and the girl in the bed beside Eunice's threw a pillow, which landed with a *flump* in the middle of the floor.

Wilf rolled over as quietly as she could, but all she could do for the longest time was stare pointlessly into the silent dark. She kept thinking about walls—how to get over them, how to tunnel beneath them, how to break them down—until finally she fell into a feverish half doze. She dreamed, eventually, of many things: of bricks and doors and tall gates topped with razor-sharp points, but everywhere they were closed, locked, shut tight. She did not dream of a key.

18

TESS SAT ON HER PEW IN THE OLD CHAPEL AND TOOK THE VIEWER out of her pocket. She let it sit in her palm for a moment or two, its markings reflecting what light there was, and thought about the theories she'd been forming over the past day or so. Could they be right? Was this viewer not just a way to see between worlds, but a way to *move* between them? Could she use it to help her rediscover the ability she'd lost, or forgotten—and if she could, where would she go? Who might she find? Question piled upon question and Tess squeezed her eyes shut against the flood of thoughts.

I'll just have to experiment, she told herself in a calm no-nonsense voice. *I've done hundreds of experiments. These ones will be no different.* Despite her best efforts, her mind fizzled and crackled, overflowing like a witch's cauldron. It took all her effort to quieten it enough to open her eyes again.

She looked down at the viewer sitting innocently in her hand. She ran her thumb lightly over its surface, feeling the metal warm to her touch, and placed her thumb right at its heart. Gently, she pressed.

Immediately it began to open, and quicker than a breath, the shimmering circle had reappeared. Faster than a thought, Tess put it to her eye. She blinked through the circle and movement on the floor caught her eye. *A mouse!* She almost drew her feet up in horror before she realized it was *Thomas's* mouse. She turned to her right, a smile already breaking over her face, and there he was, the boy from another world who already seemed so familiar. This time when he waved, she waved back.

"Hello," she whispered, smiling.

A smile was his silent reply. Then Thomas picked something up from the pew beside him and held it up for Tess to see. It was a notebook, rather battered-looking. Some words were written on its cover in an elegant looping hand.

She read the words. *Helena Molyneaux, Notes, 1936.*

Tess felt her heart flutter. "Who is that?" she mouthed.

Thomas chewed on his top lip. "My mother," he replied after a moment or two. He put the notebook on his knees and began to flip through it. Finally he reached the page he wanted and then he held it up.

On the page Tess saw a diagram and instantly she knew what it was because it reminded her exactly of the conversation she'd had in the bower seat with Mr. Cleat the day before. She saw ten straight lines piled on top of one another, just like sheets of paper in a stack. Then the note-taker—Thomas's mother? Tess supposed it had to be—had drawn an *x* on one of the sheets in the middle, with arrows pointing away from it, both up and down. Tess's eyes widened as she stared at the diagram and her thoughts began to coalesce.

An event, Tess reasoned. *One big enough to have an effect on neighboring realities, just like Mr. Cleat was talking about. This is his Interdimensional Harmonics.* She held her breath and continued to examine the page. Written beside the diagram, on the same level as the *x*, was the word *Tunguska* and a date: *1908.* She peered at it, wondering, *Wasn't that the year of the explosion in the Rus Empire? Is Tunguska the name for it—or perhaps the name of the place?*

She met Thomas's eye and nodded, giving him a small smile. If he was surprised that she seemed to understand the diagram, he didn't show it. Instead he flipped through his mother's notebook again until he found another page. He held it up and Tess missed a breath. Her mouth fell open as she stared at the page and Thomas's expression turned solemn.

On the new page of Thomas's mother's notebook was a drawing of something that looked a lot like her device. It wasn't *exactly* right—perhaps it had been made by a person who'd only ever considered it as an idea—but it was close enough.

And underneath it were written two words in Helena's handwriting: *The Star-spinner.* Beneath that was a newer note, written by Thomas. *IT'S CONNECTED, SOMEHOW, WITH THE EXPLOSION,* Tess read.

Tess's hand shook. *Connected?* She jerked the viewer—the Star-spinner—away from her face and stared at it, watching the crackling light of the void without looking through it. *It doesn't change anything,* she told herself, trying to dampen her sudden fear. *You have to know.*

After a minute or two she peered through again and found Thomas. He seemed worried, as though he'd expected her not to come back, and he smiled when he saw her.

"Your parents?" Tess asked. "Can they help?"

Thomas's answer was short. "Dead," he said, and then he looked away. Tess felt sick. When he looked back at her again, Tess mouthed, "Sorry," but Thomas didn't—or couldn't—reply.

He wiped his face, taking off his glasses to rub his eyes. Eventually he put them back on and sniffed, blinking at Tess. She felt a yawn building and tried to hold it in, unsuccessfully. He followed her example a second or two later. "Come back soon?" he said, his eyes soft with hope.

Tess made a face, balancing her notebook on one knee as she wrote. *LESSONS START TOMORROW. LATIN! I'LL COME AT NIGHT.*

Thomas stuck out his tongue, looking disgusted. "Latin!" Then he grinned. "I'll be here," he said.

Tess nodded just as the light began to sputter. "See you tomorrow!" she called, and Thomas's grateful smile was the last thing she saw before it went out completely.

Thomas went upstairs, bringing his mother's notebook with him, and slid it back among its shelf-mates. Then he settled himself on his sleeping mat and looked at the spines of his mother's collected notes, sighing. He wished again that he'd been able to bring all of them.

Since he'd retrieved the books from the house, he'd spent a long time just looking through them, thinking about how clever his mother had been—and his dad, too, for he was to be found in these books as well. On several occasions his square, firm hand would appear, writing a question or observation, correcting a formula, leaving a doodle. A page in one of the notebooks had a pen-and-ink sketch on it, one which his mother had drawn of his father as he'd pored over something or other, and Thomas had studied it for hours.

That notebook was now beneath his pillow.

He sat cross-legged in the light of a candle and thought. Moose sat on his knee, gazing out into the darkness, and Thomas stroked his back.

"I was so sure they'd sent her," Thomas whispered, and Moose's ears twitched. "So sure, Moose. I've been waiting so long for a message, keeping an eye on their stuff, watching the Oscillometer like a hawk"—his gaze flicked to the gently hissing machine on his desk for a brief moment—"but when I saw her coming, I thought, *This is it!* I thought, *They're not actually gone.*" He rubbed angrily at his leaking nose, squeezing his eyes shut behind his glasses, but the tears came anyway. "But they *are* gone, Moose. They really are." He wiped his face on his sleeve and tried not to sob. "They'd never leave me without saying anything, they'd never just *go* and not try to let me know they were all right. They'd never just forget me."

After a few minutes he lifted his face and sniffed, the ache in his chest so painful it felt like the air he was breathing had claws. "But Tess has proved one thing. Mum and Dad were right all this time. They *knew* this was possible, what Tess and me are doing." Moose turned and scampered up Thomas's sleeve until he came to rest on his shoulder. "I'll make sure they aren't a laughingstock anymore. Whatever Tess needs, I'm going to help her—and then together we can figure out how to prove my parents were the best scientists the world has ever known."

He reached into his shirt pocket and took out a few crumbs of cheese. Moose crawled onto his outstretched palm to nibble at them and Thomas felt his heart slow and the pain in his chest gradually lessen. "You were the best present they ever gave me," he whispered, running a gentle finger down Moose's back. The mouse responded by putting one tiny paw on Thomas's thumb and the boy smiled.

Finally Thomas blew out the candle and they lay down to sleep. High above the heads of the boy and his mouse, dashed across the face of the clear night sky, a web of stars was sparkling; in another world, in which the stars had been scattered in a different configuration across the heavens, a girl and her spider were dreaming of them.

19

"No! No! That's clearly the ablative case, you foolish girl!" Mrs. Thistleton smacked the chalkboard with the palm of her hand, making a cloud of whitish dust puff into the air. The words beneath her fingers got smudged, but Tess hardly cared. "*Amico magno!* Pay attention!"

Tess's head ached. She stared at the copybook on the desk in front of her, wondering how on earth she was going to make sense of the mess of scribbles when—or if—she ever read these notes again. Her mind groaned beneath strange words like *nominative, declension,* and *vocative,* and it struggled particularly with one Mrs. Thistleton had used for her a few times already—*obdurate.* She'd been afraid to ask what it meant, but she had a feeling it was something extremely unpleasant.

"Can I please take a break?" asked Tess. "I need a drink of water."

"You *may* take a break," Mrs. Thistleton growled, turning back to the board, "at half past twelve and not a second before." She picked up the duster and cleared some space amid the chalked nonsense. "We'll begin again with the nouns of the second declension—and I hope you're paying attention this time."

"What's the *point* of this?" Tess muttered, flipping to a fresh page in her copybook. "It's not like anybody even speaks Latin anymore." Mrs. Thistleton froze at these words.

"I'll pretend," she said, without turning around, "that I didn't hear you say that."

Tess stifled a sigh and picked up her pencil as Mrs. Thistleton began to drag her chalk across the board. It squeaked in protest and Tess felt a silent kinship with it. Under the neckline of her cardigan Violet stirred and Tess reached in a finger to stroke her, hoping Mrs. Thistleton wouldn't notice. *We wouldn't want to cause a distraction now, would we?* Tess thought with a small grin.

"Now, most of the second-declension nouns and adjectives are masculine—some are neuter, but we'll deal with those in a moment," Mrs. Thistleton began, busily writing. "Their endings are commonly *-us* and *-er*, but . . ."

Tess's pencil stilled as she stopped listening. This was

making even less sense the second time around, and she knew there was no point in taking any more notes. Keeping her eyes on Mrs. Thistleton, she slipped the Star-spinner out of her pocket and placed it in her lap, underneath the table and out of sight. Its warm weight felt comforting, like a purring cat.

As Mrs. Thistleton droned on, Tess let her thoughts wander. She ran her thumb along the Star-spinner's edge, her mind focused on explosions in faraway worlds.

When something moved under her hand, she barely registered it for a second or two. Then she jerked upright in the chair, trying to look down at the device without being noticed. The Star-spinner had separated into an upper half and a lower one, and the top half of the object had begun to move counterclockwise, like someone screwing off a lid. Tess pushed and it clicked, the tarnished marker moving one place to the left.

Tess fought to keep calm. *The Star-spinner,* she thought. *Of course it makes sense that it spins. Why didn't I think of it before?* She tried to memorize everything—exactly how the device had started to move, the fact that there was no light, nor any sign of the void, how much pressure it took to get it going, and anything else she could remember. It was all slipping out of her head already and she wondered if she'd ever be able to do this again.

I have to do this again, she told herself. *And I have to tell Thomas!*

Then Tess noticed the complete silence in the room. She looked up, panicked, expecting to be met with Mrs. Thistleton's silent angry glare—but the sight that greeted her was even stranger than that.

Before her was a long table piled high with books. The high semicircular window was the same but the wheeled chalkboard and Mrs. Thistleton were gone. A strange haze hung over everything like a half-light or a veil.

And at the far end of the table, his head resting on an open book, there was a sleeping man.

He had a mustache and thick dark hair with a wide stretch of pale scalp at the parting, and a pair of gold-rimmed spectacles were sitting by his elbow. Tess had no idea who he was.

She ducked under the table, where she tried to breathe quietly and think even more quietly still. She dug her fingers into the carpet, her heart thumping hard at the discovery that her flesh met no resistance—her fingers passed right through the pile as though it weren't there. *Or,* Tess realized, *as though I'm not.*

Just then the man gave a loud snore, which turned into a cough—which, to Tess's horror, turned into him waking and sitting up. She could hear his groan as he leaned to stretch out his back and the scraping of his spectacles against the table as he picked them up.

"Nature calls," the man muttered, apparently to nobody. He slipped his feet right out of his untied shoes and padded away in his stockings. Tess shrank, her heart beating so hard it shook her rib cage, but the man didn't notice her as he left the room. She didn't move until she heard the distant lavatory door closing behind him, and then she scrambled out from underneath the table. She blinked as she looked around; everything was out of focus.

But she could see enough to know that besides the fact that Mrs. Thistleton wasn't in it and it was messier than she would have stood for, this room looked just like her office. The room was full of books, piled on the table and in heaps on the floor, as well as thickly stacked on shelves along two walls.

As quickly as she could, Tess walked to the end of the table the man had just been sitting at and glanced at the book he'd been reading. It was in a language she couldn't understand and she frowned at it. A stack of thin notebooks stood beside the book, and their owner's name was written on the top volume. Tess recognized the ornate handwriting immediately.

Helena Molyneaux de Sousa, Notes, 1938.

Tess felt faint. *Helena Molyneaux! That's Thomas's mother!* Her head began to cloud over, the thudding pain between her ears reaching an unbearable pitch. This didn't make any sense, but before she could properly start to think about it, she heard the sound of the lavatory door unlocking.

She dropped to her knees and scuttled under the table again, desperately looking for a better place to hide. Her gaze fell on the man's empty shoes, and as she watched, a mouse hopped up onto the toe of the left one. It began nibbling contentedly at the shoelace and after a moment or two the mouse's tiny black eyes found her. It remained completely calm, as though spotting a tousle-headed girl crouched awkwardly on the carpet with a tarantula on her neck was a completely normal thing in this household. Tess watched the mouse for a moment or two, feeling herself relax.

So that's where I am, Tess thought, giving the mouse a small grin. *I wonder if you can go and fetch Thomas?* Her heart lifted a little and instinctively she reached for Violet—but then her breath caught in her throat as she realized the spider was gone.

Tess sat for three juddering heartbeats, trying to think. Her eyes raked the patterned carpet—could Violet have fallen? Gone exploring? Could the journey to this world have *harmed* her somehow? There was no sign of her anywhere and Tess's panic began to build again. She shoved her hand into her cardigan, feeling around frantically, but Violet was nowhere to be found. *It's not like her to just wander off, especially not in a new place,* Tess told herself. *Even if it does look remarkably like the old place.*

She fought to control her breathing. *Logic,* she told herself. *Come on.* She squeezed her eyes shut and began to flick through the things she knew for sure, one by one. *There is more than one reality. I have the Star-spinner, which lets me see between worlds—and maybe do more than that. I used to be able to go from world to world as a kid, until I forgot about it.* Her eyes popped open. *And I forgot about it because of Violet.*

Miss Ackerbee's voice filled her memory and Tess remembered the day everything had changed. In her mind, she was once again in Miss Ackerbee's parlor, listening to her explain how Violet had been the thing that had kept Tess tied to one world, had made her stop flitting between realities. *So if that's true, perhaps she can't come through. If she's my anchor to the world—to my world—perhaps she stays behind and I go.* She chewed the inside of her mouth. *And maybe she can bring me home.*

Tess gazed at Thomas's mouse. Its nose quivered and it cocked its head to one side in a gesture that looked so intelligent and friendly Tess felt a squeeze of loneliness. *I miss you,* she told Violet, inside her mind. A hot tear spilled down her cheek. Impatiently, she brushed it away, trying to focus.

Somewhere close by, she heard the man whistling and there was the sound of a kettle being filled with water. *Let him stay away for a few minutes longer,* Tess pleaded inside her mind, and squeezed her eyes shut.

She began to build Violet from memory. Her legs, her body, her cluster of shining eyes, the feel of her movement, until the image of the spider was so clear it felt that Tess could reach out her hand and Violet would come crawling into it. She could sense the gentle tickling tapping of her feet, just reaching Tess's palm . . .

Then she opened her eyes again and set the Star-spinner moving, turning its upper half back until it clicked into place once more. The discolored marker settled back into its original position but nothing else happened. Queasy disbelief filled Tess's mouth—but at the same time as she saw the man's stockinged feet reentering the room, she felt the air around her refocusing and Violet, the *real* Violet, clinging to the sleeve of her cardigan. The man's feet vanished and the wave of relief was so great that Tess scrambled upright, whacking her head into the underside of Mrs. Thistleton's table.

"What on *earth* are you doing on the floor, Tess?" Mrs. Thistleton said.

"Sorry—s-sorry, Mrs. Thistleton, I dropped my spider—I mean, I dropped my pencil," Tess babbled. She hauled herself back into her chair, amazed at the sense of *rightness* that settled over her once Violet was safely ensconced in her usual spot. It was so profound it even outweighed the throbbing of her wounded head. *My anchor,* she thought, wishing she could get away with giving Violet a kiss. *Miss Ackerbee was right about that.*

Mrs. Thistleton watched all this, the tip of her nose lifting as she showed her distaste, and after a moment she shook her head and began to gather her things. "Since it's practically half past twelve," she said, "perhaps we can call it a morning. I'll leave you to get some lunch, Tess, and I'll see you back here at one sharp." She bored through Tess with her gimlet-eyed stare. "I trust you'll be more receptive to my instruction once you've had a chance to refresh yourself," she continued.

"Um," Tess began. "Yes. Of course. I'm sure I will."

Mrs. Thistleton heaved a sigh so deep it made the paperwork on her desk flutter. "I truly have a Sisyphean task on my hands with you, child," she muttered, sweeping toward the door. "If you learn a single thing in this room, it will be a miracle." Tess listened to the clacking of her heels as it slowly faded away, only allowing herself to slump in her chair once the sound had completely gone.

A small smile grew on Tess's face as she thought about the things she'd *already* learned in that very room—none of which Mrs. Thistleton had anything to do with—and she got to her feet, settling Violet at her neck. Her excitement began to build at the thought of what Thomas would say when she told him what she'd done—but then she realized she had to stifle it. A long, boring afternoon lay ahead, and Mrs. Thistleton would surely suspect something if Tess spent it grinning at her.

She settled her face, stood up straight and made for the door. "Better go and get some grub, girl," she whispered to Violet. "And before we know it, we'll see Thomas again. Just you wait!"

20

"WELL, ISN'T THIS A PRETTY PICTURE," CAME MRS. THISTLETON'S voice, closely followed by the *whish* of a curtain being pulled back. Sunlight fell across Tess's face and she jumped, her eyes pinging open, and as she did so, she realized she was lying sprawled across the bed, mostly out of her blankets. It took all her willpower not to feel for the Star-spinner, to check whether it was all right.

"What?" she mumbled, trying to focus. She reached for a blanket and threw it over herself, hoping she had everything properly concealed.

"Good morning," trilled Mrs. Thistleton sarcastically, leaning over Tess's bed with her hands clasped at her waist. "Mr. Cleat and I *did* worry so when you didn't emerge for breakfast. Not sickening for anything, I hope?" Mrs. Thistleton freed one thin, cold hand and pressed it against Tess's forehead, from which Tess instinctively knocked the probing fingers away. Mrs. Thistleton straightened up, a look of distaste on her face as she refolded her hands, one into the other. "You *are* quite warm," she said. "But perhaps that's what lolling about until midmorning will do for a person. I wouldn't know," she finished with a sharp disapproving sniff.

"Midmorning?" said Tess, squinting at the clock with one shortsighted eye.

"It's almost *eight!*" crowed Mrs. Thistleton. "What else would you call it?" Before Tess had a chance to answer, Mrs. Thistleton began to stride across the floor toward the door. "Well, now that I've established you didn't expire in your sleep, I'll leave you to freshen up. Sadly you'll have to do without breakfast, which isn't the ideal way to start a day of lessons, but—"

"No breakfast?" said Tess, sitting bolt upright. "What?"

"In this household, there are a few simple rules." Mrs. Thistleton turned on her perfectly polished heel. "One of them is if you are not present for breakfast at seven, you do not eat."

"But why can't I get something now? I'm sure Millie could—" Tess began, but Mrs. Thistleton cut her off.

"You've done more than your fair share of ordering that girl about," she replied. "No, you'll just have to do without, I'm afraid. Now, do hurry up, won't you?"

Tess blinked at her. "This is unfair," she said miserably.

Mrs. Thistleton simply pursed her lips in reply and had disappeared through the door before Tess could say anything else. Instead she flopped back down on the bed, landing among her pillows with a *flump,* and threw her arms over her face.

A gentle tickle on her upturned palm made her roll over, searching carefully for Violet. The spider settled as Tess turned to face her. "A fine mess, girl, isn't it?" Tess whispered. "Goodness knows when I'll get to see Thomas again at this rate." Her head began to pound with the knowledge that she must have slept right through the night. She couldn't bear the thought that Thomas might have spent hours waiting in the chapel before finally giving up on her. She hoped he wouldn't be angry if she managed to see him later. Violet stroked her hand with her usual tenderness and Tess tried a smile—but the heaviness settled back around her again at the thought of facing Mrs. Thistleton.

She pulled on some clothes and was buckling up her second shoe when her stomach gave a painful growl. She tried to quell it with the promise of a distant lunch, but it did no good whatsoever.

As she was putting the Star-spinner into its usual place, Tess remembered how it had felt a few days before when Mrs. Thistleton came uncomfortably close to discovering it. She slid the device into her folded experiments notebooks, then slipped the lot into her vest. Tess wriggled her body until the notebook and device settled just at her waist. The elastic of her vest kept the bundle from falling too far and her cardigan concealed the tiny bulge it made under her dress. She looked at her reflection in the mirror, satisfied that the Star-spinner was as hidden as she could make it. Then she put the note from Miss Ackerbee, which she was never without, into her pocket.

Finally she held out a hand to Violet and the spider crawled up her arm so gently that Tess could barely feel it. She settled against Tess's collar as Tess made her way downstairs, crossing the wide hallway in the direction of Mrs. Thistleton's office, the door of which was standing open. As she walked, Tess noticed Mrs. Thistleton's voice coming from the kitchen; she was giving orders of some sort, her tone cold and shrill. *She's probably telling them to make sure not to feed me, no matter how hard I beg*, she thought with a hot flash of irritation.

She noticed something else, too, something sitting on Mrs. Thistleton's desk, shining in the light coming in through the half-moon window. Something she'd never once had a chance to touch since arriving at Roedeer Lodge.

Tess hesitated for a moment, listening, and then a burst of courage spurred her on. She hurried into the room and toward the telephone.

She put one hand on its shiny black receiver, wondering how it worked. She'd never made a telephone call before; she'd never had a need to. A small label at the bottom of the apparatus, protected by a worn layer of clear plastic, read *CLEAT 4518* in neat handwriting. A corner of the plastic was lifting and another, more yellowed piece of paper lay beneath it. Finally her determination outweighed her fear and she took her hand from the receiver in order to rummage through her pocket.

Quicksilver, Tess thought, searching for Miss Ackerbee's note—the note with her telephone number written on it. *All I have to do is—*

"And what have we here?" came Mrs. Thistleton's voice, shattering Tess's plan like a hammer hitting glass. "Turn out your pockets, young lady!"

"But—" Tess tried to protest, facing her.

"I said *turn out your pockets!*" Mrs. Thistleton's face became a rather alarming color as she approached Tess, her pace across the hall tiles quickening.

"It's just this!" Tess retorted, holding out the piece of paper. Her insides churned with disappointment, sorrow, loss and a hundred other things, as she knew full well this was the last time she'd see it.

"A likely story!" crowed Mrs. Thistleton as she strode into her office, reaching out her hand to snatch the paper as she drew near. "I'll have it all, please. Everything in your pockets, emptied out. Now!"

Tess struggled to keep her composure as she pulled her cardigan pockets inside out, their meager contents spilling onto the floor. A crumpled hanky, a few stones and a long-forgotten acorn rained down around her feet.

Mrs. Thistleton took it all in, her sharp black eyes flashing as she nudged aside the detritus with the toe of her shoe. Her chest heaved with her angry breathing. "Your dress, too, please," she said. Her eyes never stopped moving, her gaze raking through the pile of Tess's rubbish as though she wasn't seeing what she wanted to.

Tess quivered but did as she was asked. Her dress pockets were pulled inside out, yielding nothing but a broken pen and a discolored coin. Mrs. Thistleton seized upon that, and it vanished into a pocket of her housecoat. All the while, Tess could feel the weight of the notebook-wrapped Star-spinner at her waist, and she pleaded with the bundle not to fall out of her vest.

"You don't have any need for this, Tess," Mrs. Thistleton said, holding up the paper. Her beetle eyes were triumphant as she tore it through the middle, cutting Miss Ackerbee's neat handwriting in half. Tess bit her lips tight, stifling a shout.

"You didn't have to do that," she said after a moment,

keeping her voice as steady as she could and fixing Mrs. Thistleton with a glare.

"You'll find," Mrs. Thistleton replied, turning away and crushing the halves of Miss Ackerbee's note in her fist as she went, "that I did. Take your seat, please, while I dispose of this rubbish. We will begin lessons promptly." She strode out of the room, leaving Tess alone with the telephone—but she knew there was no point in touching it now.

Tess turned back to look at the telephone anyway, her eyes burning. Something flared in her chest as she did, and she didn't know if it was frustration or anger or simple *hatred*, but she reached out to the label that read *CLEAT 4518* and ripped it all the way off, hoping to tear it in two just as Mrs. Thistleton had destroyed her last link to home.

But instead what she saw revealed beneath the torn-off label stopped her in her tracks. It wasn't the number that surprised her, as it was the same—*4518*. Rather, it was what came before it, which Tess could only guess must have been the name of the people who had lived in this house long before Mr. Cleat had ever come here.

That name, written on the age-yellowed label, read *de Sousa*. All Tess could do was stare at it.

"All right then," came Mrs. Thistleton's voice, sudden enough to make Tess jump. "Let's begin." She made her way around her desk as she spoke, taking her seat before she noticed Tess's dumbfounded expression. She raised a questioning eyebrow and then she saw the strip of paper in Tess's fingers.

"This house belongs to me." Tess's voice sounded strange to her own ears, like it was coming from someone else's throat.

"I beg your pardon?" Mrs. Thistleton sounded genuinely confused and her smirk faded, replaced with a frown.

Tess looked at her. "Or was it my parents' house?" She placed the label on the desk with trembling fingers. "I thought nobody knew who they were. Is that a lie?"

Mrs. Thistleton picked up the label but didn't look at it. She toyed with it instead, turning it around and around in her fingers. "I'm not sure what you mean," she finally said.

"This was their house!" Tess shouted. "That's their name on the telephone!"

Mrs. Thistleton recoiled as though Tess had slapped her. "How *dare* you." She tossed the label back on the desk and folded her arms.

"This house used to belong to someone called de Sousa, just like me." Tess's chin began to wobble as her flashing anger drained away, drowned out by her fear and uncertainty. "Was it my parents' house? Why did Mr. Cleat bring me here? *Please.* Tell me the truth."

Mrs. Thistleton gave her a cold look that lasted for a long

moment. "You need to learn a little self-control, my girl," she said. "Not to mention manners. I shudder to think what they taught you at that home."

Tess's anger roared again. "Don't *talk* about Ackerbee's like that!" she yelled, clenching her fists.

Mrs. Thistleton got to her feet and leaned across her desk. "You will not *raise* your *voice* in this *house!*" she shouted. Trembling with rage, her face pinched and white, she hauled in a breath through flared nostrils. "I'll thank you to keep a tight rein on your temper while you're under this roof, young lady," she said eventually. "Or you know the price you'll pay."

"What are you talking about?" Tess said, the words interrupted by a sob.

Mrs. Thistleton took her seat again, tucking a stray strand of hair behind one ear before meeting Tess's gaze. Her eyes were like black diamonds. "If you prove too much of a handful for me, then we'll have no option but to send you away. Mr. Cleat has already had me prepare a list of suitable boarding schools for you, just in case." She paused to lick her lips before continuing in a near whisper. "And if you're forced to leave Roedeer Lodge—for whatever reason—then you know what will happen to your beloved Violet. Your only friend in the world, it seems."

"That is *not* fair," Tess said, struggling to keep her voice steady. "And you're not touching my spider." She placed a protective hand over Violet, who was cowering just below her chin.

Mrs. Thistleton drew her lips thin. "Well, we'll see. You know what to do if you want to keep her safe."

Tess stared at her for a moment before pulling out a chair and flopping into it. Mrs. Thistleton nudged a textbook toward her, and Tess pulled it the rest of the way.

"Good," said the governess, turning to her chalkboard. "Now, let's get started."

Mrs. Thistleton's cold smile was a spike in Tess's brain. She clung to it, hoping it would keep her awake long into the night, long enough not to miss any more chances to see Thomas. *There'll be no more sleeping through,* she told herself. *Not when I have so many answers to find. And not now that I know what I'm going to do.*

THOMAS SAT IN THE DARKNESS OF THE OLD CHAPEL, CURLED UP ON
the pew he'd come to think of as Tess's, hoping that tonight she'd come. He'd been eaten up with worry since she'd
missed their last meeting—had something happened? He felt
as though Tess was a friend—probably his only friend besides
Moose—but he thought about how strange it was that he'd
never heard her voice. He didn't even know her full name.
And if she never returns, Thomas thought, the small grin fading
from his lips, *I never will.*

He shuddered away the thought and turned back to his
book, an old one he'd retrieved from his bedroom on a
previous raid. It wasn't one of his favorites but he could remember his mother reading it to him when he was younger
and sometimes he could still hear her voice in certain words.

Just as he'd reached the bit where the family opens an unexpected delivery to find a fully grown penguin inside, the silver-blue circle of the Star-spinner appeared beside him like a light being switched on. He smiled when he saw Tess's face inside it, her dark eyes apologetic. She pushed her glasses up her nose and blinked at him.

"I'm so glad to see you," he said, speaking slowly.

Through the circle, Tess's face relaxed into a relieved grin. "Me too."

"Are you all right?" Thomas mouthed.

Tess nodded. "I was asleep," she said, leaning on her free hand and miming lying on a pillow. He laughed, and when Tess met his eye again, she held up a message.

YESTERDAY I CROSSED INTO YOUR WORLD BY ACCI-DENT. I WANT TO TRY AN EXPERIMENT TONIGHT TO SEE IF I CAN DO IT AGAIN.

Thomas felt his jaw drop as he read. He read it again and stared at Tess through the window between worlds.

"That's impossible!" he said.

Tess said something in reply with a laugh. Thomas thought it might have been "I did it anyway." Her eyes danced with nervous joy and he felt his own heart begin to race.

"How?" he said, and Tess shrugged.

"I'll show you," she said, her eyes opening wide, as though she could hardly believe her own words.

Thomas blinked at this. Then he picked up his pen and

paper, shaking his head slowly as he wrote. *IF YOU END UP SOMEWHERE HORRID, AMONG DINOSAURS OR SUCH-LIKE, DON'T EXPECT ME TO COME AND SAVE YOU. ALL RIGHT?* Tess met his eye once she'd finished reading and they shared a grin.

"Good luck," he mouthed, and Tess nodded.

"See you soon," she told him. Then the silver circle went dark.

Tess set the Star-spinner down on the pew and took Violet from her head-top perch as gently as possible, despite the spider's reluctance. She placed her beside the lantern Millie had stolen for her.

"I won't be long, girl," she whispered to the spider. "You'll hold the fort until I get back, won't you?" Violet looked uncertain, her shining eyes like liquid night in the flickering shadows. "I love you," Tess said, her voice tight.

Tess picked up the Star-spinner. Her heartbeat thundered in her ears and her throat felt too tight to swallow, but she forced her fingers to remember what they had done the previous day. *This time it'll work properly*, she told herself. *I have the window open.* She went through each step as though she were reading from her experiments notebook, and like it had been waiting for this moment, the Star-spinner moved. As soon as Tess held it and began to adjust the "face," the device's upper half started to pivot. The first marker clicked into place and Tess steadied her grip.

For a heartbeat, nothing happened at all.

Then the bright blue circle at the center of the Star-spinner seemed to suck her in, growing large enough for Tess to tumble in headfirst. As she was swallowed by the void, an overwhelming sense of light and air swept through her, as though every fragment of her body were separating. She felt herself expanding outward in all directions like a gigantic net, spreading across an unfathomable darkness in which she could see nothing, hear nothing, *feel* nothing, and a light exploded across her eyes and gradually formed itself into a distant sun, slowly burning.

Tess turned her head to see the immensity of herself. She was a constellation, a starspun web, a lacework of light strung with pearls, stretching to infinity. She laughed and it rang forever. She had never known such lightness and joy and had never felt such freedom. She never wanted to go back.

The sun she'd seen was, she now realized, one of a network of similar suns laid out before her. Each one was surrounded by a swirl of stars so that the suns appeared as pupils in eyes as immense as galaxies. As Tess drew near, something flickered across her nebula mind like a tongue of lightning. *My father,* she thought. *My father. Somewhere out there is my father.* She faltered, just for a moment, in her flight.

Then a sun sucked her in and down, and she began to whirl, tighter and tighter and *tighter* until she exploded into herself in a collision of light and energy she could feel right down to her atoms—and when she opened her fully human eyes again, all she could see was a dark-haired boy looking down at her with concern.

"Are you—are you all right?" he said, but Tess couldn't answer for a long confusing moment. She couldn't find her mouth, couldn't feel her tongue, didn't know how to breathe. She coughed, spluttering like a landed fish, until she gradually got her wind back. Her heart slowed to a normal pace. Her brain refocused, and she could finally see where she was.

The tiles on the floor. The wooden pew a few feet from her nose. The ceiling above her head a delicate shade of blue, dotted here and there with bright golden stars. She blinked and sat up and Thomas backed away, watching her with wide, careful eyes.

"I did it," Tess said, looking at him. She felt heavy, like every molecule of her body had gained a core of stone. A crushing sense of loss filled her mind, but with every passing second she found it harder and harder to remember . . . What *had* she seen?

"You most certainly did," Thomas replied, shaking his head in admiration and disbelief.

Tess looked at the Star-spinner, still in her hands. It glowed happily, the viewfinder clear. She glanced through it, but all she could see was night. She turned back to Thomas and saw herself reflected in the lenses of his glasses.

Then she lurched forward, reaching out for him, and they met in a tight, fierce hug on the tiled floor of the chapel, holding one another for a long moment.

"It's all right," he whispered. Moose scampered onto his owner's head and Tess caught a glimpse of him out of the corner of her eye. It made her laugh and finally the children let one another go.

"Thank you," Tess said as she and Thomas sat back on the floor, close enough that their knees were touching. She looked around the chapel again. The windows were shuttered and candles burned in several wall sconces. The door was locked and tightly barred against the night. She let her gaze linger on the painted golden stars and how the wooden boards met in the middle, dovetailing perfectly into the shape of an eight-pointed star. *Another one,* she thought. *That's one too many coincidences for my liking.*

"Who built this place?" she asked, still staring at the ceiling.

"My father," Thomas answered, looking up. "I remember him painting this ceiling when I was knee-high."

"It's wonderful." She dropped her gaze from it and after a second Thomas did the same. "It's almost exactly like the pattern at the heart of my Star-spinner. And it looks—well, it looks a little bit like what I saw on my way here."

Thomas blinked at her. "Really?"

Tess nodded. "Your dad was a clever one."

Thomas shrugged. "Not just him. My mum was the one with the real training—she studied astrophysics, only they wouldn't give her full credit for her work because she was a woman." He grimaced. "So Dad became interested too and it was something they loved to work on together. Until the accident."

Tess blinked hard. "I'm so sorry," she said. Thomas just nodded, not looking at her.

"What about your parents?" he asked.

Tess frowned. "I'm a foundling," she said. "Nobody knows where they are, or who they are, or if they're alive."

Thomas's eyes were sympathetic as he turned to her. "That's awful," he said.

Tess sucked her lips tight. "So, your mum and dad. They worked on Interdimensional Harmonics then?" she asked after a moment, hoping to change the subject.

Thomas frowned. "No. Well, they didn't call it that. What does it mean?"

Tess tried her best to explain. "Trying to send messages

between the worlds, basically. With radiogram waves, Mr. Cleat said."

Thomas nodded, his eyebrows shooting up. "Yes! Well, my parents called it Oscillation Theory. They built a machine, the Oscillometer, to listen for interference from other worlds." Tess listened to this dumbfounded, yet also somehow unsurprised, and let her gaze drift back to the ceiling.

"The same house," she breathed. "The same place. The same work being done, the same research, but in two different worlds. It's all very strange."

"Well, my parents were de Sousas," Thomas said. "It stands to reason."

Tess sat rooted to the spot. She looked away from the ceiling and stared at him. "What did you say?"

"My parents," Thomas repeated, looking uncomfortable. "They were de Sousas." He licked his lips nervously. "Have—have I said something wrong?"

"I thought your name was Molyneaux," Tess said, and then she remembered the notebook she'd seen when she'd made her not-quite trip to Thomas's world. *Helena Molyneaux de Sousa.* "So that *was* your mother's notebook I saw. Helena Molyneaux de Sousa!"

"Mum's married name," Thomas said with a half grin. "She didn't always use it."

In the midst of Tess's excited confusion, she remembered

something else Thomas had said. "What do you mean, it stands to reason? What does—that your parents would be scientists, researchers, interested in this sort of thing?"

"Because de Sousas always are," Thomas said with a nod. "At least as far as Mum and Dad knew. They'd made contact with, I think, two or three other realities, and that name kept coming up. The family has some connection with Tunguska—probably, Mum and Dad thought, with the original blast site, the biggest one." He gave her a nervous frown. "But I suppose you put a bit of a spanner in the works with that theory, eh?" He laughed, but there was nothing in it except anxiety. "Unless you're going to tell me you're a de Sousa too?"

Tess took a deep breath and stuck out her hand. "Teresita Mariana de Sousa," she told him. "But everyone calls me Tess."

22

"So THIS IS A LOT TO TAKE IN, ALL AT ONCE," Thomas SAID. "*You're* a de Sousa?"

"It can't be that much of a surprise," Tess replied. "I mean, look at us."

Thomas did and he straightaway saw what Tess meant. "I suppose we are a little bit alike," he admitted.

Tess snorted. "Alike? We could be identical twins. If boys and girls could be identical twins, I mean. We even have the same *glasses*."

Thomas leaned closer, peering at her. "Ah. Yes." Then he sat back. "They look better on me, though," he said in an undertone, and Tess gave him a halfhearted kick.

"What's more, whoever lived in my house—Mr. Cleat's

house, I mean—before him was a de Sousa too," she said. "I don't know who exactly. There's lots I don't know yet."

"That makes sense," Thomas said. "In the worlds my parents knew of, this house was always owned by a de Sousa. It's like a fixed point, they said."

"Like a pin driven through several sheets of paper. Sticking the worlds together."

Thomas nodded thoughtfully. "Something like that, I suppose."

Tess chewed on her lip for a moment. "I just wish I knew why he brought me here. Or there. You know what I mean."

"Probably not for anything good," Thomas said. "But he might have done you a favor. I bet he'd kick himself if he knew."

"What's that?" Tess gave a curious frown.

"My parents always said there had to be a reason why our family is at the heart of all this, in all the worlds they knew of. They always felt we had the potential to travel between realities, just waiting to be uncovered, and I'm pretty sure it's something to do with the house. Maybe our natural ability is strongest here. Who knows?"

Tess frowned. "But I used to be able to do it by myself, as a baby." She paused, looking at him. "At least, that's what Miss Ackerbee believed. I forgot how as I got older and more attached to Violet."

Thomas blinked. He didn't speak for a moment or two. "Well then, you've got a gift my parents would've marveled at." He took a long breath before continuing. "They used to hope that one day one of us would do what you've just done. I wish they'd been here to see this. To meet you."

Tess smiled. "Me too."

Thomas's chin wobbled. "Anyway. They're not."

"So who looks after you?" Tess said. "You don't live out *here*, do you?"

Thomas brightened. "More or less. Do you want to see?" He sprang up from the ground and extended a hand to help Tess to her feet. "Come on," he said. "Up here."

He hurried to the ladder at the back of the chapel and Tess followed him as he climbed to the workroom. His sleeping mat and blankets were on the floor, his radio burbled softly into the empty air and the Oscillometer hissed. Moose poked his head out of Thomas's pocket and looked around, his nose trembling. Thomas pushed a crumb of cheese into his pocket and Moose nibbled on it, content.

"There isn't a window," Tess observed. "I'd really like to see out if I could."

"Look up," Thomas said, walking to the wall. He began to crank a handle and Tess heard the smooth running of gears—and then, like an eye awakening, a segment of the domed roof overhead opened. She watched as the night sky began to appear and she was so entranced by the sight that she barely noticed Thomas coming to stand beside her again.

"It's so different," she said, her eyes full of stars.

"What is?" Thomas frowned and looked up.

"Your sky," she said, pulling her gaze away from it and focusing on him. "Even the air smells different here."

Thomas surreptitiously tried to sniff his own armpit. "I haven't had a bath in a while," he admitted. "It's probably—"

"No!" Tess laughed. "I don't mean that. It's not you. It's *everything*."

"Come up here then," Thomas said, moving past her. "Get a proper look." He climbed on a desk and then hauled himself up a short iron ladder to the gap in the roof. Very soon he had his head and shoulders out through the dome. "Come on!" he called, turning back to Tess. "You're missing it."

He moved over to make room for her as she joined him on the topmost rung, and they looked out together over the city. Its lights shone, but dully, as though they were muted, and beyond it mountains rolled against the sky.

"This is Dublin. My city. There's the sea," Thomas told her, pointing to where the darkness took a mouthful out of the land. A black ribbon flowed into it, cutting through the heart of the city. "And that's the Liffey running into it."

"We call it the Plura," Tess said with a smile. "I used to live right by it. I miss seeing it every day."

"Where *did* you live?"

"Near Carlisle Bridge. On Shelmalier's Quay. We could see the Victoria and Albert Memorial at the bottom of Sackville Street from the common room window." Tess smiled at the memory.

"Sackville Street," Thomas muttered, gazing out over the city again. "I wonder. I think I know where you mean, even though all those places have different names here. That quay? What did you call it?"

"Shelmalier's Quay. Don't you have that?"

Thomas shook his head. "But I think you might be talking about O'Connell Street," he said. "It's not far if we had my bike. I could get it if you like."

Tess's heart thumped. "Do you really think we could?"

Thomas sighed. "Well. Technically there's a war on, so we probably shouldn't. We're supposedly neutral"—he waved at the city—"which is why you can still see our lights. Across the water they're under a total blackout. Trying to confuse the Jerries, you see."

Tess frowned politely. "The Jerries?"

"The Germans. They use city lights to navigate at night, for bombing raids. Poor Liverpool just got pummeled. London's been flattened—they've been at it since last year. We're not supposed to be helping either side, but sometimes I really do wish they'd just turn the lights out." Tess couldn't miss the fear in his voice.

She looked out at the shining city. "This really is a different place."

Thomas turned to her. "And you *really* don't have the war? It's all anyone talks about here, even if we have to call it the Emergency."

Tess shook her head. "The last war we had was a hundred years ago, over the price of grain or some such nonsense."

Thomas nodded sagely. "This one's a bad one. Nearly as bad as the last one." He looked grim.

"The last one? When was that?"

"Oh, about twenty-five years ago," Thomas replied. "I don't remember it, of course. But my parents did. It kicked off a lot of interest in the theories about other worlds, too. The Great War, they called it. Nothing great about it if you ask me, though," he added in a mutter.

"What did a war have to do with any of this?"

Thomas thought about how to reply for a moment or two. "Well, I can only tell you what my mum and dad told me. They always said big world-changing things—like the Tunguska bang in 1908, for instance, or the Great War, or even the Spanish flu, which happened around the same time—caused *distortions* in reality. And that sometimes little rifts can happen, like rips in a piece of cloth if it's stretched too far."

He paused to gather his next sentences. "And so things

can get lost in the rips. Things like people, and time, and objects. In the chaos, nobody really notices it happening; it's only afterward, when things have calmed down, that you hear about the battalion of men who just vanished off the battlefield, or the lady whose house was bombed and who swears she fell into another world before somehow being shoved back into her own horrible reality again."

He pushed his glasses up his nose. "People like to pretend it's because folk are making things up, but really it's because the worlds get closer at times like these, when the realities go off-kilter a bit and things start to get mixed up. Tunguska was the first time it really happened, and study into other realities started then. By the time the Great War began five or six years later, there was already a network of underground scientists and enthusiasts invested in it."

"That's sort of what Mr. Cleat said too," Tess replied. "It began with the big explosion—the Tunguska thing. He said it became fashionable after that."

Thomas let out a mirthless chuckle. "I wouldn't say 'fashionable.' But each to their own." He looked back at the house and his expression turned cold. Tess followed his gaze, but all she could make out was a light burning in a turret window. As she watched, the light was turned off. Thomas cleared his throat. "Come on, let's go. It gets cold up here."

They climbed back down the ladder and Thomas closed

the roof. His room was surprisingly warm and cozy and Tess wanted so badly to curl up on his sleeping mat and close her eyes—but something was pulling at her. She kept expecting to feel the tap of Violet's feet on her skin and she missed the spider's gentle weight on the back of her hand.

"Who was that?" she asked, trying to keep her focus. "In the window of your house. Who turned out the light?"

"Mackintosh," Thomas said, his voice low and dark. "My *guardian.*" The word oozed unpleasantly. Tess remembered the stocking-clad man and shuddered.

"I think I met him, yesterday. Is he the reason you live out here?"

Thomas tightened his lips in a joyless grin and looked at her. "We don't get on. It's easier if we stay out of one another's way. Plus I like this old place."

Tess gave a knowing nod. "He and my governess, Mrs. Thistleton, should probably have afternoon tea. It sounds like they'd be best friends."

Thomas grinned properly, but only for a second. Then he crossed the room and dropped to his knees to pull open a cupboard. Tess glimpsed rows of tinned food, packets and cans and a biscuit drum. "So what'll you have? I've got sardines and corned beef and cheese and—"

"I should be getting back," Tess said softly. "I don't think I can stay much longer."

Thomas turned to her. His eyes were lost in the gleam on his glasses. "But—I thought you'd stay. For a bit, at least." Moose peeped out over Thomas's shirt pocket, his shining eyes fixed on Tess and his nose quivering like a plucked string.

"I have to get home to Violet," Tess said, looking at Moose with a painful tug in her chest. "She's in danger without me. But you'll see me again soon. I promise."

Thomas got to his feet. "I hope so," he said. "Moose and I get lonely out here sometimes."

Tess gave him a knowing, sympathetic look as she pulled up the trapdoor and began to climb down the ladder. Thomas followed. When they were both standing in the chapel, Tess took the Star-spinner out of her pocket and Thomas's eyes went wide.

"Do you want to see it?" she asked, holding it out.

Thomas backed away. "No thank you. Too much power for me, I reckon."

Tess cradled the Star-spinner to her chest, feeling awkward. "Until tomorrow then."

"Until then," Thomas said. "Take care."

"And you," she replied, turning the Star-spinner back until the markings clicked into their original positions.

She just had time to meet Thomas's eye before the void sucked her through and she was gone.

23

IN A SMALL, PLAINLY FURNISHED ROOM, A WOMAN LAY SLEEPING. Her bed was simple, the frames on her wall containing nothing but sprays of dried flowers. Her hair was in a long tight braid and her sharp-featured face was, in sleep, as relaxed as it ever became. The grayish light of early morning soaked through the net curtains, making everything seem dull.

On the woman's bedside table lay her locket, empty where there should have been a portrait of someone dear, and beside it she had placed the thin gold band she wore on her ring finger.

Another table sat beneath her window. It held a tall, narrow box that its owner liked to pass off as her sewing machine, but the mechanism this box contained was no such thing. A steady gentle hiss emanated from it and an urgent *scritch-scritch* noise could barely be heard beneath it, like a counterpoint melody.

The woman stirred awake a minute or two before her alarm went, as was her habit. She frowned, licking her dry lips, and then her eyes opened. It was only then she heard it: the *scritch-scritch.* Her body went rigid as she tried to listen. She perched on the edge of her bed like a bird about to take flight.

After pulling her robe from the back of a nearby chair, she got to her feet and bent down to take the cover off her machine. What sat there looked like a wireless radio and her knowledgeable eyes took one look at it and knew that it was receiving something of importance. A needle-thin pen was moving over a roll of paper, *scritch*ing as it went—a change she'd been hoping for since the child had come to live here. Confirmation that everything she'd worked for, all the things she'd dreamed of, were going to come true.

If she had anything to do with it, at least.

She settled into her chair and pulled open a drawer in her table, revealing a book that, she felt sure, nobody else in the house would have the faintest idea how to use. It was a book of codes used to send messages. She opened it, smoothing it out on the correct page. Picking up a pencil, she made some light marks on the page, notes to help her to say—

"Mrs. Thistleton?" came a voice outside her door. The woman jumped, turning irritably toward the sound.

"Yes?" she snapped.

"Forgive me, ma'am, but there's a problem in the kitchen. The milk wasn't delivered and the butcher's just been but he didn't bring *half* enough beef and—"

"Yes, yes, all right. Cora—is that Cora?"

"Yes, ma'am," came the sheepish reply.

"I'm just dressing, girl. I'll be down presently."

"Thank you, Mrs. Thistleton," the girl said, and the woman waited to hear the sound of her feet moving away before she bent over the book again.

Be ready, she wrote. *Thirtieth. Protocol S.* She left the pencil in the book to mark her place before putting it back in her drawer and replacing the cover on her machine.

As she finished dressing, she looked at her reflection in the mirror of her wardrobe door. She smoothed back her tight chignon, straightened her collar and allowed a brief gleam of satisfaction to brighten her eyes. *We've played the child right into our hands,* she thought, *and I've played him into mine.*

She locked the bedroom door behind her and hurried to the kitchen to attend to her duties, but the hiss from her machine filled her ears. She counted the seconds until she could get back to it again and until she could use it to send the most important message it had ever broadcast.

It's happening, she thought. *The time has come at last.*

"You're looking a bit green around the gills," said Mr. Cleat as Tess entered the breakfast room. He put aside his newspaper and looked at her with concern. "Everything all right?"

"I'm fine," Tess said, taking her seat. Her head ached; she was exhausted and she felt cold to the bones. The night before had taken a toll on her, but of course nobody could know anything of that.

"I can't imagine you're tired from the work you've been doing in my lessons," Mrs. Thistleton remarked. "What have you been up to?"

"I didn't sleep very well last night," Tess replied, reaching for the toast. The thought of eating made her want to retch, but she knew she needed the energy.

"Shall I send for the doctor?" Mrs. Thistleton asked, turning to Mr. Cleat.

"Let's just give Tess the day off and see how she feels later." Mr. Cleat reached across the table to put his hand over Tess's and she struggled not to pull her fingers away. "Does that sound like a good plan?"

Tess squinted at him as she swallowed a mouthful of toast. She nodded.

"Good, good," Mr. Cleat said, patting Tess's hand once or twice before withdrawing his own. "Now, I'll leave you in Mrs. Thistleton's care and I'll see you both for lunch."

"Lunch?" Mrs. Thistleton gave Mr. Cleat a curious look but he didn't glance in her direction. "To what do we owe the pleasure?"

"I have an experiment I want to carry out and I was hoping Tess would help me. This might be the perfect day for it." He met Tess's eye. "That is, if you're feeling a bit more energetic later?"

Tess swallowed another mouthful of toast and jam. Her stomach roiled but didn't rebel. "Of course," she said, even though the thought of it made her feel uneasy.

"Splendid. Get some rest this morning. Back to bed, I think. And we'll see you at one. Right," he continued, "I'm away to the city. Enjoy your leisurely morning, ladies." And with that, he was gone.

Tess put the rest of her uneaten toast back on her plate and stood up. She felt like something dragging itself along the bottom of the sea; everything seemed to weigh heavily on her. She turned to leave the room.

"Don't think I shan't be checking on you," Mrs. Thistleton said as Tess's hand touched the doorknob. "If I find you've been malingering, I'll be straight to Mr. Cleat about it."

Tess paused, considering how to respond, but her brain refused to form a sentence. She just turned the knob and pulled open the door, making her way out of the room on aching legs. Getting upstairs seemed like a struggle too far, but she knew she had to try.

As she crossed the front hall, Millie emerged from a servants' door weighed down with an armload of laundry. "Miss," she said, her eyes widening in surprise. "Are you all right?"

Tess nodded, but she felt Millie's hands go around her shoulders anyway. The laundry was left in a neat pile on the bottom step.

"No, you mustn't do that. If she catches you—" Tess began.

"If she catches me, she can go and blow her hot air at someone else," Millie said firmly, helping Tess up the steps one by one. "That's it, miss. You're doing well. Come on, now."

"Millie, will you please call me Tess?"

"All right, miss—I mean, Tess. That's it. Just one more turn and we'll be there."

As they walked, Tess thought of something. She could hardly believe it had never occurred to her before. "Can I ask you a question, Millie? Where is this place? I mean, we're not far from the city here, are we?"

Millie bit her lip. Tess felt her stiffen and her grip on Tess's shoulders tightened. "We were told not to tell you if you asked, miss. I mean, Tess. You weren't to know."

"Why not?"

Millie sighed. "I was never sure. I suppose it's in case you tried to run away."

"I don't know why he wants to keep me prisoner here," Tess said.

"Nor I, miss. Tess," Millie replied, giving her a fond squeeze. "It's not right," she continued in a whisper.

They reached Tess's bedroom door. "So," Millie continued in a more normal tone, "let's get you settled and then I can get back to work. Come on, miss."

Tess let Millie lead her into the room. The older girl bent to undo Tess's laces and pull off her shoes, and as she stood up, she leaned close to Tess's ear. "We're in Fairwater Park, miss. North of the Plura? Near the old Kingsbridge train station."

"I've heard of it," Tess replied. "Thank you, Millie."

"Don't mention it," Millie said. "Please."

"The message I wanted you to send to Ackerbee's," Tess whispered, looking Millie in the eye. "*Quicksilver.* Have you sent it yet?"

"I wanted to talk to you about that, miss. Tess," Millie corrected herself, looking red and flustered and apologetic. "You see, Kate, the girl who was going to send the message for you, well, her sister's taken ill. So Kate's been called home to help and she won't be back for a few weeks at least."

"That's all right," Tess said, taking off her glasses. "I was going to ask you to wait a bit, actually; I'm not finished traipsing through the garden yet." She pulled her legs up onto the bed as she lay down and gave Millie a grin as the maid began to arrange the blankets over her. Millie smiled back, her eyes kind. "I don't know how to thank you, Millie," Tess whispered.

"Getting one over on that old windbag is more than enough thanks," Millie muttered, tucking the bedclothes tightly around Tess. "I'll see you in an hour or two, miss. I'll bring you some soup. Feel better, now."

"Thank you, Millie. See you then," Tess replied, and Millie threw her a wink.

Left alone, Tess tried her hardest to stay awake, to keep an eye out for Mrs. Thistleton, to make sure the Star-spinner was hidden, to think about Thomas and how all the strange pieces of her life might fit together, but the next thing she knew there was an odd grating sound close to her ear. She jerked awake and turned her head to see what had caused it.

"Whoops!" came Mr. Cleat's voice. "Tess, you almost had your own eye out!" He laughed but there was no amusement in it. Tess caught a glimpse of something in his hand and she pushed herself up onto her elbows.

"Is that—is that a pair of scissors?" she asked, blinking. She reached for her glasses and put them on. She stared at Mr. Cleat. "What are you doing?"

"It's that experiment I mentioned," Mr. Cleat said. "I needed a sample of your hair and I didn't want to wake you to ask for one, but these rusty old scissors gave me away before I could make the cut." He squeezed the handles a couple of times, making the blades *whir* back and forth with the same grinding noise that had woken Tess.

She put her hand to her head. "My *hair*? What for?"

"Just to demonstrate something to the members of my Interdimensional Harmonics Society," Mr. Cleat replied. "We've been working on a machine, one that can detect harmonic signals from objects, and I wanted to show my colleagues that a sample from me and a sample from you would be exactly the same." He gave Tess a level stare. "That's all right, isn't it?"

"No," Tess said, her eyes wide with shock.

Mr. Cleat pouted. "And here I was thinking you'd be happy to volunteer in the interests of science."

"I'm sorry," said Tess, edging away from him.

Mr. Cleat held up his hands. He didn't drop the scissors. "All right, all right, I'm not going to force you. Forgive me, won't you?" He inclined his head toward Tess, as though bowing. "No offense was meant. I hope none has been taken."

"No." Tess licked her lips. "No, of course not."

"Wonderful. Well, I hope you're feeling better. Will you be coming down to lunch?" Tess managed to nod. "I'll leave you in peace then," Mr. Cleat said. He whirled the scissors around one finger and shoved them into a pocket before turning and leaving the room.

Tess drew her knees up and rested her forehead on them, wrapping her arms tightly around her legs. Her heart gradually began to slow but her thoughts whirled faster and faster. Eventually her mind settled and she realized she was filled with an infuriated rage.

He was about to cut my hair, she told herself. *Without asking!* And what would have happened if he'd put it in his infernal machine? It would have proved exactly the opposite of what he was trying to demonstrate—she and Mr. Cleat were from different worlds, so their samples would have different harmonic readings. For a moment she enjoyed imagining his embarrassment, thinking about Mr. Cleat slapping his machine and apologizing for its malfunction in front of his ridiculous Interdimensional Harmonics Society . . .

But then a second thought began to creep up through the cracks of the first and her smile faded. *But that's assuming he's telling the truth,* she told herself. If Mr. Cleat wasn't being truthful, Tess realized, she might have walked herself into a trap. *If all he wanted was to see what I'd do, then I've given myself away.* Her heart began to pound. *Because if I had nothing to hide, I would have let him have my hair . . .*

Violet crawled up the blanket and Tess cupped her in one hand. "I know, girl," she whispered miserably. "I know. I've made a huge mistake, haven't I?"

24

COME ON THEN, TESS THOUGHT. WHERE ARE YOU? SHE WAS perched on a high stool in her lab, where she'd been for over an hour. *The Secret Garden* lay beside her on the bench, underneath her experiments notebook, but all she'd managed to note were some random doodles. Now she was using her magnifying lens to zoom in and out on the back of her own hand, marveling at how it was harder to truly see something the closer you got to it.

It had been three days since she'd last seen Mr. Cleat for longer than a few moments at a time, and just over a week since she'd last been in the lab. However, as soon as she'd walked through the door, she'd realized that *someone* had paid it a visit in her absence and she could take a guess at who. Things weren't as she had left them: her lab coat had been left hanging on a hook near the door and she'd found it lying across the back of a chair; some of the things in her top drawer had been disturbed, as though pushed aside by a questing finger. She reached for the Star-spinner, a tiny bulge at her waist, and gave it a gentle squeeze. *I won't let him find you,* she told it.

"What a surprise!" came a voice behind her, and Tess fixed a smile in place before turning around. "How nice to see you back in here. I did wonder whether you'd lost your taste for science."

Tess gave Mr. Cleat an incredulous look. "Not at all. Mrs. Thistleton's been keeping me busy, but I have this morning free."

Mr. Cleat inclined his head. "What's on your agenda, then?"

Tess reached into her cardigan pocket and took out a small envelope, trying her hardest to appear meek. "I wanted to give you this," she said, holding out the envelope.

Mr. Cleat grinned. "Oh?" Three long strides had him in the room and by her side. He took the envelope but didn't open it. Instead he gave her a curious look.

"It's what you wanted," Tess replied.

Eagerly, Mr. Cleat tore the seal and looked inside. "Ah," he said, smiling an embarrassed-seeming smile. His enthusiasm faded a little, but he gave Tess a warm look all the same. "Your hair?"

A lock of hair lay inside the envelope—but it wasn't Tess's. It was Millie's, and she'd darkened it as much as she could to try to match Tess's shade by soaking it in strong black tea and letting it dry on a sunny windowsill. It still didn't look quite right, but Tess was hoping Mr. Cleat wouldn't notice. He hadn't seemed to. "I'm sorry I didn't give it to you the other day," Tess said. "I wasn't feeling too well, I suppose." She smiled, and hoped it looked heartfelt.

"Please don't apologize, my dear. I was in the wrong. I shouldn't have woken you so abruptly." Mr. Cleat smiled back and Tess bit her tongue. *That's not all you shouldn't have done,* she thought.

"In any case, I don't need it now. The time for that experiment has passed, sadly. The members of my Society are looking for proof that these outlandish theories about other worlds and realities are actually *true.*" He sighed, tucking the envelope of hair into his pocket almost absentmindedly, but Tess had a feeling it was anything but.

"I was hoping the experiment on your hair would act as a control, you know—a demonstration that two people from the same reality would have the same vibrational frequency." His gaze grew cooler. "But I met my fellows in the Society yesterday evening, and they're looking for a greater exhibition than that. No, a couple of clumps of hair won't satisfy them any longer."

"Oh really?" Tess looked guileless. "So what are you going to do now?"

Mr. Cleat sighed, looking away from Tess as he spoke. "The existence of other realities, Tess, is something I take for granted. Sometimes I find it hard to remember that other people don't. Mrs. Thistleton, for instance, thinks I'm a fool; she hardly believes the ground under her own feet is solid until she stands upon it. It's people like her I'm trying to convince. And the only way to do that is to give them something they can see and feel." He paused, raising his eyebrows. "To actually send something between worlds right in front of their eyes."

"But how are you going to do that?" Tess asked, clutching the edge of her desk so hard her fingertips ached. "I thought you said it was impossible."

Mr. Cleat smiled. "No indeed. I don't believe it to be impossible at all. I'm firmly of the opinion that if it's possible to send a radiogram signal far enough that it can be picked up by someone in a neighboring reality, then it's possible to send other things too. People, perhaps." He licked his front teeth. "Machines."

"Machines?" Tess tried to keep her tone bright and interested. "You work with those, don't you?"

"I do," he agreed. "I work with large engines, Tess, which power steamships and airships and the new faradic trams you might have heard of—they run right through the heart of our own city. My father did it before me; it's the family business. But the machines I'm talking about now involve significant investment on the part of some of the members of the Interdimensional Harmonics Society, and I must show a return on that investment or fall foul of their graces."

Tess squinted at him. "You mean—they'd be upset with you? For wasting their money?"

"I couldn't have put it better myself," he said with a chuckle.

"But why do you care so much?" she asked. "Why is all this so important?"

Mr. Cleat settled himself more comfortably on his stool as he searched for a way to answer. "I know you'll know what I mean," he began, "when I say it's important to feel that you belong somewhere." He looked sidelong at Tess. She nodded and he continued. "It's the same with me. I think all of us who grew up without parental figures might share that feeling. We can seem rootless. Am I making sense?"

Tess nodded again, giving an encouraging smile, and Mr. Cleat narrowed his eyes just a little. "My interest in all this began with my father, who was taken from me when I was around your age. My mother sadly passed away when I was so young that all I have left of her are some letters and a tattered photograph." He paused but Tess remained silent. In her hair, Violet stirred as if warning her to be cautious and Tess tried to relax. *Breathe,* she reminded herself. "I began to cling to the things my father had loved—machines, engines, money, and Interdimensional Harmonics most of all. I vowed that I was going to get to the bottom of the things that had eluded him and I was going to leave my name—*his* name—all over them as a living testament. This is it." He waved his hands around, taking in everything. "This house. This Society. This quest, which I'm determined to see through."

Tess gulped, waiting until her voice was steady before she spoke again. "What quest?"

"To change the course of history, Tess. Not only in my own reality, but in another. Perhaps in *all* of them. To design and build machines that, when sent between worlds, will start and finish wars, or solve problems that have no other solution. I'll be paid astronomical sums of money to do this work, of course, but that's not important." He waved his hand dismissively, as if Tess had accused him of being greedy. "There happens to be an ongoing war in a nearby world; I want to start there. The bombers I've built will—"

"Bombers?" Tess couldn't help but interrupt, thinking of the dark terror in Thomas's voice as he'd spoken to her about cities being flattened by things called bombers. Cities whose names she couldn't remember. Cities that were real to him.

Mr. Cleat smiled indulgently. "Flying machines, Tess, that

can destroy things on the ground. Nothing for you to be worried about. They'll do you no harm—but of course you'll see that for yourself. You'll have the seat of honor at my exhibition. Indeed, the night couldn't go ahead without you."

"Wh-what night?" Tess hoped her fear sounded like excitement.

"It's not far away now," Mr. Cleat replied carelessly. "Oh, and by the by—do you still have that old book of mine? Or rather of *yours*. I seem to remember giving it to you."

Tess blinked, then turned to fetch *The Secret Garden*. She held it up. "I can't seem to put it down," she said. "I'm not sure why."

"Are you enjoying the story?" Mr. Cleat asked, a smile hovering on his lips.

Tess looked at him apologetically. "Not really," she admitted.

"You and that book have something fundamental in common, you know," Mr. Cleat said. "I'd wager my considerable fortune that it's the reason you seem so drawn to it and it to you."

Tess turned the book around so that its front cover was facing her. "Something in common?" she said. "I'd never heard of it before I saw it in your library."

"Nobody in this world has ever heard of it," Mr. Cleat continued, his voice low and prowling. Tess froze as she listened but remained still. "It was published by a company that doesn't exist, written by an author who doesn't exist—or, if she did, she became a nun or a physicist or a farmer instead, who knows." Mr. Cleat paused, as if waiting for Tess to respond, but Tess found she couldn't. She just kept her eyes fixed on the cover of the book and tried to take comfort from Violet's gentle movements in her hair.

"I really don't know what you mean," she said, looking back at Mr. Cleat and fixing him with the widest, emptiest stare she could muster.

"I don't think that's true," he replied. "I'll leave you to think on it. Maybe you'll conclude something different once you've considered it a little." He stood up, pulling his waistcoat straight and settling his tie, gazing at Tess all the while. "Speaking of which, I'm away to a Society meeting. I'm sure they'll be interested to hear how your reading's going," he said, nodding his goodbye.

Tess watched him leave. She didn't breathe again until he'd closed the door behind him and his footsteps had faded away.

25

"So you see, I had to come and warn you," Tess said. She sat in Thomas's workroom, her knees drawn up to her chest. Moose sat on her outstretched hand, nibbling happily at a lump of cheese. Thomas stood by one of the desks, apparently lost in thought.

"It might not be *here* he's talking about," Thomas finally said, turning to her. "Mightn't it? There could be a war in another reality. That could be what he meant."

Tess shrugged. "I suppose. But are you willing to take that risk? He's threatened to send bombers through. Right *here*. And if I've learned something about this whole business, it's this: when you travel, you stay in the same place. By which I mean—"

"You move from world to world, but your *geographical* location stays the same," Thomas said, finishing her thought. "As in if you use the Star-spinner in *your* chapel, you arrive here in mine. If you used it in *your* version of the house, you'd arrive in my version of it."

Tess sat up straighter, the movement spooking Moose enough for him to scamper off her hand and onto her knee instead. She stroked him apologetically as she tried to get her thoughts into words. "And if I were to travel to the building in *this* reality where Ackerbee's is in mine . . ." She let the sentence trail off as she looked hopefully at Thomas.

He turned to her. "You'd arrive at your home," he said, his eyes shining. Then his face fell. "Without Violet, of course."

Tess frowned. "There is that problem."

"But you could still send your *own* message," Thomas continued. "Tomorrow night, we can do it. Meet me here. I'll have the bike ready and we'll speed there and back in no time."

Tess's eyes shone behind her glasses. "I can write a note saying *Quicksilver* and where I am, and put it through the letter box," she said. "And then in the morning it'll be there. Miss Ackerbee will see it and she'll know it's from me. And then they'll come." She closed her eyes, imagining Miss Ackerbee and Rebecca on their battered tandem bicycle; she saw their faces as they jangled the bellpull of Roedeer Lodge, and

Mrs. Thistleton's expression as they told her they were there to take Tess home . . .

"They'll probably have a fight on their hands," Thomas said.

Tess sighed. "Yes. They probably will."

"Mr. Cleat won't just give you up. Not if he thinks you're useful to him, which of course you are." He frowned, chewing thoughtfully on the inside of his cheek. "I just wish we knew exactly what he was planning."

"Yes. And when he's planning it," Tess said. "All he'd give away was that it was 'soon,' whatever that means."

"Well, he's hardly going to hand you his entire dastardly plan, is he?" Thomas said with a grin. "Even I would give him more credit than that."

Tess grinned back at him, shaking her head ruefully. "I'd better be going," she said. "It's after two in the morning and I'm going to need some sleep if we're going to attempt our own dastardly plan tomorrow night."

"Right. So we're agreed? Operation Quicksilver is a go?"

Tess snorted. "If you must call it that," she said.

Thomas rubbed his hands together. "Brilliant. I haven't taken the bike out in ages. It'll be great to have a midnight flit."

"You make it sound like we're going on a picnic or something," Tess said. She scooped up Moose and handed him to Thomas before hauling herself to her feet. She couldn't wait to be back home again in Ackerbee's, where this would all seem like a bad dream . . . *But what about Thomas?* said an inconvenient thought. *If you leave Roedeer Lodge, how will you see him?* She looked him in the eye, and he seemed troubled too. "Are you sure this is a good plan?" she asked in a quiet voice.

"You need to be gone from Roedeer Lodge before Mr. Cleat does whatever he's going to do," Thomas replied. "Even if it makes things tricky for us for a while."

"But I don't want—"

"Let's not worry about it now," Thomas said. "We'll find a way to see one another. I promise. Now go on. Get back and sleep. And I'll see you tomorrow."

Tess sucked on her top lip. "Right. Tomorrow. Take care, won't you?"

"And you," Thomas said, giving her a hug.

Tess made her way down the ladder and stepped through the void as easily as into the bathtub; it held no fear for her anymore, though the intensity of the journey remained. Every time she traveled, she wondered if all of her came back—sometimes, particularly when lying awake late at night trying to calm her feverish mind, it felt as though some of her particles got lost along the way with every crossing.

Stepping into her own derelict chapel, Tess shivered. She put the Star-spinner back inside her vest and hurried to the top pew to collect Violet. "Hello, girl," she crooned as the spider made her careful way up her sleeve. "Let's go, eh?"

Tess quickly made her way over the field, across the gate and back to the kitchen door of Roedeer Lodge. She had barely locked the door behind her when she heard a tiny noise in the darkness. It seemed to come from beside the cold fireplace, against the kitchen's back wall.

"Psst!" it sounded again, and Tess froze, her eyes searching the shadows and her heart beginning to thud. Then a figure stepped out of a darkened corner. "Miss! It's just me!"

"*Millie!*" Tess whispered, her voice strained. She leaned against the doorframe, weak with relief. "You startled me!"

"Sorry," Millie answered, coming close enough to take Tess's hands. "I needed to talk to you and I saw you weren't in your room. Miss, there's something I think you need to hear. Rosaleen—my cousin, remember, who works in Mr. Cleat's club—well, she was able to tell me that Mr. Cleat has something big in the works. Something to do with his Harmonics crowd. Something that's going to take place here—a demonstration, I think she called it. She said there was talk among the Society members that there'd be a child involved—a girl with a key, or something like that." Millie frowned. "I can't quite recall. But anyway, whatever sort of demonstration it is, I wanted you to know."

Tess felt her breath catch in her throat. *Mr. Cleat's experiment.* This had to be what he'd been hinting at in the lab.

My front-row seat. "Do you have any clear idea what's going to happen? He mentioned it to me, too, but wouldn't tell me much."

"Search me, miss. Rosaleen didn't really know either. She's too interested in who's starring in the latest flick to really care about Mr. Cleat and what he gets up to," Millie said impatiently.

"How does she know about it?"

"Mr. Cleat was looking to get some of the girls who work in the club to come up here to the Lodge for the night, as serving staff and the like. The Society members apparently aren't too pleased—but as most of them are invited to the event, there shouldn't be a problem with nicking the people who keep the place running." She paused for thought. "Apparently Mr. Cleat's not too popular with his precious Society at the moment, so this demonstration is supposed to give him back a bit of credit. That's Rosaleen's opinion anyway." She sniffed dismissively. "It's all under wraps, what he's going to do, but he wants a full quota of staff on duty."

"When is it supposed to be happening? Do you know?" Tess's heart was thundering. Whatever Mr. Cleat was planning, she was certain the 'child' had to be her—and she wanted no part of it.

"This Friday, miss," Millie said. "And it's to run late, into the small hours of Saturday."

"This Friday?" Tess felt weak. The plan she and Thomas

had made *had* to work, then, as imperfect as it was. She needed to be gone from here before Mr. Cleat could stage his demonstration. It had to work and there were only days to get her out. She hoped Miss Ackerbee could pull enough strings in that time to set her free. *She doesn't seem to have tried too hard up to now, though,* the tiny doubting voice inside her mind whispered. *What makes you think she'll come through under time pressure like that?*

"Miss? Are you all right?" Millie asked.

"Call me Tess. And yes"—Tess tried to smile—"I'm fine, Millie. Thank you so much for this. You've been such a help."

"Not a bother, Tess," said Millie, beaming with pride. "Now we'd best get back to our beds before there's war." She began to walk away but Tess reached out and took her by the hand. Millie stopped short, surprised. She turned to Tess with wide eyes.

"Whatever's going on this Friday, you shouldn't be here either," Tess said. "I don't know what it is exactly, but what Mr. Cleat has told me sounds bad. Do you have anywhere you can go?"

Millie smiled, but it was a veneer of bravado. "My mother lives in County Carlow, miss. I mean, Tess. I can't get there—not on a few days' notice, at least. I have Rosaleen in town, of course, but she can't take me in on a whim. And she'll be here on the night anyway. So I'll have to stay, but don't worry about me. I've seen worse, I'm sure."

Tess's mind filled with fire, great billowing gusts of it. "I'm not sure you have," she murmured.

"Don't worry about me, miss. Nobody pays the slightest bit of attention to me, where I go or what I do. So don't you fret." Millie squeezed Tess's hand companionably, then let it go. "That's not to say I'm not grateful for your kindness, Tess." She smiled shyly and Tess smiled back.

"You're my friend, Millie," Tess said. "That's what friends do."

"Has Prossy fallen *asleep*?" Wilf whispered. Prissy shrugged, then nudged Prossy sharply with her toe. Prossy gave an indignant snort, then sat up, her hair askew.

"What?" she demanded. "I was paying *complete* attention."

"To the pillow perhaps," Wilf said, rolling her eyes. "Now. What's next?"

Eunice held a handwritten sheet of paper closer to their candle. "Plan: To Exit Ackerbee's Undetected," she read. "I have an idea for that, actually."

"Oh?" Wilf said, sitting forward.

"Mrs. Stubbs keeps a skeleton key in the kitchen," Eunice said. "I can borrow it for a while and then we can just let ourselves out of the front door."

"How on earth do you know what Cook keeps in the kitchen?" Prissy asked.

Eunice shrugged. "I like to eat. And I'm nosy."

"Won't she miss it?" Wilf asked, wrinkling her nose. "I should think a skeleton key is something you *would* miss."

"It's up on a high shelf above the stove," Eunice said. "I don't think she even remembers it's there."

"Right. Well, let's try that then. Eunice, you can retrieve the skeleton key from Mrs. Stubbs as soon as possible." Wilf's voice was bright. "And as for the rest of us, let's figure out a way to get to Fairwater Park."

"We could save up for the tram fare," Prossy suggested. "I've got about three shillings in my sock drawer."

"Or we could just walk," Prissy said. "It'd take a while, is the only thing."

"I think the tram's a better option, except I don't have *any* money." Wilf rubbed her head, thinking hard.

"We could ask the others. I mean, everyone. Surely between the whole house we'll have enough for four tram fares." Eunice looked at the others in turn. "We all want Tess back. Nobody will say no."

"Just let's get a move on," Wilf said. "We've only got until Friday to do this. If we're to have any chance of getting into that park, it's got to be the night of the party. I *have* to see Tess and find out if she's all right. And if she wants to come home, we're going to be the ones to help her."

"We will have time for a canapé or two, though, won't

we?" Prossy said, looking dreamy. "It's not every day we get to go to a garden party. I'm quite looking forward to it."

Eunice sniggered, which set the others off. Very soon all four girls were laughing as quietly as they could—but it didn't stop a thrown hairbrush, which smacked Wilf on the head. Somehow that just seemed funnier. "Will you lot *shut it*," hissed someone in the corner of the dorm. "Or find a different place to have these coven meetings! I'm going to have a word with Miss Ackerbee, see if I don't, and we'll soon find out what *she* thinks of your ridiculous plan."

"She'll have to pay her own tram fare, if she wants to join us," said Prissy, wiping her eyes. "I'll be blowed if I'm stumping up for her."

This set the four of them giggling again. The hairbrush thrower tutted loudly and flung herself back into her bed, stuffing her head inside her pillow until eventually the dorm fell silent once more.

26

TESS ENTERED THE CHAPEL WITH HER CARDIGAN BUTTONED UP, HER sturdiest boots on and a small burlap sack she'd begged from Millie. In it, Millie had placed a flask of soup, some bread wrapped in waxed paper and a large bar of chocolate. With any luck she, Moose and Thomas *would* have time for a picnic when Operation Quicksilver was done.

"Here we are, love," she whispered to Violet as they approached their top pew. She set down her lantern and Violet dutifully crawled out onto her fingers, ready to be deposited beside it. "I know you don't like this bit but I'll be back as soon as I can, I promise."

She kissed her finger and tapped Violet gently with it, and the spider settled beside the soft light. Then Tess got to her feet and fished the Star-spinner out of her pocket. She took a deep breath and ran her thumb over the metal fronds, feeling them warm to her skin, feeling her own pulse vibrate through it, and—

"Ah. Here you are, Miss de Sousa. Good of you to join us." The voice cut Tess to the heart. She turned, overcome with shock, to see Mrs. Thistleton emerging from a doorway tucked behind the rotting lectern. "We were wondering when you'd make your appearance." Behind her stumbled a sobbing Millie, her face shining with tears in the lamplight. Mrs. Thistleton held her tightly by the wrist.

"Wh-*what?*" Tess feared she might throw up as she looked from one to the other.

"I'm sorry, miss!" Millie called. "She made me! She said— *Ow!*" Mrs. Thistleton yanked her forward and she reeled, losing her footing entirely on a loose floorboard and pitching headfirst down the altar steps. Her head smacked painfully off the floor tiles.

Tess pocketed the Star-spinner and dropped to her knees to haul the other girl up into a sitting position. "Are you all right?"

Millie seemed dazed but her eyes were bright. "Get away from here," she said. "Go!"

"That's quite enough," Mrs. Thistleton said, coming to stand behind them. She'd positioned herself, Tess noticed too late, between the girls and the door. Tess turned her head to peer through the dark hole in the wall from which Mrs. Thistleton and Millie had emerged. *But what's out there?* she thought. *Thomas once mentioned a tunnel—is there one here, too?* For a split second she prepared to run, and then she remembered Violet. Her eyes flickered to the top pew; Mrs. Thistleton was standing in front of it, a knowing smile on her face.

"What's happening?" Tess said. "I don't understand."

"All this can be over quite quickly if you simply hand over the device," Mrs. Thistleton said, her words so calm they almost seemed bored. As she spoke, she flexed the fingers of her left hand, on which she wore a thick leather glove.

"Wh-what device?" Tess swallowed hard as soon as the words were out of her mouth, looking away from the glove to stare into Mrs. Thistleton's bone-white face.

"The one"—Mrs. Thistleton bent forward at the waist, tilting her head a little as though she were speaking to a baby—"that you had in your hand just a moment ago. The one you've been using to wriggle through holes in reality for the past few weeks. *That* one, Tess."

"I—I don't know what you're talking—"

"Spare me," Mrs. Thistleton said, straightening up. "Hand it over now or things will be worse for everyone. Believe me."

Tess blinked away tears of frustration and fear. "This doesn't make any sense. You don't even *believe* in any of this."

Mrs. Thistleton smirked. "Did Norton tell you that? The *dear*. I shall have to have a word with him later. Now"—her face settled into its usual scowl—"the device, please."

"No," Tess said, trembling. "I won't."

"One last chance, Tess," Mrs. Thistleton said, her voice low.

"And I've already told you," Tess snarled back. *"No!"*

In one swift movement, Mrs. Thistleton turned to the top pew. She lifted Tess's lantern with her ungloved hand, tipping it sideways to knock the candle out of it, and with the gloved one she grabbed Violet, shoving her into the empty lantern so quickly that the spider had no chance to react.

Mrs. Thistleton turned back to Tess as she snapped the glass door of the lantern closed, a triumphant light in her eyes.

"Let's begin negotiations again, shall we? How about you reconsider what I'm asking you, Tess? The device in exchange for your spider." The candle, lying on its side on the floor near Mrs. Thistleton's feet, still burned; there was light enough for Tess to see Violet inside her glass prison, her legs searching for a way out.

Mrs. Thistleton lifted the lantern slightly, peering into it. "Tarantulas are remarkably strong for their size," she said conversationally. "I'm sure you know that. But," she continued, turning to face Tess, "I'm sure I'll enjoy finding ways to hurt it if need be."

"Don't hurt her," Tess said, her vision blurring. "Please."

"You can stop all this if you just do as you're asked," Mrs. Thistleton said. "Be reasonable. I'm asking you for such a little thing. Is it really worth your spider's life?" She sneered. "And without her, doesn't that spell the end of your career as a world-wanderer anyway? You don't want to risk that, surely."

Tess stared, dumbfounded. *She knows about Violet being my anchor, too? How?*

"You'll find, my dear, that it doesn't do to underestimate those you feel are *beneath* you," Mrs. Thistleton said, her voice tight with disgust. "Housekeepers, mere governesses even, are capable not only of great things but of great thoughts. Sometimes it is the most humble among us who wield the true power." She began to swing the lantern. Tess watched as Violet staggered about inside it, fighting to find her balance. "So what's it going to be?"

Tess reached into her pocket, keeping her eyes on Mrs. Thistleton all the time. *If I pretend,* she told herself. *Pretend to be about to give it to her. Distract her with it. Then grab Violet and run . . .*

Mrs. Thistleton's eyes glittered in the low light. Without dropping her stare from Tess, she leaned to one side, just enough to reach the tall windowsill beside her. She placed the lantern on it, and as Tess watched this, her courage failed. Violet was gone, as completely as if she'd been thrown into the darkness.

"That's it," Mrs. Thistleton said, the beginnings of a smile on her face as Tess withdrew her hand from her pocket. "Now hand it over and you'll get your spider back. You have my word."

"Here's what I think of your word," Tess muttered before turning to Millie—or where Millie had been. Unseen by Tess and Mrs. Thistleton both, she had fled—and with her had gone Tess's last hope of getting out of this situation with both her Star-spinner and her spider intact. Her mouth fell open in dismay.

"Dratted girl," Mrs. Thistleton muttered, glancing at the chapel's open door. "I hope she hasn't gone running to Mr. Cleat in order to try to save her job. Her severance papers are already on his desk and now she's sealed her fate—she'll never gain a position in Hurdleford again." She focused on Tess once more. "A shame when friends let you down, isn't it?"

"I hate you," Tess said, staring up at her governess.

Mrs. Thistleton shrugged. "And I you, child. Yet here we are. And if that device is not in my possession by the count of five, I shall smash this lantern against the wall. Sturdy as your spider is, I doubt very much whether it will survive the experience."

"Violet is not an 'it,'" Tess said through clenched teeth. Her fingers tightened around the Star-spinner and Mrs. Thistleton moved as quickly as a snake to haul Tess to her feet.

The governess's gloved fingers wedged themselves beneath the device, forcing it out of Tess's grip.

Mrs. Thistleton held up the Star-spinner, turning it this way and that as if to admire it. "Such a *tiny* thing," she said. "And yet how it will change the world."

At that moment, the candle at her feet gave out, plunging the chapel into darkness. Mrs. Thistleton pocketed the Star-spinner and reached up to retrieve Violet, all the while keeping Tess's arm in her iron grip.

"Now," she said, into Tess's ear, "let's go home."

Through the darkness of a deserted Fairwater Park, a young girl was running.

A young girl struggling to see through her tears, whose brain was ringing with hatred for the woman who'd made her betray her friend. Millie's memory was filled with Tess's wide disbelieving eyes, and the thought of what might be happening to the young miss right at that moment kept her feet flying. There was enough starlight to make out her destination—a padlocked pedestrian gate in a shady corner of the park, little used except by some of the staff of Roedeer Lodge.

Her breath tearing through her aching lungs, Millie

reached the gate and climbed it. She landed heavily on the pavement outside and started to run down the leafy lane that led toward the city. Eventually, as the River Plura came into view, she had to stop for breath and she leaned against a lamppost as she tried to compose herself. Millie's destination lay right at the end of the quays, at the heart of the city; it was a place she'd never been, but she was sure she could find it. Tess had described it often enough.

I've got to find her, Millie told herself. *And whether Miss Ackerbee's angry with me or not, whether she turns me out with a flea in my ear, I've got to try.* She blinked hard. *And then I'll just have to fend for myself.* She'd never seen Mrs. Thistleton angrier than she'd been earlier that evening, when she'd cornered Millie and made her tell her everything she knew. She'd threatened Millie with the sack but—as the girl now miserably realized— she was going to sack her anyway. She'd betrayed Tess for nothing.

"You'll stop crying right this minute," she told herself, wiping her eyes with her apron. "And you'll go and get the job done."

The silent city lay before her and Millie set off into it, her courage clenched in her fist.

27

MILLIE STOOD ON THE DOORSTEP OF ACKERBEE'S HOME FOR LOST and Foundlings and tried to compose herself. The building's tall, narrow façade was unmistakable, but a light had been left on inside its porch, and the brass nameplate beside the door gleamed. If Millie had been in any doubt about whether she'd reached the right place, that would have put an end to it.

She took a deep breath, steadied herself and then pulled on the bell. Faintly, she heard it jangling inside the house and bit her lip at the thought of how early—or late—it was. She hated having to cause such a disturbance, but she knew she had no choice.

Several minutes passed before Millie saw a light in the

hallway. Through a glass panel beside the front door, a woman's tired face peered out at her in confusion. Seconds later, Millie heard the door being unlocked and a heavy bolt being drawn back.

"Are you looking for Ackerbee's?" said the woman, opening the door wide. She smiled wearily at Millie, her brown eyes warm and welcoming.

"I'm looking for Miss Ackerbee herself," said Millie, finally finding her voice. "There's something I need to tell her."

"You're in luck then, for I am she," said Miss Ackerbee, stepping back to admit Millie into the hallway. "Do come in. You look like a large cup of cocoa would do you good."

Millie stepped through and Miss Ackerbee closed the door behind her. In the shadows at the far end of the hallway, Millie saw another woman, her tousled copper-brown hair coming out of a loose plait, hurrying toward them. She wrapped a dressing gown around herself as she came.

"Is everything all right?" she asked, looking at Millie. "Does someone need help?"

Miss Ackerbee nodded. "Everything's fine, Rebecca dear. Perhaps you'd join us in my parlor while I chat with this young lady. Can I tempt you with cocoa? I was just about to go to the kitchen for some."

"Please, let me take care of it," Rebecca said. "You get our guest settled." Miss Ackerbee nodded at Rebecca and led

Millie through into a room with a long low couch, a chair and a small table in one corner and a desk in another. Millie felt herself begin to shiver, in both relief and shock and also with simple exhaustion, and she allowed Miss Ackerbee to lead her gently to the sofa.

"Now," Miss Ackerbee said once Millie was settled, "can you tell me what the trouble is?"

"It's Tess," said Millie simply.

Miss Ackerbee's eyes opened wide and she sat forward. She took one of Millie's hands in hers. "I didn't dare hope," she said in a quick, tight voice. "Is she all right?"

Millie didn't know quite how to answer. "She was, last I saw her. But, Miss Ackerbee, I don't know for how much longer. She's in trouble, you see." Millie paused to think, trying to make sure she was remembering Tess's message properly. "She told me to tell you one thing, one word. It was *quicksilver*. I don't know what it means."

Miss Ackerbee bent her head for a moment, and when she looked back at Millie, her eyes were wet. "I know what it means, my dear. I know. Thank you."

Rebecca came into the room with a tray bearing three steaming mugs of cocoa and a plate piled high with choco-late biscuits. Miss Ackerbee let her set the tray down before turning to her.

"This brave girl has come here with a message from Tess,

my dear," Miss Ackerbee said. "I feel we should be ready for action."

Rebecca slid to her knees on the floor in front of Millie. Her face was drawn with worry. "We've been writing to the post office box he left us with," she said. "But there's never a reply. Is she getting our letters?"

Millie shook her head, her face twisting with distaste. "No, ma'am. There hasn't been anything. She's keeping them from her, and keeping her letters from being sent too."

Miss Ackerbee frowned. "She?"

"I think this is a conversation best had with a cocoa in hand," said Rebecca, handing them each a mug. "Let's get started."

After Millie had told Rebecca and Miss Ackerbee as much as she could, she was ushered upstairs toward the dorms.

"Please," she whispered. "Really, there's no need—I have a cousin who has a position in town. I can go to her and—"

"Nonsense," insisted Miss Ackerbee. "You've come all the way here to help one of my girls and now I'm to turn you out into the night? I won't have it. You must get some rest and then we'll make sure you're delivered to your cousin. Until then you're safe here."

"Well—thank you," Millie replied. She *was* exhausted, that much was true. But she wondered how safe she was here really. The memory of Mrs. Thistleton's face, twisted with rage, loomed in her mind, but she shoved it away and tried to stay calm as Miss Ackerbee led her to an empty bed.

"You'll be fine here till morning; do make yourself at home," she whispered. "And try to get some sleep, my dear. I can't thank you enough for what you've done for us, and for Tess, tonight." She patted Millie on the shoulder and left her to it.

Millie was slipping off her second shoe, getting ready to place it carefully on the floor beside the first, when she heard the *whish* of a match being struck. Then the corner of the room pooled into light, a gentle glow from a candle showing her several wide-awake faces. Four girls in various stages of dishevelment sat crowded onto a single bed. All of them were looking at her, and Millie shrank a little under their scrutiny.

"We heard the bell—was that you ringing?" one of the girls began in a loud whisper. "Do you know Tess?" asked another, and "What's happened to Tess?" asked a third, all at the same time. Millie's mouth fell open as she wondered who to answer first, but no sound managed to come out.

"Hush," said the fourth, a tall, strong girl with a long yellow plait down her back. "Let her get used to us first." Millie blinked at them all for a moment or two. "Now," the girl with the plait continued, "that should be quite long enough. Time for introductions. I'm Proserpina, but everyone calls me Prossy. Pleased to meet you."

Another girl sat forward, similar in build to the first, but dark where the other girl was fair. "I'm Priscilla. Call me Prissy." She looked at Prossy and then back at Millie. "And no, we're not related. Just in case you were wondering."

A small girl was next, her black hair in a profusion of tight, neat braids. "I'm Eunice," she said, holding out her hand to Millie, who stretched across the bed she was sitting on to shake it.

"And I'm Wilf," said the fourth, a pale girl with her dark hair in a neat bun. "We've been missing Tess so much. Has something happened to her? Only, Miss Ackerbee mentioned her to you just now."

Millie looked at them each in turn, all hanging on her next word. "I'm Millicent, but Tess calls me Millie" was all she could say.

"Then you're Millie to us, too," said Prossy, smiling warmly.

Millie returned the smile, some of her shyness falling away. "Thank you, miss," she said.

"Oh, for goodness' sake—none of that 'miss' stuff, please," scoffed Prissy. "You're not in service here." Then she paused thoughtfully, taking in Millie's clothes. "Speaking of which—where *were* you in service? The place they're keeping Tess?"

Millie nodded. "Roedeer Lodge, miss—whoops," she said, feeling her cheeks burn. Prissy simply nodded encouragingly. "It's in the grounds of Fairwater Park," she continued.

Prissy turned to Wilf. "Well done, you," she said. "You were right."

Wilf nodded, looking grim but pleased. "Is Tess all right?" she asked, and Millie looked at her. She took a moment to get her thoughts straight and then told the girls what she knew—how Tess had been doing experiments of some sort in the old chapel at Roedeer Lodge and how Mrs. Thistleton had trapped Millie into telling her where Tess went at night. How she'd been dragged there to witness Tess's fate.

"I was stupid to think Mrs. Thistleton wouldn't know something was happening," Millie said mournfully. "No housekeeper worth her salt doesn't notice missing matches and pilfered candles and suspicious creaks after dark and lanterns bobbing over the garden. I should have thought of that." Millie paused, shaking her head. "It's my fault," she said miserably. "She was caught because of me."

"Look, that bit can't be helped," said Prissy, giving Millie a friendly pat on the arm. "This Thistleton creature sounds like a pill. It's not your fault. You've done what you can to get Tess's message out. That's all she could want."

"But that's not enough. We need to try to get her away from there," Millie said, looking back up at the girls. "And we only have until Friday. Tomorrow, really."

Wilf nodded. "Yes. We know about the party," she said.

"It's more like some sort of demonstration," Millie said. "Mr. Cleat's bringing all his Society crowd. I really don't know much else about it, besides that it had Tess worried for some reason. And then when Mrs. Thistleton attacked her . . ." Millie paused, shuddering at the memory. "She's important to them, that much I know. They need her for something. And whatever it is, Tess wants nothing to do with it."

Wilf took a deep breath, trying not to think about what might have happened to Tess—and to Violet. *Focus on getting them back,* she told herself in as fierce a voice as she could muster. "You've told Miss Ackerbee and Rebecca all of this?"

Millie nodded. "Tess had wanted to call for help but she had something she needed to do first. I never asked her what; that was her business. But after tonight, her message couldn't wait anymore."

"And what did Miss Ackerbee say she was going to do?" Wilf's large green eyes were narrowed and her whole body seemed pointed, like a nocked arrow.

Millie tried to think. "She mentioned something about a lawyer. She's going to telephone in the morning and—"

"No," Wilf said, dropping the word into Millie's sentence

like a guillotine. "No more lawyers. They take too long. This is up to us. We've got to get her back, right now."

"We can't go *now*, ninny," said Prissy. "How are we going to get there? How are we going to get *in*? It's not like you can just walk into Fairwater Park."

"Well, actually, I think I *can* get us all in," said Millie, straightening up. "And in a way where we won't be noticed. Do you all have a black skirt? And a white blouse?"

"Do we have what?" said Prossy, looking faintly disgusted.

"Something that would pass for a maid's uniform," said Millie. "There'll be loads of extra staff on Friday for this event Mr. Cleat's planning. Nobody will pay the slightest bit of attention to a few new faces. We'll blend right in." Millie's bright expression faded a little. "Or at least, you will. I hope nobody at the Lodge spots me."

"I'm sure we can manage to beg, borrow or steal the right clothes," said Prissy, shrugging. "And we'll hide you somehow, Millie."

"I'm sure I'll think of something," Millie said distractedly. She slumped a little, tiredness overwhelming her. "All I know is Tess didn't want anything to do with whatever Mr. Cleat's planning. I want to be there to help her stop him and maybe to get her away, if we can."

"So do we," said Eunice in a determined tone. Then she yawned and rubbed her eyes. A wave of yawns traveled around the group.

Millie yawned so widely her ears popped and she realized the truth of the matter: there was nothing to be done for Tess now. If what she'd gleaned from Mrs. Thistleton was accurate, Tess was important for whatever was to happen on Friday. They had to hope she'd be as safe as she could be in that horrible place until then.

"At least we've got a plan," said Wilf, looking at them each in turn. "We have a way out of here, thanks to Eunice, and now thanks to Millie we have a way into the park. It's better than nothing. And though I wish we could go sooner, we'll make our move at the right time."

"Friday it is," said Prissy, crawling onto her own bed. "Sleep well, everyone."

"Sweet dreams," added Prossy, already pulling the covers over her head.

Wilf blew out the candle and soft darkness filled the room. "Millie?" she said after a moment or two, just as Millie's eyes were adjusting to the dark. "Thank you."

A sleepy chorus of thanks came from the other beds, all except Prossy's—soft, contented snoring had already begun from her corner of the dorm.

"It's what friends do," whispered Millie into the night.

28

THOMAS HAD WAITED IN THE CHAPEL AS LONG AS HE COULD, BUT he'd eventually crawled upstairs, his mind heavy with worry. The radio was whispering something about the sinking of the *Bismarck*, which had happened a couple of days before; the Oscillometer was hissing steadily. Still Tess did not come. Moose ran from one of Thomas's hands to the other, the movement soothing like a metronome, and just as Thomas realized he was being lulled to sleep, he pulled himself to his feet, gently placed Moose on the top of his head and began to climb down the ladder.

He found his torch, ignoring his own worried mind. *Something's happened.* She wouldn't have missed this, not for anything. Maybe she was sick, or something had gone wrong with the Star-spinner, or—worst of all—she'd been prevented from coming. Thomas was filled with a sense of dread. Stuck here, he could do *nothing* to help Tess.

But maybe Mackintosh knew something that would shed some light.

Thomas slipped Moose into his coat pocket as he hurried to the vestry. He dropped into the tunnel and, for the first time doing this journey, felt afraid—afraid of the shadows, of Mackintosh's pasty face leering out of the earthen walls around him, or that a uniformed soldier with a rifle leveled at his heart would come charging toward the light of his torch . . .

Thomas flattened himself against the tunnel wall, trying to calm his breathing. *Come on, you dolt,* he told himself. *You've done this journey a thousand times. And you're going back to your house. It's Mackintosh who should be running scared, not you!* He squashed his eyes shut, remembering the reading of his parents' will, and their inexplicable decision to name Mackintosh, their distant acquaintance, as Thomas's guardian. There was no one else who could take him and Mackintosh was willing to move into Thomas's home, so things were smoothed over quickly, and before he knew it, Thomas had lost his family but gained a disinterested caretaker—someone who seemed to care more about his parents' work than looking after their son.

He has no right to anything they owned, Thomas reminded himself. *And Tess is the only family you have. This is up to you now.* Moose popped out of his coat pocket, as if he could hear Thomas's thoughts, and the boy smiled as he stroked the mouse's head. "I mean, it's up to us, Moose. Right?"

Moose sniffed the air, his ears twitching, and Thomas took heart. He made his silent way into the scullery of his home, creeping out of the kitchen and across the lobby. The house was bathed in silent darkness but with every step he expected the lights to be thrown on and Mackintosh's voice to shatter the night.

He'd made it to the bottom of the stairs before he fully realized how far he'd come.

Thomas looked up. The stairs were the same as he remembered, their richly patterned carpet balding near the edges, and he hoped he could remember all the creaky spots. The first landing held a glowing lamp. Thomas was thankful for it as he began to climb, holding his unlit torch like a sword so firmly his knuckles paled around its grip.

He has my dad's Oscillometer, Thomas thought. *The big one.* The machine in the observatory was merely a working copy; Thomas's father had built a full-scale machine in the house and it had been kept in his workroom upstairs. It wasn't something that could be easily moved, so Thomas knew Mackintosh had to be using the same room. Maybe it could tell him something useful. Maybe he'd be able to send Tess a message, though he wasn't sure how to work the machine. Maybe he'd even find Mackintosh himself and force him to rescue Tess, somehow . . .

Thomas shook those thoughts away as the door to his father's old workroom loomed before him. The door at the end of the hall had been his parents' bedroom; Thomas assumed Mackintosh was in there and so trod as quietly as he could on the floorboards until finally his hand was on the doorknob.

A huge snore from the bedroom made Thomas jump. His heart raced as he heard Mackintosh turning over in bed and he tried to twist the knob while Mackintosh himself was making noise in the hope one sound would mask the other.

And finally he'd made it. He clicked on his torch and swept it around, swallowing back against his suddenly tight throat. Everything looked different now; for a start there were no framed photographs of his mother or of Thomas himself, and the Oscillometer—so large it took up most of the room—looked like it wasn't being maintained as well as it had been when his parents were alive.

Similar to its smaller cousin in the observatory, the large Oscillometer hummed and hissed placidly, its needle bobbing gently in the main dial. A stack of paper beside the machine was slowly growing, being quietly churned out as every twitch of the needle was recorded by a narrow pen scratching across the surface of the paper; Thomas carefully picked up a handful of this record, trying to spot a pattern or any sort of recent activity, but he was eventually forced to replace it, having learned nothing.

There wasn't anything here he could use. The disappointment was crushing. He just didn't know enough about how the machine worked to send a message—and even if he could, how would he guarantee Tess would get it? Just as Thomas convinced himself to go back to the observatory and get some sleep, the torch beam fell on a nearby table with some open books on it.

He made for it, keeping the light focused on the books all the time, and realized as he drew near that he was looking at Mackintosh's logbook. Excited, he bent to examine it. Nothing much had happened for the past few weeks, besides that he'd been in touch with a person named Sharpthorn—whoever he was. *Or she, I suppose,* Thomas reminded himself, running his finger down the page.

Under the date, there was a message from Sharpthorn. *Be ready,* it said. *Thirtieth. Protocol S.*

Thomas didn't know what this meant, but something about it made him nervous. Could *thirtieth* be a reference to Friday's date? He supposed it had to be.

But what on earth could *Protocol S* mean? He cast about for something that might help—a dictionary, a book helpfully labeled *Codes*, anything at all—but came up short. There were lots more logbooks and a few dusty old textbooks, which Thomas didn't think would be of any use. As an afterthought, he put down his torch and struggled to heave out the bottom logbook in the pile, on which a golden figure 1 was embossed. He flipped the book open and after a moment saw that he'd hit the jackpot. There was a loose sheet taped inside the front cover—a legend, or a key, which Mackintosh must have needed when he was new to the study of Oscillation Theory. Thomas scanned it as quickly as he could.

"Protocol S," he whispered, finding it almost three-quarters down the page. "Destruction of Device and/or Elimination of Wielder."

It took him a long moment, blinking into the dark, to realize what this meant. *The device is the Star-spinner,* he thought, his panic rising. *And the wielder—that must be Tess.*

The clattering of a key turning in the lock made Tess jerk awake. She'd dozed off sitting on the floor of her bedroom, Mr. Cleat's copy of *The Secret Garden* on her lap. Despite what she now knew about it, something in the pages gave her comfort. It felt as close as she could come now to leaving her own world.

"Lunchtime," Mrs. Thistleton announced, striding across

the room with a tray in her hands. She placed it on Tess's dressing table beside her untouched breakfast tray, the porridge long congealed and the cup of tea as cold as stone. "You'll have to start eating soon, you know," Mrs. Thistleton said, sweeping up one tray and replacing it with another. "Starving yourself won't get your spider back."

Tess ignored her, focusing all her attention on the thick iron nails that had been hammered into the frame of her window, keeping it closed tight. The nails had split the paintwork and driven long cracks into the wood, but Mrs. Thistleton hadn't cared about that. All she'd cared about was keeping Tess under lock and key until Mr. Cleat decided what to do with her.

And all Tess had done was sit on the floor pulling strips off the wallpaper, dreaming up ways to get out of here.

"I'll take your convenience, while I'm at it," Mrs. Thistleton muttered, picking up Tess's chamber pot. "We can't have the room smelling foul when Mr. Cleat comes calling, can we?"

Tess stiffened and blinked at the sound of his name but made no reply.

"Yes, he'll be here to speak to you this afternoon. So you'd best eat your lunch or he'll be asking you why." Tess maintained her silence, glaring out at a bird that had the cheek to perch on a branch outside her window, singing to its heart's content as though nothing in the world had turned upside down or rotten or wrong. "All right, you stubborn little mule. Have it your way," Mrs. Thistleton sighed before leaving the room. The key clanked home in the lock and Tess was alone once more.

Eventually she pushed herself up off the floor, her body sore from sitting so uncomfortably. She tossed Mr. Cleat's book onto the coverlet and perched on the side of the bed to uncover her lunch: an unappetizing-looking stew piled high with boiled potatoes and complete with a layer of grease on top. Despite everything, her stomach growled at the sight of the food and so she picked up her cutlery and made the best of it.

She was just draining the last of her lukewarm milk when the key was once more shoved into the lock and turned. This time there was a polite knock on the door before it was opened but there was no pause to allow Tess to speak before the person entered.

"Ah, Tess. There you are," said Mr. Cleat, as if there were any possibility Tess could be anywhere else.

"I want to see Violet," Tess said, wiping her mouth on a napkin and throwing it onto the tray. "And I want to get out of here."

"Of course you do! Of course," Mr. Cleat said, closing and locking the door behind him. He pocketed the key and then stood in the middle of the room, his hands clasped behind his back. Then he noticed the book lying on the bed. "Ah. You're still enjoying my old tome, I see," he said with a grin.

"Not really," Tess said as rudely as she could. "It's terrible. I just like throwing it against the wall every now and then, wishing it was you."

Mr. Cleat shook his head, wagging his finger playfully at Tess. "Now, now. No need for that. It's hardly *my* fault you chose it out of the hundreds of books in my library and proved that you were everything I hoped you'd be," he said. "It resonated with you. You answered its call—and all without even knowing why or what it meant. It was almost poetic."

He knows, Tess thought. She clenched her teeth as a further realization washed over her. *He's known since before he ever met me, and there's no point pretending anymore.* "If it's really from another reality, how do you even have it?" she asked, forcing herself to sound calm. "How do I know *anything* you tell me is the truth?"

"Well now, that's a good question," Mr. Cleat said, settling into a nearby chair entirely without invitation. "My father bought it for me from a dealer in cross-world objects, Tess—a person who buys and sells things that get lost between the worlds. They're rare, and expensive, and they don't always stay where they're put, which is a risk you take when you buy them. But this one, for whatever reason, has stuck around." He deftly crossed his neatly trousered legs before continuing. "I believed my father when he told me where he got it. And the fact that he died a short time later from a disease contracted in another world proved to me he was telling the truth." Mr. Cleat's expression hardened.

"What?" Tess said, frowning as she tried to understand.

Mr. Cleat sighed, seeming to think about what to say next. "My father died from a strain of flu that killed millions of people in an adjoining world between the years 1918 and 1920. It didn't strike here, yet my father and several others lost their lives to it. All the deaths I've been able to examine from this particular cluster have one thing in common: they were all traceable to a cross-world object. That book," he said, looking at it, "was my last gift from a dearly loved father. It also killed him."

"And you think killing people on another earth is going to make you *feel* better for losing your father?" Tess said, her disbelieving anger sharpening her words. "I never *knew* my father. It doesn't mean I want to take other people's fathers away."

"Perhaps you're a better person than me then. Who's to say?" Mr. Cleat uncrossed his legs and leaned forward, his fingers interlaced, and stared at Tess. "But what would you do to see your father again, Tess? If it were possible, that is. Tell me, *what would you do?*"

29

"WHAT ARE YOU TALKING ABOUT?" TESS SAID. "I CAN'T SEE MY father again. It doesn't *matter* what I do."

Mr. Cleat rubbed his chin, giving her the smug smile of a person who thinks they know best. "The thing about multiple realities, Tess," he began, "particularly multiple realities between which people have learned how to travel, is that things can get lost. However, they can also be found. Again and again if need be." He held out his hand, fingers outstretched as though he were holding up an invisible plate. "Imagine each fingertip is a world," he said. "In each world is a version of you. Of me. Of our good friend Mrs. Pauline Thistleton. And of your father, your mother, everyone you've ever known. Theoretically, at least."

"Theoretically," Tess said. "You love that word."

"But isn't it worth finding out?" Mr. Cleat said, staring at her incredulously. "I can't believe I'm hearing this from you, Tess, the most promising scientist of your years I've ever met. You don't even want to *think* about what I'm saying?"

Tess drilled into Mr. Cleat with her stare. "I had one father," she said. "And one mother. Other versions of them aren't *them.* And other versions of your father aren't *him.*"

Mr. Cleat dropped his hand, giving her a cool look. "I think that's my decision to make," he told her.

"I am not going to help you," Tess said, her words slow and deliberate. "I'm not going to help you bring across the worlds things that can drop bombs or cause pain. I will *never* do that. It doesn't matter what you offer me, it's not going to change my mind. So you'd better just give up. You're wasting your time."

Mr. Cleat chuckled mirthlessly, shaking his head. "Even if I could help you find your home, Tess? And I don't mean that silly house by the river. I mean the place you were born." Mr. Cleat's icy blue stare was enough to rob Tess of her breath. "Because the world in which you were born, Tess, is the one where all of this began. The world that experienced the Tunguska blast in all its ferocity, where in 1908 a meteorite hit the ground with so much force that it threw up an ash cloud thick enough to block out the sun. All other known worlds, including this one and our war-torn neighbor, suffered but an echo of that cataclysmic event, Tess, but your world is dying, gradually going dark and turning to a lump of blackened stone." Tess blinked and her mind flashed to the Star-spinner. *The tarnished marker,* she thought. *Is that—is that the key that leads to my home?* Mr. Cleat spoke again and it broke her concentration. "If you want to see it before it's too late, now is the time to act."

"I don't need your help to find it," she retorted.

"You do if I have your device," Mr. Cleat said, sitting back in his chair. "And your spider. You can hardly go without them, can you?" He pressed his lips into a thin line. "And if you don't help me tomorrow evening, you'll never see either of them again."

A roar was building inside Tess, but she forced it back. "How do you know all this? About me, and my—where I was born?"

Mr. Cleat rubbed a hand through his hair. "You've been spoken of since you were an infant, Tess, in the jangling wires and hissing frequencies and tapped-out codes that link the worlds. People have been looking for you in all known realities almost from the moment you were born. You were a legend, some said; a fabrication, said others. Few of us actually believed in the truth of you, a refugee from a dying world, the girl whose father risked all he had to save." He paused, pursing his lips thoughtfully for a second before continuing. "And of course he ran to save his own hide, too—to keep himself out of the clutches of those who wanted to use the device he'd built for their own ends."

Tess blinked. "Wait. The device he'd built?"

Mr. Cleat raised his eyebrows. "You mean you hadn't guessed? I'm surprised. Yes, Tess. Your father was—*is*—the architect of the Star-spinner. He forged it from materials excavated from the Tunguska blast site on his world and yours, from metals and other things that fell from the stars." He shrugged. "The exact science is beyond me. All I know is that it works."

"But it can't do what you want it to," Tess said, desperately hoping she was right. "It can't take your bombers through to a different reality. It just takes me—one person at a time."

"That's because you haven't conducted the correct experiment yet," Mr. Cleat told her. Then he frowned. "You know, I may have been wrong about you after all. A great scientist needs to be someone with imagination, Tess—a person who sees beyond the obvious to what is *possible*. A person who asks questions that don't seem to have answers. You've had every chance to do just that and yet you've been content to focus on yourself." His eyes narrowed. "A lot like your father, perhaps."

"That is *not* fair," Tess said, fighting back tears.

"Well, let's prove me wrong then," Mr. Cleat said. He sat forward once again. "How about this for a deal? If you don't do precisely what I require tomorrow evening—and I do mean *precisely,* because there is a lot at stake—then I'll be forced to take extraordinary measures. It doesn't bring me any joy, believe me. But I'll do what I have to do."

"Just tell me," Tess said, through gritted teeth and smeared glasses.

Mr. Cleat stared her down for several long seconds, his eyes sharp as scalpels. Finally he began to speak in a low and deliberate tone. "Tomorrow night I will have at my disposal five bombers. These are flying machines, as I've told you before, which have the power to reduce anything on the ground to a smoking crater, killing anyone unfortunate enough to be in their path. Currently their pilots are a bit nonplussed with me as I've refused to give them exact coordinates for their mission. I can't, of course, as they'll be flying where our coordinates will be meaningless. But I can change my mind and give them coordinates at any time. I can give them the exact location of a lovely old building on the corner of Carlisle Bridge, overlooking the River Plura, right here in our fair city of Hurdleford. Many young ladies live there, I'm told. A rather happy place by all accounts."

Tess held her breath, trembling as he spoke. With his next words he froze her still. "And it might interest you to know that the lives of every single person in that building depend on your agreeing to help me." He paused, leaning closer, his eyes sharpening with every word. "You've already said I can offer you nothing to change your mind, so the only recourse I have left is to take something away. I'm forced to tell you this, then: if you persist in your stubbornness, you'll never see your beloved Miss Ackerbee, nor anyone from her blasted Home, ever again."

"Yes. Yes, I quite understand. But please—won't you just give me a chance to explain? I have it on good authority that a child is in danger." Miss Ackerbee paused, listening to the voice on the other end of the phone. "Whose authority? An eyewitness—a child named Millicent, who had been employed in the household."

Rebecca winced as she watched Miss Ackerbee's facial expression changing with every word that came down the telephone line.

"A simple charwoman-in-training? I hardly think it's fair to discount her testimony because of her position!" Miss Ackerbee's gaze flicked to Rebecca's face; her fury could burn holes straight through the wall. "She knew the child well and she witnessed the ill-treatment firsthand."

Please, my dear, Rebecca begged inside her head. *Let it go.*

Miss Ackerbee's mouth drew tight against her teeth as she listened. "I simply cannot believe you're unwilling to take this complaint seriously." She paused again. "Childish imaginations? Sir, I have worked with children for almost twenty years. I know exactly— Sir? *Sir?*" Her mouth dropped open as she stared at Rebecca. Slowly she replaced her telephone receiver. "He hung up," she said.

"I know, love," Rebecca replied sympathetically. She folded her arms across her middle. "They're not going to listen to you. The time for asking nicely is over, I think. It's time to *do* something instead."

"But what *can* we do?" Miss Ackerbee said, taking off her spectacles and pressing her hands against her eyes. "The law can do nothing. The *police* can do nothing. Nobody will touch a rich, well-connected, apparently law-abiding man, not even when I try to explain that one of my girls . . . that *my* girl . . ." Miss Ackerbee broke down and Rebecca hurried to her. She hugged Miss Ackerbee tightly and Miss Ackerbee clung to her in turn.

"Aurelia," Rebecca whispered. "She is our girl. *Our* girl. The only person who loved her more than we do was the man who left her here." She paused, readying herself for what had to come next. "And we trusted her once—it's time to trust her again."

Miss Ackerbee pulled back to look into Rebecca's face.

"What do you mean?" she said, a small hiccupping sob interrupting her words.

"We raised that girl to be clever. We raised her as nobody's fool. But also she *came* to us that way. She has formidable courage that belongs to nobody but her, and she chose to face this challenge head-on once already. It's not the law she needs; it's *us*. And her friends." Rebecca held a hopeful breath. "She doesn't need a police van to knock on the door and take her away. She needs help to get the answers she went there to find. We owe her that."

"We owe her safety," Miss Ackerbee said, her eyes filling with fresh tears. "Her father crossed *worlds* to leave that child on our doorstep, and this is what becomes of it."

Rebecca's eyes shone. "Exactly, Aurelia. *Exactly.* Imagine how proud of her he'd be."

Miss Ackerbee gave a tiny tired nod, closing her eyes just as they overflowed. Rebecca watched hopefully as expressions flitted across Miss Ackerbee's face.

Then Miss Ackerbee cleared her throat and straightened up. She cleaned her face, blew her nose as daintily as possible and reached out to find her spectacles.

She put them on like a queen readying herself for battle.

"What then is our plan?" she asked, and Rebecca smiled.

"For that," she said, "I think we need to have a word with Wilhelmina."

30

THOMAS SAT IN THE OBSERVATORY WITH THE WINDOW OPEN. THE darkness had long ago given way to the pinkish gray of dawn and he wrapped himself loosely in a blanket, hoping the cool of the morning would keep him awake. He hadn't slept much in the twenty-four hours since Tess had vanished; he'd dozed a bit during daylight hours but through the night he'd waited for any sign that she was coming. There had been nothing.

Moose sat on Thomas's blanket-swathed knee, gazing out at the day. "I know," Thomas whispered to the mouse. "It's daytime again and she's not here. And there's nothing we can do except hope, is there, boy?" Moose quivered, his ears changing direction as he listened, and then he scampered for Thomas's head. His tail dangled in Thomas's eyes as the mouse changed position, tiny claws prickling the boy's scalp.

"What is it, Moose?" Thomas asked. He looked up, trying to catch a glimpse of his mouse, and then he heard it—a squeaking noise from the chapel below. His heart leaped into his throat.

The vestry trapdoor, he thought. *The tunnel! Could it be Tess?* He knew he'd mentioned the tunnel to her. Maybe she'd had to use the Star-spinner in her own house, which meant she would have arrived in Thomas's, and it had been safest to come to the chapel that way. *But if it isn't . . .*

Thomas tossed off the blanket and slid across the floor. Moose clung to his head as Thomas began to climb down the ladder, intending to go just far enough to see into the chapel, but as his shoes touched the rungs, footsteps rang out in the chapel—*heavy* footsteps, coming fast.

"That's not Tess," Thomas muttered, leaning down to look. He almost lost his grip when he saw Mackintosh striding up the central aisle, his face a mask of fury. His cheeks were crimson and his teeth were bared and his bulge-eyed gaze was fixed on the boy.

"No!" Thomas shouted. "Get *away!*" He scrambled back up the ladder and began to fiddle with the bolts that held it in place. They were supposed to release in a trice if there was an emergency—but there had never been an emergency before and Thomas hadn't kept them oiled. His fingers shook and slipped as he tried to undo them, even just enough that he could drag the ladder up into the room, out of Mackintosh's reach . . .

"Give it up, lad," Mackintosh growled, landing on the bottom rung of the ladder with the grace and solidity of a sack of coal. He gripped the sides and began to climb. "You've got nowhere to go."

"Get out of here!" Thomas sobbed, pushing himself away from the hole in the floor. Moose scrambled for his shoulder, tucking himself tight against Thomas's neck. "You're *never* supposed to come out here!"

"Oh, right? A bit like you're never supposed to go into my *office.*" Mackintosh's head was through the hole and still he climbed. Thomas cast his gaze around, hoping for something to throw, but there was nothing. Even his sharp-edged tins of food were in the cupboard, all the way across the room.

"Nothing in that house belongs to you," Thomas said, getting to his feet. "It's not your office. It was my father's workroom and you've got *no* right—"

"Give it a *rest!*" Mackintosh roared. His gaze landed on Thomas's desk, with his radio and Oscillometer and the pile of his mother's notebooks. "I'll have those back and all," he said, striding toward them. "You've got no need for this stuff, boy—it belongs with me."

Thomas stood in his path and Mackintosh stopped, a mocking grin on his face. "Like that, is it?" the man said.

"Those were my mother's," Thomas said, sticking out his chin and trying not to fall down. "Which means they're *mine* now." He raised his fists and Mackintosh laughed.

"I don't have time for this," the man muttered, grabbing Thomas by the upper arms in a grip so tight that Thomas cried out. Moose, squeaking wildly, ran down Thomas's arm and up onto Mackintosh's sleeve quicker than a blink, but Mackintosh threw the boy, hard, against the nearest wall.

Thomas landed awkwardly, his head whacking against a wooden pillar, and just before he blacked out, he heard Mackintosh's voice. "Get off me, you rotten vermin!" the man yelled, pulling Moose off his sleeve and flinging him to the floor. He raised his boot to stamp and Thomas knew no more.

"Nobody mentioned *headdresses*," muttered Wilf, settling hers on top of her too-tight hairdo. "I mean, there's looking ridiculous in public and then there's this." She examined her reflection in the dusty mirror. She and what seemed like a hundred other girls were crammed into the basement of something called the Interdimensional Harmonics Society, which, Millie assured them, meant they would soon be on their way to Roedeer Lodge. The room was abuzz with preparation, loud voices shouting instructions and not a small amount of excitement. Wilf, for her part, merely felt so nervous she could vomit.

"Oh, do budge up," snapped Prossy, shuffling over to crowd Wilf out of the mirror. "At least you don't have three feet of hair to tuck in somehow. There simply aren't enough pins in the world." Her plait was wound around her head like a crown and her headdress sat on top of it like a raft atop a golden sea.

"What's wrong with your leg?" asked Wilf, frowning at Prossy's movements. "Have you hurt yourself?"

Prossy finished pinning on her headdress and turned to Wilf with a mischievous grin. "Look at this." Casting a glance around, she pulled Wilf to one side and gathered up her long black skirt. Before Wilf could protest, Prossy had lifted the skirt up high enough to display one leg encased in a long, thick sock—and a hockey stick, which was shoved down inside the sock. She had tied a ribbon around the neck of the stick just above her knee, keeping it tight to her upper leg.

Wilf's mouth dropped open and Prossy dropped her skirt, settling it neatly. There was no sign of the stick besides the fact that Prossy couldn't bend her knee much as she walked. Somehow she was managing to make up for it by taking long strides and talking a lot.

"What do you need that for?" Wilf asked, aghast.

"She's not a 'that'; she's my best gal, Hortense. Never leave home without her," Prossy said sagely, patting her thigh.

Wilf didn't have a chance to reply before a door opened at the top of the room, drawing her eye. A woman stepped through it with a bosom like a galleon in full sail. "Girls!" came her loud, crisp voice, followed by a barrage of sharp claps. The room fell silent and everyone turned to face her.

"Now, ladies," she began, "you'll form two neat lines and we'll assemble outside where Mr. Cleat has arranged a fleet of steam cars for us . . ." The woman's voice droned on but Wilf allowed herself to tune out. *Mr. Cleat.* This was really happening. In less than an hour, she'd see Tess again.

"Quick march, girls! One, two! Let's get going!" The woman ("Mrs. Hayden," Millie whispered) led the way through the downstairs floor of the Society building. Wilf tried not to look around too much. She figured a girl in service—like she was supposed to be—would be far too well trained to be nosy, but she couldn't help seeing some things, like the framed portrait of Mr. Cleat on one of the walls in the lobby. She gave it an evil glare.

Then the girls were being ushered two by two into one of three steam cars parked outside, each vehicle gently hissing. Prossy stepped up into the steam car with her good leg, drawing the one with the hockey stick behind it. Wilf threw her a grin and she returned it.

"I still can't believe Miss Ackerbee is letting us do this," Wilf said as they found seats near the back. She remembered the worry in her housemistress's eyes as Millie had outlined her scheme for infiltrating Fairwater Park.

"I reckon Miss Whipstead talked her round," Prossy replied. Wilf nodded, her own worry returning. When they'd been summoned to Miss Ackerbee's parlor the day before to brainstorm a plan, Wilf had surprised herself by feeling relieved. She should have guessed; it was impossible to keep a secret in Ackerbee's.

Today, Miss Ackerbee and Rebecca had seen them off, giving hugs and kisses and whispered wishes of good luck, smoothing shoulders and tucking back locks of stray hair as though they were off on a school trip. Wilf had thrown a glance at the house as they'd walked away; the upstairs windows had been lined with watchful girls, each pair of eyes willing them on. She'd lifted a hand to wave and a forest of hands had waved back.

And now Wilf found herself chugging up the quays alongside the Plura in a steam car, not knowing what to expect next. It was a bright day, sunny and warm, and the river sparkled. They passed the Gossamer Bridge, and Wilf realized she'd never been this far north of the city before.

"We'll see Kingsbridge Station soon," Millie's cousin Rosaleen said, turning round in her seat to talk to them. "After that it's not far to the main gate of Fairwater Park."

Wilf nodded and gave Rosaleen a grateful grin. Rosaleen turned round again, settling herself in her seat before Mrs. Hayden caught sight of her.

"So what's the plan for when we—" Wilf began, muttering out of the corner of her mouth to Prossy, but her words were drowned out by the roaring of an engine—a *petroleum* one, by the noise it was making—swooping overhead. It was overwhelmingly loud and it was belching out a thick black cloud. The steam car seemed to jerk to one side as everyone leaned to look out of the windows at the same time.

"What is that?" said Prossy, her eyes round as she searched the sky. Wilf pressed her nose against the glass as another engine noise ripped through the air above their heads. She saw the riveted belly of a silver machine passing over the steam car before roaring out over the water. It flew upriver, following the course of the Plura. The machine was long and thin, tapering near the end, with two straight stretched-out wings on either side. At its nose flickered a propeller, chopping at the sky. As Wilf watched, a second machine joined the first and they accelerated away, banking and turning as they reached the furthest point that Wilf could see on the horizon before finally vanishing from view.

"Whatever they are," she said, turning to Prossy with fear in her voice, "they're heading for the park."

31

TESS WAS SITTING IN A CHAIR BESIDE THE TALL COPPER BATH SHE'D just vacated, surrounded by a haze of lemon scent. One of the housemaids sent to attend her was gently combing out her hair, which squeaked clean between her fingers. The other had brought a dress—"a gift from Mr. Cleat, miss"—and laid it out on the bed. Tess glared at it with loathing. It was a pale pink spun-sugar nightmare, like a cake with sleeves. A pair of polished shoes and two white frill-edged socks lay beside it.

I have to look the part, she thought, the words like a stinging nettle inside her. *And he's the one in charge of the show.*

Then unexpectedly the second maid began to agitate the water in the bath. Tess turned to watch what she was doing, and she heard the whispered voice of the first maid in her ear.

"Millie never came back, miss. After the other night. We reckon she went to fetch help."

The second maid stirred the bathwater again, creating more splashing noises to mask the sound of their words. "Try not to worry," the first maid said. Tess gave them both a grateful look but then they all jumped as Mrs. Thistleton's voice sounded outside the door.

"Enough lollygagging in there," she barked. The maids stood to attention as the housekeeper unlocked the door and entered.

"You and you," she snapped at the maids. "Set about getting that bath emptied. And you," she said to Tess. "Get dried and dressed and take care not to snag that gown." As the maids busied themselves carrying pitchers of water out of Tess's bath, Mrs. Thistleton stared Tess down.

"Mr. Cleat is relying on you this evening," she said. "As am I. And if you think you'll refuse to do what's needed, then do know this: Millicent's position here in Roedeer Lodge will depend on your cooperation. If you want to see her thrown out into the streets of Hurdleford without a penny to her name, by all means disobey."

"Millie?" Tess replied, frowning in confusion. "But I thought—" She bit back the rest of her words, remembering what the maids had said.

"You thought what?" Mrs. Thistleton said.

"Nothing," Tess replied. "Yes, Mrs. Thistleton. Of course. I won't let you down."

"I should think not," Mrs. Thistleton said, turning on her heel as the maids returned, ready to carry out the empty bath. "Yes indeed, I should certainly think not."

Mrs. Thistleton followed the maids out of the door and locked it behind her. Tess sat for a moment longer before tossing the wet towel on the carpet and setting about getting into the ridiculous dress. It pinched and pulled and made her itch, and she didn't dare look in the mirror.

Instead she looked down at her reflection in the black patent leather shoes and thought with a heart-wrenching lurch of Violet. The shoes were a little like her eyes. Tess just couldn't get used to the lack of her; nothing was the same. Tess's eyes grew hot and gritty, and she closed them tightly.

She took three deep breaths, in and out, and opened her eyes again. They narrowed with determination. *It's time to get out of here and get her back,* Tess told herself. *I've had quite enough of doing what Mr. Cleat wants me to.*

She looked around. The door was locked tight. The window was still nailed shut. For a minute she considered smashing the glass, but she quickly discounted that; it would raise the alarm too quickly.

Her thoughts were interrupted by a noise, like the drone

of a far-distant engine. She frowned, searching for the source—and then her eyes fell on the empty fireplace. The droning sound was coming down through it.

She dropped to her knees by the hearth and hauled in a breath. Holding it, she stuck her head into the fireplace and looked up.

The wide chimney gave way to a rectangular patch of blue sky. The sky was partially blocked by something with a pattern cut into it, but it looked like there was a large enough gap to let the smoke through. *I could fit out through it too,* she thought. *Couldn't I?*

Before she had time to lose her nerve, Tess tucked her glasses inside her vest for safekeeping and began to climb.

Thomas opened his eyes. For a moment all he could see was darkness and he blinked until the view settled into something he could make sense of: shadows under a cupboard. Floorboards were cool beneath his cheek and a breeze blew gently over his hair from somewhere close. *The observatory,* he thought, beginning to drift down into sleep again. He took a deep breath and winced as a sharp pain stabbed him, jerking him back into wakefulness.

After a few seconds more his arms began to throb where

they'd been caught in Mackintosh's crushing grip and his memories began to click back into place.

He threw me, Thomas remembered. *I clattered my head. And then—Moose . . .*

He forced himself to sit up, grimacing as his head pounded with dull, bruising pain. Rubbing his temple, he squinted around the room, and after a few moments' searching he found his glasses, which had slid across the floor. He slipped them on but things still looked a bit skewed.

"Moose?" he called, his voice cracked and weak. *"Moose!"* he shouted, ignoring the ringing pain it caused in his skull. Desperately he searched the expanse of floor for the body of his friend but there was no sign. Tears sprang to Thomas's eyes. "What has he done with you?" he whispered.

Suddenly a movement on top of his desk caught his eye. Thomas glanced up and saw the tip of a tail just vanishing from view and straightaway he fought to get to his feet, using the pillar he'd hit his head against to pull himself upright. Hardly daring to hope, he searched the desk for his mouse— and then there he was, peeking out from behind a portable stove. Thomas whooped out a laugh of triumph.

"Moose!" he called, stretching out his hands to scoop the mouse up, but instead of running for his owner's fingers, Moose squeaked and scampered backward, his entire body quivering with fear. He disappeared behind the stove and only gradually reemerged, just his nose poking out and the barest hint of light glinting off his eyes. "Boy, it's me," Thomas said, his chin beginning to wobble. "It's me, Thomas." Slowly he moved his hands closer, but Moose retreated and Thomas closed his eyes as a tear forced its way through.

Stop it, he berated himself, but then he began to sob as the loss crushed him like a giant pair of iron jaws closing over his head. He rested his elbows on the desk, put his forehead in his hands and cried. Everything he loved was gone: his home, his parents, Tess—and now Moose, his last friend. He didn't know if Moose would ever trust him again, if things would ever be the same. Mackintosh and his cruelty had destroyed the bond they'd shared, and Thomas felt like a piece of him had been broken off.

Finally he straightened up, reached beneath his glasses and scrubbed his eyes dry. He drew his sleeve across his face and tried to think—and then he glanced at his watch.

Friday, May 30, it read, the little windows in its face that displayed the day and date almost invisible behind a fresh crack across the glass from when he'd hit the pillar. "And it's almost five in the afternoon," he whispered. *Which means there are only a few hours left until those bombers come through. It's happening tonight.*

"I've got to try to do something, Moose," Thomas said. "I can't help Tess and I can't do much to help myself. But I can try to help the city." He looked over at his radio; it had been thrown onto its side. The Oscillometer was gone, as he'd expected it to be, along with the stack of notebooks; he didn't spare any time to mourn that loss, as there was nothing he could do about it. Faintly he heard the sound of a radio news bulletin beginning and he tried to take heart. "He hasn't cut the power, boy," Thomas told Moose. "And I bet he didn't know about the transceiver."

Thomas hurried to a set of drawers built into the wall and pulled one open. Inside sat a radio transceiver, which he hoped was still working. "No time like the present," he muttered, gathering it up. A few minutes' work had it assembled and for a second he stood with the mouthpiece in his hand, unsure what to say or whether he was doing the right thing.

Then the pictures of bombed buildings he'd seen in the newspapers flicked across his mind. He remembered a newscaster's voice describing the swathes of terror unleashed by the Luftwaffe, German planes sweeping in a wave of flame across Europe, and he checked he'd set the transceiver to the distress frequency. Finally he clicked the button to transmit his message.

"Hello," he said. "Hello. This is a mayday." His voice wobbled with nerves and he took a moment to steady himself. *Don't give up now!* He cleared his throat. "Mayday, mayday, mayday. This is an emergency. If anyone can hear me, an attack on Dublin is coming tonight. It will be an aerial bombardment. Mayday, mayday, mayday." Thomas released the transmit button, hoping for a response, but all he could hear was static.

He licked his lips, breathed deeply and started again.

Tess clung to the bricks inside the chimney, coughing so deeply it felt like her lungs were going to turn inside out. She tilted her face to the sky, forcing herself to keep going. *Come on!* she told herself. *You're nearly there!* Her toes dug into cracks in the stonework as she made her way up. The chimney narrowed as it rose and for a few moments Tess stuck fast, panicking at the thought of becoming wedged inside it, but she summoned the last of her strength and hauled herself up, and up, and *up* until she could smell fresh air. She sucked it down, breathing it in like she'd never breathed clean air before, and tried to calm her racing heart.

Finally she reached the lip of the chimney. It was covered with bird droppings and soot and the gap between it and the cast-iron chimney cap was frighteningly narrow. Gritting her teeth, she forced herself through it, falling out onto the roof tiles before rolling onto her back to catch her breath. She reached into her vest to pull out her glasses, put them on with soot-blackened fingers and looked at herself; every inch of the too-fussy outfit Mr. Cleat had picked out for her was destroyed, right down to the ridiculous socks.

She allowed herself a laugh, which turned into a torrent of giggles, which ended in a coughing fit. When she finally managed to catch her breath, she heard the drone of engines again—except this time it was much louder.

So loud, in fact, that Tess felt a wave of fear.

She got to her knees and then to her feet, clinging to the chimney she'd just climbed up. Her legs wobbled as she looked around, the wind tossing her long, loose hair like a whip.

And then, so suddenly that it made her scream and lose her grip, a gigantic machine roared overhead, low enough that Tess could feel the terrifying *thrum* of its engine inside her chest and the sucking air in its wake. She braced her feet against a gutter and looked up, her back flat against the sloping roof, and saw the terrible silver belly of a bomber pass right over her head.

32

Tess trembled from head to foot and scrambled for what cover the chimney could provide. She huddled behind it as roaring machines flew overhead, their long silver bodies like monstrous fish and the wheels of their undercarriages so low it seemed like they were going to skim the roof. The sound of the propellers was like nothing Tess had ever heard. She squeezed her eyes tight, terrified of being sucked off the roof.

Finally there were no more and Tess opened her eyes to peer out from behind her chimney. As she watched, the bombers flew away from the house in a wide arc, going so far that they almost vanished from view. Then they circled back over the park until their noses were pointed for Roe-deer Lodge once more, the noise of their engines growing louder as they approached. They began to bank, flying in tight formation toward the ground, and Tess looked at the lawn in front of Roedeer Lodge, where they seemed to be about to set down.

Then, in the center of the lawn, the small, dark shape of Mr. Cleat appeared. He raised his hands to the sky, beckoning the planes to land, and they followed his instructions.

Tess watched the planes land at the end of the lawn, rolling to a halt in a semicircle around Mr. Cleat. Eventually their engines were switched off and their propellers fell still and the sounds of the evening resumed all around her.

Tess watched Mr. Cleat applauding, and the cockpits of the bombers began to pop open one after the other as the pilots emerged. They dropped straight to the ground, helmets under their arms, to shake Mr. Cleat's hand. After a few moments they clustered companionably in the center of the lawn.

Then Tess held her breath as the straight-backed figure of Mrs. Thistleton appeared. She strode toward Mr. Cleat and the pilots, her course fixed and immovable, and stood at a polite distance until Mr. Cleat eventually turned to look at her. He walked toward her and they began to speak, their heads close.

"What are they saying?" Tess muttered to herself. *She's probably telling him I've gone missing,* she realized. *Gone, from a* locked room. Her heart began to thud. *They'll guess what I did. I have to get down from here!* Mrs. Thistleton gave a brisk nod and walked away, back toward the house.

Quickly Tess tried to think. She looked around, evaluating her meager options, and tried not to panic. About ten feet in front of her stood one of the house's front turrets. Tess knew there were windows in the turrets, but she didn't know whether they could be opened from the outside. She crawled out from behind the chimney and slid forward a little, controlling her fall with her feet. She could see that ivy grew on the wall just beneath her, but it was well out of reach. Her nerve failed as she looked; the drop to the ground was just too much.

That simply left one option—to go across.

She was lying on the pitched roof that ran along the front of the house, between the two front turrets. Above her stretched the great copper-covered expanse of the house's main roof; flat in the middle, it didn't have any openings that Tess knew of, nor any means of getting to the ground. But all along the pitched roof to her left were windows to the maids' quarters. *Not that any of them will be in their rooms at this time of day,* Tess thought, beginning to edge her way over. *But there's nothing else for it.*

Slowly she crept toward the nearest window. It was set into the roof, its panes secured with a simple metal lock, and

Tess braced a foot against the gutter to look through it. She caught a glimpse of her reflection and grimaced. She looked like some sort of ill-intentioned woodland sprite; her face and clothes were filthy and her hair stuck out around her head like the fronds of a thistle. If she'd seen something like that peering in her window, the last thing she'd do would be to throw the pane open in welcome. *I'd be more likely to fling the chamber pot at it,* she thought grimly.

She rapped gently on the window anyway in the hope that someone would recognize her and take pity. The small, neat room inside the window remained completely empty, its three plain beds with their spotless sheets looking so inviting that Tess almost wept. The door at the far end of the room stood open and Tess could just about see the narrow servants' staircase that led down to the kitchen.

Tess blinked as suddenly a torrent of running legs went past, all of them making for the stairs, each of them clad in black and white. For a surprised second she could do nothing and then she came to her senses and began to bang, as hard as she could, on the window.

"Help!" she shouted. "Help! *Out here!*"

The flow of maids didn't slow and Tess began to despair that anyone would hear her. She pummeled her fists on the glass, hard enough that she was afraid the window would break—and then unexpectedly all the banging made the flimsy lock slip, causing one of the panes in the window to pop open very slightly. She nearly lost her balance, she was so surprised, and clung to the window frame for a moment or two, trembling.

The gap wasn't nearly wide enough to get a finger through, Tess discovered once she'd gathered herself—but it *was* wide enough to wriggle the arm of her glasses into. Quickly she took them off and did just that. Then she spent several long, frustrating minutes trying to use the arm to flip the lock up and open. Eventually, after some maneuvering, the lock slid free. The window popped fully open and Tess let out a hoot of triumph.

She put her glasses back on and clambered into the room, landing on the rug in a cloud of black soot. She got to her feet and hurried to the washstand, rinsing away the worst of the grime from her face and hands. She dried herself on one of the pristine towels, turning it gray in the process.

She took in the room again, wondering what to do next. It looked as though someone had shaken out an ash box all over the floor, and Tess cringed at the mess she'd made. Even though it couldn't be helped, she felt guilty.

Then her eye fell on one of the room's small wardrobes and an idea began to brew inside her mind. *What's the best place to hide when you really don't want to be found?* she thought with a grin. *Right in plain sight.*

She crossed to the wardrobe and pulled it open. As she'd hoped, it held a spare uniform, and in less than a minute her ridiculous dress was lying in a crumpled heap on the floor. Moments later, out of the attic bedroom a new maid crept, one with unkempt hair, no socks and a skirt that was rolled up three times at the waist. She ran down the stairs after the others, hoping not to be noticed.

But first she had a spider to find.

Thomas broadcast his distress call until he grew hoarse. Nobody replied, but he didn't give up, not until his voice began to crack and the ringing in his temples grew so painful that he simply had to rest. He let his head droop and dropped the transceiver mouthpiece, leaning his hot forehead in the palm of his left hand. He closed his eyes.

After a few minutes he heard the faint sound of scuttling claws on the tabletop. He stiffened but didn't move, letting Moose come to him when he was ready. Instead Thomas focused on breathing in time with the pulsing throb in his head; it was easing now.

Then he felt the tiny tickle of Moose's whiskers on his skin and he opened his eyes. The mouse had emerged from his hiding place and was sitting beside Thomas's outstretched right hand, sniffing at it as though checking that it was really him.

"Hello, boy," Thomas whispered, and Moose scampered up onto the back of his hand. Thomas used his left hand to stroke Moose's back and the mouse turned to him with trust in his shining black eyes. "I missed you." Moose swiveled his ears as if to say *Me too*.

Thomas settled Moose on his shoulder as he leaned back in his chair. The open panel in the observatory ceiling loomed above him and the sky was beginning to turn purplish blue in preparation for night. He stood up and crossed to one of the roof ladders, climbing it until he could see out through the aperture, and watched as the lights of Dublin began to come on. It was then he knew for certain that nobody had heard his warning and that there was nothing more he could do.

Thomas gritted his teeth and felt his eyes flood with hot frustrated tears. "Turn out the lights!" he yelled into nothingness. *"Turn out the lights!"* But nobody could hear him, not all the way up here.

A sob choked off his words as he tried to shout his warning a third time, and something inside Thomas's chest broke. He climbed back down the ladder and sat on the floor of his father's observatory, looking around at the things his dad had gathered and built, wondering how much of his parents still lingered here.

His eyes opened wide as he remembered something and

he pushed himself up from the floor. He hurried to his sleeping mat and dropped to his knees, shoving his hands beneath the pillow—and there it was. The one notebook he'd managed to keep out of Mackintosh's hands. He held it close, then slipped it beneath his jumper.

Moose flitted down his sleeve and perched on the back of his hand. The mouse made a pleading gesture with his front feet and the boy looked into his sparkling eyes as he spoke. "I don't think I have any chocolate left, Moose," he said with a grin, "but let's have a look and see what else we can turn up. After the day we've had, I reckon a midnight feast is the least we can do for ourselves."

Moose straightened up, looking pleased, as Thomas got to his feet. Then the boy and his mouse laid out a blanket on the floor and raided their food cupboard for everything they had that was sweet and tasty and they sat and ate together beneath the stars, waiting for the bombs to start falling on their city.

33

TESS SIDLED OUT OF THE KITCHEN AND INTO THE CROWDED LOBBY
of Roedeer Lodge, trying to keep out of the way of anyone
who might decide she needed a job to do. She fully expected
at any moment to run straight into Mrs. Thistleton—but so
far she'd avoided so much as catching a glimpse of her.

The house was *full* of people—maids and guests alike—
who were going back and forth between the lobby and the
lawn. The gates to the lawn were thrown open now and
Tess could see a collection of garden furniture set out on
the grass: tables with candles on them, each surrounded by
spindle-backed chairs, and furthest away a long table with a
pristine white cloth laid on it right beneath the nose of one
of the planes.

She shuddered at the sight and hurried away.

Mrs. Thistleton's room was somewhere upstairs, Tess didn't know exactly where. Starting her search for Violet there seemed to make sense—the chances were that Mrs. Thistleton was somewhere in the house shouting orders at someone, which meant Tess wasn't likely to be caught. She passed her own bedroom door and on impulse tried the knob; it was still locked. She hurried away, wondering, *Does anyone know yet that I'm gone?* Her heart began to race. *What did Mrs. Thistleton tell Mr. Cleat out on the lawn, then?*

There was a staircase at the end of the hall beyond her room, one little used except by staff, which led to the next floor up. She'd just begun to climb it when she heard a voice that stopped her in her tracks.

"Hey! You there. Hang on!" it called, and Tess froze. She turned to see a maid hurrying after her carrying a tray, which she held out for Tess to take. "As you're going that way, you might as well bring this for me. Mrs. Thistleton's tea? She's at the near end of the next corridor up, first door you'll see as you step off the stairs."

Tess nodded, though her stomach did a full roll inside her. "Yes," she managed to croak. "Of course."

"Don't sound so nervous, love," the older maid said, her voice warm and reassuring. "She'll probably tell you that your hair needs a good brushing, but that's the worst it'll get this evening. She'll be too busy to tell you off." She beamed a wide smile. "Plus if you're a girl from Mr. Cleat's Society, she can't touch you anyway." The woman leaned in, whispering conspiratorially, "Maybe take your time going up so's the tea has a chance to cool right down, if you know what I mean." She gave Tess an exaggerated wink. "Nothing's as bad as taking a mouthful of tea when it's piping hot. Am I right? Downright dangerous, that is." She chuckled mischievously and hurried off down the corridor.

Tess waited until the maid had vanished from sight before continuing. Her hands shook badly and she tried to stay calm. *I've done nothing wrong,* she told herself in a stern tone. *And I'm going to get my Violet back.* She glanced down at the tray. *And if Thistleton comes for me again, I'll throw this at her and run.* Sooner than she liked, her sooty shoes had taken her almost all the way up the stairs. She hesitated before taking the final step and then she emerged into the low-lit hallway, her eyes on the door the maid had described.

She walked to it and balanced the tray in one hand. She pulled her lips tight and knocked on the door with the other hand, standing back and lowering her head as she waited for a response.

"Come through," came Mrs. Thistleton's voice, and Tess obeyed, her heart juddering like an earthquake. She risked a glance as she walked in; Mrs. Thistleton was lying on her bed with a cloth over her eyes and Tess sucked in a deep breath of relief.

"My tea, is it? Thank you. Just leave it on the side, won't you?" Mrs. Thistleton said in a kinder tone of voice than Tess usually heard her use. Tess walked to the dressing table and set the tray down as gently as she could. "Dratted migraine. It would show itself *now*, on this most auspicious of evenings," the housekeeper muttered. Perhaps that had been what her discussion with Mr. Cleat had been about then. *Nothing to do with me, after all.*

Tess gave a mumble of sympathy, taking the opportunity to look around the plain, simple room. Besides the dressing table, all she could see was a table beneath the window with a covered sewing machine on it, and a low chest of drawers against the far wall. There was no visible sign of Violet anywhere, and Tess knew that with Mrs. Thistleton in the room she had no chance of taking a proper look. The crush of disappointment was so profound she felt like picking up the tea tray again and flinging it on the floor.

"Now," Mrs. Thistleton said, so suddenly that it made Tess's spine contract. "Will you take a message to Miss de Sousa, please? Tell her she'll be needed on the front lawn in thirty minutes, and I'll be down to escort her at that time."

"Yes, ma'am," Tess replied, trying to disguise her voice as much as possible by rasping out her words, as though she had a bad case of laryngitis.

"Speak up, won't you? Are you one of Mr. Cleat's girls from the club?"

"Yes, ma'am," Tess said in the same strange voice.

Mrs. Thistleton sighed. "I thought as much. Never mind about Miss de Sousa then. I'll look after that job myself. Thank you. That will be all."

"Yes, ma'am," Tess repeated a third time as she started to walk away.

Thirty minutes, she thought as she pulled Mrs. Thistleton's door gently closed. *Thirty minutes is all I have to find Violet and the Star-spinner and get them out of here.*

She swallowed her fear and ran for the servants' stairs as quickly and quietly as she could.

Millie, Prissy, Prossy, Wilf and Eunice stood in the center of Tess's bedroom, transfixed with horror as the doorknob turned suddenly before falling still. After a few quiet seconds had passed, they risked letting out their breath.

"Who was that?" Wilf whispered, and Millie shrugged.

"Could've been anyone," she replied. "Probably not Mrs. Thistleton herself, though—she'd have her own copy of this key. Just one of the maids looking for something, I'd say."

"I'm glad you locked that door," said Wilf, her heart beginning to slow.

"Speaking of which," Millie said, looking worried, "we'd better get finished up here and put our key back in the kitchen before someone misses it—and us. Mrs. Hayden will soon figure out we're not gone to collect crockery at this rate."

Prossy put Tess's experiments notebook back in the pocket of the cardigan she'd found draped over a chair, and Prissy pulled herself away from her close examination of the nailed-shut window. The girls took one last sad look around Tess's empty room and prepared to leave.

"Look here," came Eunice's voice from the far side of the room. "Does this seem strange?" She was kneeling on the fireside rug.

The others hurried to her, Prossy taking care not to clunk about too much on her hockey-stick leg. "That's a rum one," she said, staring at the floor. "What do you think, Priss?" In a semicircle around the fireplace was a pattern of soot. The kindling was still neatly set in the grate, but it was dusted with a shower of black powder, like a cake covered with icing sugar.

"Either a bird came fluttering down that chimney and somehow managed to make its way back up again," Prissy surmised, "or that's how our girl made her way out of here."

"Through the *chimney*?" Wilf said, almost forgetting to whisper. She knelt, sticking her head into the black grate, and looked up. All she could see was the same patch of distant sky that had called to Tess—but it was getting dark now and the chimney looked none too inviting. "Tess!" Wilf called, as loudly as she dared. "Are you up there?"

"She'll be gone by now, you daftie," said Prossy as kindly as she could. "She's hardly going to hang about in there any longer than she has to, is she?"

"I'll bet I know where she is," said Millie suddenly as Wilf pulled herself out of the fireplace. "The chapel! There's a tunnel out to it from the scullery. We can go without being spotted."

"Well, why didn't you say so before?" said Prossy, her face alight with glee. She turned for the door and saluted as she strode forward. "Let's get going!"

They left the room, locking it behind them, and made their way downstairs. Trying to look busy, they hurried across the crowded, noisy lobby and had almost made it to the kitchen corridor when Wilf stopped in her tracks so suddenly that Prossy walked right into her, losing her balance on her immobile leg. She grabbed at Eunice as she started to fall and the two struggled to keep on their feet.

"What on earth's going on?" Prossy muttered, steadying herself.

Wilf stood stock-still. A familiar face was looking at her from the far side of the overfull room—a familiar face so surprised to see her that his monocle fell right out of his eye. Beside him stood a confused lady in a purple gown with what looked like most of an ostrich on her head.

"Dr. Biggs," Wilf hissed, feeling her face turn pale. "We've got to run!"

"*Run?*" Prossy replied. "With a wooden leg?"

"Just hurry!" Wilf said, and took off. The others followed as quickly as they could, given the pressing crowd and the fact that girls in service were never supposed to run, even in cases of emergency.

"I say!" Dr. Biggs called. "Wilhelmina! *Stop that girl!*"

Wilf lowered her head and doubled her pace as several curious pairs of eyes stared at her, but nobody had time to grab her before Millie pulled her into the kitchen and the door mercifully closed behind them.

34

Keeping close to the wall, Tess crept along the corridor that led down to the kitchen. The entire lower floor of Roe-deer Lodge was thronged with people: fur- and jewel-clad ladies in evening gowns, arm in arm with men in dress suits; groups of young businessmen with loud voices and pomaded hair; and one or two younger ladies with bright, curious eyes. As well as all the guests, it felt like to Tess, the entire house was stuffed with staff. She'd never seen so many maids, running to and fro with trays and plates and table linen, and if the noise from the kitchen was anything to go by, there were at least four extra cooks on duty and none of them could find a single thing to agree on.

A woman stopped in front of Tess and waved an empty

champagne glass in her face. Tess simply blinked in surprise and the woman fixed her with a withering look.

"Well?" she said, shoving the glass at Tess, who—not knowing what else to do—took it from her. "About time," the woman snapped before turning up her nose and wafting off on a cloud of overpowering scent. Tess stared at the delicate glass in her hand and put it behind her back.

Then she looked at the far side of the corridor and noticed a door set into the wooden paneling of the wall. *A broom cupboard?* Tess frowned. She'd gone past here a hundred times, but somehow she'd never seen this door before. She glanced around; nobody was paying her any attention.

So she made for the cupboard, opened its door and pulled it closed behind her.

In the darkness Tess tried to catch her breath and calm her mind. She sat down beside an empty mop bucket on wheels. *This is pointless,* she thought, overcome with sorrow. *I can't find Violet in this crowd! I can barely move, let alone search for her. Plus,* she thought miserably, *I was really sure she'd be in Mrs. Thistleton's room. I don't know where else to look.* She angled her wristwatch into a crack of light coming through the door. More than fifteen minutes had passed since she'd spoken to Mrs. Thistleton.

"Soon they'll know I'm not where I'm supposed to be," Tess whispered to herself. "Soon they'll come looking. And then . . ." Her imagination wandered as she tried to think about what would happen once they found her. *Mr. Cleat will make me use the Star-spinner for something my father would never have wanted*, she thought, squeezing her eyes tight. *And then Thomas, and everyone who lives in his city, will be in danger.*

Tess clenched her fists so hard her knuckles ached. "Stop putting it off," she muttered through gritted teeth. *There's no point hiding in here. I need to go and find Violet and that means facing Mrs. Thistleton. There's no time for anything else. And once I have her back, I need to stop all this before it's too late.* She relaxed her hands, took a deep breath and got to her feet.

Someone shouted something in the corridor outside just as Tess was about to open the door and she heard the sound of hurried footsteps. She hesitated a moment and then slid out, trying to be as unobtrusive as possible. A gong sounded as she made her way up the corridor toward the lobby and a man in uniform made an announcement in a voice loud enough to carry above the clamor. The crowd stopped and turned to him, looking expectant.

"Ladies! Gentlemen! Your host, Mr. Norton F. Cleat, begs your attendance on the front lawn. The front lawn, ladies and gentlemen. The demonstration will begin at ten p.m. sharp!"

At these words, Tess's feet stuck to the tiles. She stood like an island as people surged all around her, chattering excitedly as they went. The defiant spirit that had filled her a moment before suddenly drained out through her heels.

"It's all tosh, of course," one man said as he passed Tess, grinning widely at his friend as they strode toward the front door. "I can't wait to see old Norty fall on his face!" She was buffeted by elbows and handbags as people passed her by and then she noticed a figure in black coming down the stairs.

Mrs. Thistleton was striding toward her, eyes hard and glittering and her mouth pursed tight. "What. On. *Earth*," she muttered as she drew near. She grabbed Tess around the arm and dragged her into the nearest corner. "How *dare* you make me search this house for you. And how dare you present yourself in this fashion!"

Tess's heart roared within her as she stared Mrs. Thistleton down. "I want my spider back," she said.

Mrs. Thistleton snorted. "Your *spider*?" she spat. "If you want to have the slightest chance of ever seeing it again, you'll come with me. Right this minute. And you'll hope that Mr. Cleat doesn't take one look at you and destroy it out of spite."

Before Tess had a chance to answer, Mrs. Thistleton pulled her across the floor, out of the door of Roedeer Lodge, and forced her to walk through the gates and onto the lawn. People turned to watch but Tess ignored them all, gritting her teeth as she focused on where she was being brought—and on the gigantic machines that got closer with every step.

The bombers seemed impossibly big. Looming out of the night was a propeller blade, its tip almost reaching the ground; the other blade rose high into the sky and Tess followed it with her eyes. The pointed nose of the aircraft looked huge in the gloom and its massive body was lost to the shadows.

As Tess and Mrs. Thistleton drew near, there was a gasp from the crowd as a string of huge lights set into the lawn suddenly lit up with a series of *pops*, throwing bright white beams onto the bombers. The lights made them seem even bigger than Tess had thought, their wings long as horizons and their tapering bodies like gigantic beasts. The windows of their cockpits remained dark and Tess wondered if the pilots were already in there, watching her.

In the next breath, loud music—celebratory, like the sort that would herald the arrival of a circus—began to play. Tess jumped, as did most of the people around her, and the people seated at the tables twisted and turned in their chairs as they strove to be the first to see what was happening. Some of them chattered excitedly and a few began to applaud.

"Ladies and gentlemen—and the rest of you!" came Mr. Cleat's voice, sudden enough to make Tess jump again. Mrs. Thistleton tightened her grip on her arm but Tess ignored the pain and flicked her gaze around, searching for him as a ripple of laughter rolled through the crowd.

Another light popped on and there he was—standing on the nose of one of the planes, appearing to lean nonchalantly on the nearest propeller blade. In his hand he held a bullhorn, into which he was speaking. The music faded completely. "It's my honor to welcome you all here to my humble abode this evening. Most of you will know me, Norton Cleat; those who don't, well—it's a pleasure. Thank you all for being here. Tonight, my friends, we're going to witness the impossible."

As the applause sputtered to renewed life all around him, soon growing to a crescendo, Mr. Cleat dropped the bullhorn and jumped down, landing with fluid grace. He began to walk toward Tess, his wide smile not echoed in his hard, angry eyes.

Tess was cornered. Mr. Cleat was coming in one direction and Mrs. Thistleton held her in an unbreakable grip and everywhere around her were tables full of people oblivious to any of it. She had nowhere to run.

Mr. Cleat reached her and clamped his hand down on her shoulder, heavy and unmoving as an iron rod. She had no choice but to walk alongside him with Mrs. Thistleton until finally the three of them stood beneath the shadow of the planes. Tess tried not to tremble as she looked around; it was hard to see faces in the strange light but she knew for certain she was alone here. Nobody would help. Nobody *could* help.

"Now!" Mr. Cleat announced as a man in uniform bustled forward out of the shadows holding a large tray. On it was a cloth covering something that looked like a storm lantern. "This evening, ladies and gents, we're here to witness a miracle. A real, true, honest-to-Faraday miracle. What we're going to do here this evening has never been done before. Never, ladies and gents! Not only will it demonstrate the absolute proof that we in the Interdimensional Harmonics Society have been seeking for over thirty years—the proof, my friends, that worlds exist beyond our own and that those worlds can be opened up to us—but we will show you all how it can be done."

He paused to catch his breath, staring out at the crowd, a fervent light shining in his eyes. "I know there are believers among you; I know too that there are doubters. You will all leave here tonight with one solid fact lodged in your skulls: there are worlds, who *knows* how many, that we can gain access to with the right knowledge and skill—*and the power to do it is in our grasp!*"

Mr. Cleat raised his free hand in the air, his fist clenched, and after a second or two the cheer he was evidently expecting began to rise from his assembled guests. Tess felt him relax a fraction but then his grip on her regained its strength. He shoved her forward to stand in front of him, and he placed one heavy hand on each of her shoulders. She blinked, the bright lights making her feel dizzy.

"This young lady is Tess de Sousa. Yes, my friends: one of *those* de Sousas." A murmur began and Tess felt the weight of a hundred pairs of eyes as they strained to see her. "This is the girl with the key to the universe—the wielder of the Star-spinner!" A furious wave of chatter followed this, with people turning to one another in disbelief and a few even making notes.

"Poppycock, Cleat!" came a shout. A man got to his feet at a table a few rows back. "That's just a *fable*! There's no such thing. Whoever this poor urchin is, send her back to her gutter and leave us all to have a pleasant evening." This was greeted by a gale of laughter interspersed with booing.

"I admit, my dear Mr. Henderson, that the child is a little less—how can I say it?—*presentable* than I would have wished, but such is the nature of youth. Am I right?" More laughter greeted this and Mr. Henderson took his seat once again, shaking his head. "However, I assure you, Cornelius, that I am telling the truth. And for those who still find it hard to believe, all I can say is, Watch and wait."

He released Tess's right shoulder and raised his hand again. Instantly the planes' engines roared to life. They began to taxi backward, rolling over the lawn in perfect formation as they prepared to take to the air.

Mr. Cleat leaned down to murmur into Tess's ear. He reached into his waistcoat pocket and from it took the Star-spinner, which he held in his fingers like a pocket watch as he spoke. "If you want to save the lives of everyone you love—right down to your eight-legged friend—then you'll start doing exactly what I say from this point on, young lady. The choice"—he paused, making Tess swallow hard—"is yours."

Millie led the way through the tunnel, a lit candle held in one hand. Wilf followed close behind. Prissy and Eunice huddled together, neither of them willing to admit how scared they were, and Prossy guarded the rear with Hortense the hockey stick held high.

"How much further is it?" she asked, adjusting her grip on Hortense.

"It can't be too much longer now," Millie said. "I wasn't really paying attention last time, what with being afraid for my life and all." She shivered and quickened her pace.

"You might have let us know that *before* we clambered into a hole in the ground," Prossy muttered.

"Look!" Millie called, hurrying forward. "Steps. Going upward."

"Thank goodness," Wilf muttered. Millie handed her the

candle, climbed the steps and pushed hard at the trapdoor set above them. After a second or two, in a cloud of dust that made Millie turn away and sneeze, the door opened into the vestry.

Moments later, all five girls—plus Hortense—stood in the center aisle of the deserted old chapel.

"She's not here," Wilf said, searching the darkness.

"I don't understand," Millie whispered, her confusion clear. "I was *sure* she'd have hidden out here."

"Tess!" Eunice called. "Tess, it's us!"

Prissy walked to the back of the chapel and peered up at the ceiling. "She can't have gone up there. I wonder if—" She stopped short as something caught her ear.

"What is it, Priss?" Prossy asked, but Prissy shushed her with a gesture as she tried to listen.

"Can you hear that?" Prissy said. "It's like—*engines?*"

The girls stood still and strained their ears, and then they heard it: the deep thrumming roar of petroleum engines, carried on the breeze.

Millie's eyes opened wide. "It's starting," she said, running for the chapel door. "Come on!"

"You're not getting me down that tunnel again," Prossy muttered.

"No need for that now," Millie said, hurrying out into the night. "We've got to hurry! Whatever Mr. Cleat's been planning, it's happening. And if he's got Tess, she needs us—come on!"

With that the girls charged across the starlit field toward Roedeer Lodge, hoping with everything they had that they'd get there in time to help their friend.

35

Mr. Cleat got down on one knee beside Tess so that their eyes were level. He pointed up at the sky, which was already speckled with stars and hung with a thin rind of moon. Somewhere the planes' engines roared and Tess imagined them circling the park, waiting for their moment.

"Now," Mr. Cleat began, as though they were out on an evening stroll, "do you see that constellation right above the house? It looks a little like a cup with a long handle."

Tess blinked at it. "No," she said as disagreeably as she could, but the pattern in the stars was quite clear.

"Very good, Tess." Mr. Cleat chuckled. Then he put one arm round her shoulders and with his other hand held the Star-spinner loosely. "You need to find the bright star just above the cup of the constellation you seem unable to see.

Can you do that?" He pointed and Tess saw the star he meant. It was brighter than those around it, like a diamond among shards of glass.

She nodded. "I see it."

"How wonderful," Mr. Cleat said. "Now, you'll recall I spoke to you some time ago about the materials your father used to build the Star-spinner, and how he found them at the site of the meteorite crash in his own world. Well, that star—Polaris, Tess, the North Star—contains some of the same material as the meteorite that dealt a deathblow to your home. Your device is made from part of that star. Like calls to like." He placed the Star-spinner in her hand. "As above, so below."

"What are you saying?" Tess blinked at him.

"Lift the device, Tess." His voice was low, even gentle.

Tess choked back a sob. "I don't want to."

"Do as I ask and you'll see why your little trinket is called the Star-spinner, child. And do it quickly or you can kiss everyone and everything you love goodbye."

Tess shook her head, hating what she was being forced to do, and opened the Star-spinner's eye. Beside her, Mr. Cleat held his breath as he watched, his face bathed in the light of the void.

"Now," he told her, lifting his eyes to the sky again. "Focus it on the North Star. Do it, Tess."

She did as he asked, her fingers shaking. In the void, the

star looked even more beautiful, but Tess could barely see it through her tears.

"Set the stars spinning, Tess," Mr. Cleat said. "Turn it."

"I *won't* do it," Tess said, gritting her teeth. She tensed, preparing to fling the Star-spinner away, and Mr. Cleat grabbed her, hard. He held her still, crushing her fingers around the Star-spinner and making her gasp with pain.

"You!" he barked at the man holding the tray and its strange contents on one outstretched hand. The man nodded, whisking the cloth away—and Tess saw the lantern with Violet still inside. The spider jerked in fright, her limbs spreading over the glass like an outstretched hand, and Tess sobbed. She looked up at the man pleadingly but his eyes were shadowed. He didn't move an inch.

Mrs. Thistleton stepped forward, lifting the lantern as she went, and held it in Tess's sight line. "A reminder," she said, "of what's at stake here."

"Don't hurt her," Tess begged.

"Do what we're asking," said Mr. Cleat in a soft voice, "and she'll be fine. I promise."

He relaxed his grip a little on Tess's fingers and Mrs. Thistleton stepped out of the way, holding Violet in her lantern high. Tess, knowing she had no choice, raised the Star-spinner again and focused it on the North Star. Then, her eyes streaming with tears, she began to turn the upper half, the markers clicking into place as it moved. The device hummed with power, which seemed to increase as it notched up a gear.

Suddenly a circle of the Star-spinner's light burst forth from the mechanism, making Tess's hands jerk with the power of its movement, and was gone into the sky in a blink. As it rose, it began to grow, getting bluer and brighter with every second. The circle was centered on the North Star, held at its heart like a jewel on a neck, and inside the circle, around the fixed point that was Polaris, the stars were spinning, growing faster until they were curves of light like comets trapped in a tight orbit.

The roaring of the bombers' engines tore the air overhead. Chairs overturned as people scrambled to get out of them; screams were lost in the chaos. Guests stood on the lawn, unsure where to look—at the wildly whirling stars overhead, or the huge airplanes making straight for them, looking like they were on a collision course with one another.

But they didn't collide. The moment the planes reached the edge of the starfire ring, they vanished, swallowed into another world, a world full of innocent people who had no idea they were coming.

A world where the only family Tess had left was right in their path.

Thomas was startled by a bright blue flash, like lightning. He cowered in the observatory as he waited for the thunder—but all he heard was silence. After a few moments he sat up, confused.

"I'd better close the roof, Moose," he said, shifting the mouse onto the floor as he got to his feet. "Just in case it rains."

He climbed to the opening in the dome, and what he saw almost made him fall back down the ladder. He clung to the edge, his teeth chattering, as he looked at the hole that had torn open in the sky right above his house, trying desperately to understand. It was surrounded by a ring of bright blue fire, which looked like the light in Tess's device. A single star burned at its heart like a glittering eye and all around it other stars whirled faster than Thomas could imagine, so fast they became a streaked blur.

Then the spinning circle of stars was sucked outward, becoming something that looked like a tunnel. Thomas couldn't tear his eyes away from it, despite it being—by quite some measure—the most frightening thing he'd ever seen.

That was, until five bombers—*like Messerschmitts,* Thomas thought, *only bigger*—screamed out of the tunnel, without identifying markings of any sort and looking far more brutal than any plane he knew of. Thomas knew their bellies were filled with explosives—and then, as if to prove it, the final plane released a bomb as it roared over his parents' house.

Thomas ducked, clutching the rungs of the ladder, and waited for the *boom*. When he could look out again, half his house was in flames. Thomas slumped against the observatory roof and turned his head. Dublin lay there, twinkling in the darkness, filled with thousands of sleeping people, and there was nothing he could do. In a heartbeat, the planes had disappeared, ready to lay waste, and Thomas stood on his ladder with his fingers digging into the metal of the conservatory roof and despaired.

He pulled his head back inside and climbed down. Collapsing onto his sleeping mat, he pulled out his mother's notebook. As quickly as he could, he flipped to the page with his father's portrait on it, and Moose clambered up onto his shoulder as Thomas sat staring at it, wrapped in his blanket.

His mind was filled with Tess and thoughts of what was happening to her a world away, and then all he knew was the shrieking of the engines.

As the planes disappeared, along with the sound of their engines, the crowd reacted with uproar. People got to their feet, knocking over chairs and pulling tablecloths askew, upturning glasses and sending tableware flying into the grass. Most of the guests started running. Those that remained were wide-eyed and gape-mouthed, fixated on the gap in the stars. Mr. Cleat stared at it too, a wild grin on his face.

Of the airplanes, there wasn't a single trace.

Mrs. Thistleton was also looking at the sky, but her expression was different from Mr. Cleat's. Where he was examining the scene with rapturous disbelief, Mrs. Thistleton looked somehow disappointed, as though she'd expected more.

Tess took advantage of her distraction and made a lunge for the lantern in her hand—but the woman was too quick. She snapped back to attention, holding Violet out of Tess's reach.

"Give her *back*!" Tess shouted. "I *did* what you wanted!"

"I don't think we're through with you just yet," Mrs. Thistleton answered. "Now, Tess. Give me the Star-spinner."

Mr. Cleat looked away from the scene in the sky and turned to Mrs. Thistleton. "What?" he asked, confused. "Pauline? What do you want the Star-spinner for?"

Mrs. Thistleton grimaced and flung Violet's glass cage away, sending it spinning into the darkness. Somewhere in the distance it crashed to the ground, shattering Tess's heart. She screamed, desperately trying to see where it had landed, but in the same second Mr. Cleat stumbled back against her, treading heavily on her foot.

"The only thing that can truly destroy the Star-spinner is a weapon made of the same ores that were used to fashion it," Mrs. Thistleton said, glancing from Mr. Cleat to Tess and back again. "I searched for years, using every contact I had, spending every *penny* I had, until I had enough metal to have this forged."

She slid her hand into her coat and withdrew a long, thin dagger with a blade that tapered to a point so fine you could hardly see it. Mrs. Thistleton held it up, turning it this way and that, and Mr. Cleat and Tess couldn't take their eyes off it. "Beautiful, isn't it? And when I drive it through the center of the Star-spinner, this portal you've opened will remain for long enough to start a chain reaction that will tear through *all* the worlds."

She ran a finger up the blade before piercing Mr. Cleat with her stare again. "What's the point, *Norton,* of accessing realities only a few yards from our own when we could open a rift that would give us access to realities at the furthest edges of our imaginations?" She took a step toward him and he involuntarily stepped back, stumbling against Tess once more. She fought to hold him up as Mrs. Thistleton kept talking. "You and your foolish notions about interfering with a war the next world over. That's *beginners'* stuff! Think beyond your bank balance. Imagine what we will *learn!* How closely we'll be able to examine the structures of reality! They'll be talking about us for centuries, in worlds unnumbered!"

Mr. Cleat struggled to understand. "How much we'll learn about reality by *destroying* it?"

"It's for the greater good," she said, lunging at him with

the dagger in her hand. Tess saw Mr. Cleat's arms go up in self-defense but it was too late. With a groan of pain, he fell to the ground. Mrs. Thistleton stood over him, shaking out her dagger hand, and then she turned to Tess. Her face was pinched and cruel, her eyes sparkling with malice. "Give me the Star-spinner, Tess," she said, holding out her hand.

"I'm not letting you destroy *anything*!" Tess cried. "Get away from me!"

"That's it!" came a voice from among the stragglers who remained at the tables. "Give her what for!" Mrs. Thistleton turned to give the speaker the full benefit of her scornful stare, and just at that moment a shape came hurtling out of the darkness behind her—a shape wielding a hockey stick.

Prossy shouldered Mrs. Thistleton to the ground, knocking her flat. The dagger flew out of her hand and across the grass. Tess stood back, mouth agape, as Mrs. Thistleton struggled to sit up. Prossy dropped one knee heavily into the woman's midriff, completely winding her, and placed Hortense's head on Mrs. Thistleton's throat. Someone in the crowd cheered loudly before being drowned out by a chorus of "Shh!"

"Who in the blazes are *you*?" Mrs. Thistleton managed to croak. Prossy increased the pressure on her larynx and anything else Mrs. Thistleton might have wanted to say ended in a strangled, squeaking hiss.

"Tess's family," Prossy replied in a low murmur, leaning on the stick. Then she raised her voice. "Priss, search the ground for that ridiculous-looking knife, will you? Don't want anyone getting the wrong end of it."

Then Prissy, Wilf, Eunice and Millie stepped onto the lawn and Tess cried out in disbelief and delight. As Prissy began to search for the knife, Tess ran straight to Wilf and threw her arms around her, almost knocking her in the head with the Star-spinner.

"Oh, hello there. We had nothing better to do tonight, so we decided we'd come and pay you a visit," said Wilf, her voice muffled a little by the strength of Tess's grip.

Tess laughed and let her go. "You picked a fine night for it," she said. "How did you even *get* here?"

"Thank Millie for that," Wilf said, looking warmly at her new friend. Millie just blushed.

"I take it the sky isn't supposed to look like that?" said Eunice, staring up at the growing void. The blue sparkling ring was growing by the minute and there was no telling how big it was going to get.

"That's my fault," Tess said, stepping back from Wilf and wiping her cheeks with the back of her free hand. In the other, she still held the Star-spinner. "I've got to fix it. And there's someone—a boy in the other world who's my brother. Or sort of. I have to find him and see if he's all right."

"Right," said Wilf, frowning. "I didn't understand any of that. But carry on."

"And Violet is here somewhere. At least," Tess said, feeling something inside her being crushed with every word, "all that's left of her." She turned to Wilf, her eyes filling with tears. "Will you find her for me, Wilf?" All Wilf could do was nod, her chin wobbling, as they stared at one another in silent understanding.

"But—you'll be able to do that yourself, won't you?" asked Eunice. "When you get back?"

Tess's only reply was a sad smile and Eunice looked away. Then Tess glanced at the sky again, the sight of it making her brain reel. Behind her, Mr. Cleat gave a pained groan.

"Wait," said Wilf, looking back at Tess. Her cheeks were wet. "This is all happening too fast."

Tess took the Star-spinner in her hands. The void had closed, and the mechanism was still. She wondered if it would even work to get her where she needed to go. *I'm coming, Thomas,* she told herself. *No matter what.*

"I'm sorry," she said, looking in Wilf's eyes. She opened the Star-spinner and it shone true and steady. With that, and with her eyes still on Wilf, Tess was gone.

After a few seconds of stunned silence, a man at one of the tables got to his feet. "Bravo!" he called, clapping heartily. "I must say, jolly good show!"

36

Tess arrived into chaos, right in the middle of the lawn in front of Thomas's house. She dropped to her knees, burying her face in her hands. The pain of losing Violet and of never seeing Wilf again, or Miss Ackerbee, or any of her friends, was just too big to fit inside her. *At least they're all safe,* she told herself. *You did that much.*

Then a *boom* from the house grabbed her attention and she forced herself to unfurl. Most of the right-hand side of the building was on fire. She felt sick as she watched the orange flames hungrily devour the night, sparks flying into the sky.

"Thomas," she whispered, getting to her feet. *If he'd been inside there when the bomb hit . . .* She shoved the Star-spinner into her vest, realizing as she did so that it was all she had left of her past life; not even the clothes she was wearing were her own. Her notebook, her piece of paper with Miss Ackerbee's writing on it and her beloved Violet—they were all gone.

She shook the thoughts out of her head and started to run, away from the house and through the open fields that surrounded it in this world. The flames lit the way for her and soon she found herself at the chapel. Her side cramped with a stitch and, gasping through the sharp pain, she pushed open the door and made straight for the bottom of the ladder.

"Thomas!" she shouted. "Are you here? *Thomas!*"

From overhead, she heard the scrabbling of someone making their way across the floor on all fours and the next minute Thomas's face, wide-eyed, was staring at her. "Tess!" he shouted. "Is it really you?"

"What?" she answered, confused.

He slid down the ladder without touching the rungs and landed on the floor beside her in an ungainly heap, but he quickly bounced back onto his feet. Then, without saying a word, he grabbed Tess up in a huge hug.

"Thank goodness," he said, sounding overcome with relief. "Thank goodness you're all right."

"Thank goodness *I'm* all right? What about you?"

"I thought—I was afraid Sharpthorn had nobbled you,"

he said, loosening his grip enough to look her in the face. "I thought they'd done Protocol S on you and that you were a goner."

Tess stared at him blankly, searching his worried face for clues. "Did—did you hit your head? Because you're not making any sense."

"No!" said Thomas before throwing up his hands in exasperation. "I mean, yes! I did earlier. But that's not important." He tried to explain to her as briefly as he could what he'd seen in Mackintosh's workroom, and everything that had happened since they'd last seen one another.

"Sharpthorn," breathed Tess once he was finished. "I'll bet it's Mrs. Thistleton." She looked him in the eye. "She *did* try to nobble me, but my friends got to her first."

Thomas nodded. "I thought it might be her. And I'm glad you got away."

Tess frowned. "I don't think we've seen the last of her yet, though. Anyway," she continued, grabbing his arm, "we've got to get out of here. I'm not sure how to break it to you, but your house is on fire."

Thomas shrugged, adjusting something under his jumper as Moose peeked over his shoulder. "I've got everything I want right here. What about the hole in the sky?"

"I know. I have to close it but I've no idea how." Tess licked her lips as she tried to think. "I could reverse the steps," she said, looking up at Thomas with worried eyes. "With the Star-spinner. Couldn't I? Just do what Mr. Cleat told me to do but backward."

"Worth a try," Thomas said, shrugging.

"Then I need to find the North Star," Tess said. "Probably best to do it outside, at least that's where—"

Thomas cut her off. "No need," he said. "Come on." He charged back up the stairs, and Tess followed on his heels. As soon as their feet hit the floorboards, Thomas made for the back wall. A large iron wheel was built into it, which Thomas began to crank by hand. The wheel soundlessly started to spin—and then Tess was surprised to hear a low rumble start up all around her. She turned, trying to figure it out, and then she noticed that the patch of sky outside the hole in the roof was changing. After all that had happened, it was disorienting—but a few seconds later everything became clear.

"The—the *roof* is turning!" she said, incredulous.

"Yep," Thomas said, and even through his breathless exertion Tess could hear his grin. "The telescope isn't just for show, you know."

They shared a smile and Tess turned back to watch the view. "This is incredible," she said just as the North Star—clouded somewhat by the smoke from the house but still visible—came into view. "There it is!" she cried. "Stop!"

Thomas allowed himself a grin as the observatory came to rest. He locked the wheel into position and joined Tess at the foot of his father's telescope. "Come on," he said, climbing the stairs that led to the opening in the dome. Tess followed him and soon they were standing at the opening, the night air in their faces. It was tinged with the smell of smoke from the burning house. The fire was throwing strange orange shadows into the night.

Tess fished in her vest for the Star-spinner. "Now," she said, holding it tightly. "Time to undo all this, I think."

Thomas watched as she opened the void, but the blue light was faint. "That doesn't look good," he murmured as she raised the Star-spinner to her eye.

Tess could see the North Star sparkling amid the gusts of smoke from the fire and she gingerly began to turn the Star-spinner's face—but the markers didn't click into position this time. She soon realized it was moving too freely; there wasn't enough resistance. Then, with a sickening *crunch,* its upper face began to come loose. Tess gasped, and the next thing she knew, the blue glow of the void sputtered and went out and the whole device came apart in her hands.

Something fell out of the middle of the Star-spinner and landed with a distant *smash* on the floorboards below. Tess, her heart thundering, peered down—and there it was. A tiny circle of glass, now in a million shards, lay shining in the glow of the lamps. The void at the Star-spinner's heart was now a true void—empty of anything but air.

"*That* was unexpected," Thomas said. Moose scampered

up his arm and perched on his shoulder, his nose twitching as he watched.

"It wasn't starlight at all," Tess said. "It was a solid thing!"

Just as Thomas started to reply, the air was torn in half by the roaring sound of the airplanes overhead once more. Thomas and Tess clung to one another, searching the sky, as a blood-chilling sound wailed through the night: a long, thin, high-pitched scream, growing louder as it went. Another shriek joined the first, and then another and another.

"Those are falling bombs," Thomas gasped, holding Tess so tightly she could feel him trembling in fear. A chilling *crump* sounded out like distant thunder, followed by an orange-yellow blossom rising from the streets of Dublin. In the next breath there was a second and then a third explosion and Tess felt her throat fill with bile. *This is my fault,* she thought, numb with shock and grief.

Then a noise caught her attention—but after a panicked moment she realized it sounded completely different from the bombers. She searched for its source, looking back toward Thomas's house; there was movement amid the smoke. Just before the flat roof of the house collapsed inward, something lifted away from it and sailed off into the night. She blinked, confused, but before she could ask Thomas about it, he'd begun to scramble down the ladder. Almost before he'd landed, he was sprinting across the room.

"Watch out for the trapdoor!" Tess called, starting her

own descent, but Thomas made no reply. He reached a set of drawers on the other side of the room and began to rattle through them, muttering impatiently to himself as he went.

Tess hopped down and hurried to join him at the drawers. "What are we looking for?"

"My dad called it starglass," Thomas said, still searching. "I always thought he was being fanciful and that he didn't *literally* mean it had anything to do with stars, but he also said this glass came from Tunguska. Where the big impact happened."

Tess's eyes widened. "So does the Star-spinner," she told him. "Mr. Cleat said my dad built it, from things he found at the impact site."

Thomas stared at her. "Your dad?" Then he shook his head. "Of course it'd be your dad. Anyway, *my* dad had this starglass for years but never knew what to do with it. He just knew it was valuable." He picked something up hopefully, then tossed it aside with a grimace. "It's in a wooden box. Dad said it needed to be kept out of the light."

"Why?" Tess asked.

"No idea," Thomas answered with a shrug.

"It mightn't mean anything," Tess said, raking through the drawer beside Thomas. "It being from Tunguska, I mean."

"Maybe not," Thomas agreed. "But it *also* happens to look a lot like the stuff that fell out of the Star-spinner."

Tess felt a surge of hope in her chest. *Mrs. Thistleton said that dagger was the only thing that could destroy the Star-spinner. We have to try!* "Are you sure it's still here?" There were springs, wires, objects made of metal and plastic in the drawer, but nothing that felt like a wooden box.

"No," Thomas said. "But I can't imagine Dad getting rid of it. He barely threw anything away."

They kept searching for a few moments in silence and then Tess felt it: something smooth and cool, with four corners. "I think I have it," she whispered.

Thomas hurried to help, and together they prized the box out of his father's drawer. Tess held it up and flipped open the clasp to reveal a shard of glass sitting on a velvet cushion. As soon as it was free of the dark confines of the box, the fragment of glass began to glow blue. Tess smiled so widely she felt like she'd never be able to stop.

"This is it," she said, her fingers starting to tremble. She suddenly remembered a note she'd made in her experiments notebook—it seemed like forever ago. "Solid starlight. I *knew* it."

"Quick," Thomas said, his voice tight. "Where's the Star-spinner?"

Tess fished its halves out of her pocket with her free hand. "But I don't know how we're going to get it in," she said, frowning at the broken mechanism. The void was a perfect circle, but the new piece of starglass was larger than the old one, and irregularly shaped. "Or even if this thing will work, if we can."

"Of course it will," Thomas said. He gave Tess an encouraging nod as she brought the Star-spinner right up to the glass—but nothing moved. She tapped the metal gently off the starglass, making it chime.

"Well, that's experiment one out of the way," she said, trying to think what to do next.

Then the starglass, which had been glowing a steady blue, began to sparkle at the edges as it softened, vanishing into the darkness. Tess gasped, staring at it. In a matter of seconds, it would be gone.

"Quick!" Thomas said. "Do something!"

"I don't *know* what to do!" Tess cried.

Thomas took the halves of the Star-spinner out of Tess's hand, and in desperation, Tess simply laid the shard of starglass between them as Thomas closed the Star-spinner—and then, after a moment in which nothing happened, the starglass seemed to *melt*, becoming something that looked a lot like sunlight shimmering on water. In one breath it was there and in the next it had been sucked into the mechanism, where it shone blue and steady once again. Tess allowed herself a cry of triumph.

"Well, blow me down," Thomas said, shaking his head. "I guess being a genius runs in the family."

She looked up at him and grinned. "I guess it does," she replied, and Thomas beamed with joy, looking slightly bashful.

"Now come on," he said. "Let's get up to the roof and get this done."

TESS KEPT THE PULSING STAR-SPINNER IN HER HAND AS SHE climbed, until finally she could lean out of the observatory window. She steadied her breathing and then she placed the Star-spinner's void over her left eye.

And there it was—the North Star, as it looked in this world, surrounded by its spreading ring of fire. The ring had gone so far by now that Tess couldn't see its highest point and it was like a strange thin rainbow with only one unnaturally radiant color. The tunnel of spinning, flickering stars within it was unnerving, and Tess tried not to look too closely as she began to turn the top half of the Star-spinner back the way it had come. She met with resistance, but she didn't stop. *It's working,* she told herself, hoping Mr. Cleat was watching in his own reality and that he was screaming at the sky in frustrated anger.

"Keep going," Thomas said, though she barely heard him through the rush of her pulse in her ears. Vaguely, she was aware of Moose coming to sit on her shoulder, burying his flickering nose in her hair. She was comforted by the sensation, even if she felt like she was floating in midair and all this wasn't really happening to *her*—just to her body, far below.

Then her eye began to water and she realized she desperately wanted to blink, but she was afraid of losing her hold on the rift if she did. A piercing pain started in her pupil, shooting back into her head like a whip. She gritted her teeth against it.

"The circle is shrinking!" Thomas called. "The stars are slowing, Tess. They're stopping and the tunnel's closing. You've got it!"

And then Tess blinked. She had to. A tear ran down her cheek and her eye stung with exertion. When she opened her eye again, all she could see through the window was the North Star, rotating slowly, bringing its own world back around it. The ring of blue fire grew smaller with every second, until it vanished into the heart of the North Star once more.

Finally the Star-spinner stopped moving and Tess closed

her eyes, exhausted. The void's blue light flickered and then faded to gray once again. A shiver of shattering cracks snaked their way across the glass and all the energy drained from Tess as though someone had switched her off. She would have fallen had Thomas not grabbed her by the arm. "Hey now," he said, gently taking the Star-spinner from her limp fingers and stowing it safely in her pocket. "Let's get you down from here." He helped her numb feet to find the rungs as she descended and finally they both sprawled out on the floor of the observatory, just breathing. Moose skittered between them, never still for a moment.

"Do you hear sirens," Tess asked hoarsely after a while, "or is it just my ears ringing?"

Thomas propped himself up on one elbow. "Definitely sirens," he said, sitting up fully. "The fire service attending the damage from the bombs, maybe." He paused, looking mournful. "I hope *someone* heard my warning."

Tess looked at him. "Me too," she whispered.

"So what do we do now?" Thomas said, pulling his knees up to his chest. "You did something incredible tonight, Tess. So incredible and we can't even tell anyone." He turned to her with a half grin. "Who'd believe us? Heck, who'd *understand?*"

She returned the grin briefly but the weight of grief and tiredness soon drained her. "My dad," she finally said, realization settling on her shoulders. "My dad would've understood."

Thomas's grin faded and he blinked thoughtfully. "Mine too, I suppose." He cleared his throat and looked at his feet, and when he spoke again, his voice was quiet. "Shame he'll never know."

Tess fought hard against the wave of sorrow that flooded through her, but her chin began to wobble. Soon, to her disgust, she felt her eyes fill with tears.

"Hey!" Thomas said, sliding across the floor to put an arm round her shoulders. "No need for that. What's the matter?"

"My dad will never know either," she said, yanking off her glasses and wiping furiously at her eyes. She swallowed a hiccup. "All I wanted was to find out what happened to him and now I never can. I'll *never* be able to find him. And I'll never be able to go home." She closed her eyes, feeling them burn.

"Whyever not?" Thomas said, frowning.

Tess wiped her top lip dry and slipped her glasses back on and then peered at Thomas. "You saw the Star-spinner, didn't you? And we have no way to fix it now. But even if it was working perfectly, I have no Violet. She's gone and with her goes my anchor," she said miserably. "I can't go anywhere else, not without her. So I'm stuck here, for better or for worse."

Thomas let out an incredulous snort. "But of course you're not stuck here," he said, staring at her. "You're Tess de *Sousa*. You're a legend. Look what you've just done!" He gestured to the sky with his free hand and squeezed Tess gently around the shoulders with the other. "And even if Violet's dead, your memory of her isn't. Right? The love you have for her is as bright as it ever was. That's all you need, I'll bet."

"Well . . . ," Tess began, but stopped when she found she had nothing to add.

"Exactly my point," Thomas said, getting to his feet. "Think beyond the possible, Tess. Tonight you literally did just that. And now you're doubting yourself because of some half-garbled hearsay?" He reached down to drag Tess to her feet. "Get that machine out of your pocket. Come on."

Tess stood beside him, her knees feeling watery. She sniffed, then dug around in her pocket for the Star-spinner. It sat in her palm like a stone. The cracks across the starglass void looked like eyelashes on a pallid gray cheek. "We can do this," she murmured, staring at it. "This is *going* to work."

"Yes, it is," Thomas assured her, his tone confident. "After what I've just seen you do, there's nothing standing in your way." He clapped her on the shoulder, making her wince. "Right, then, get on with it. We haven't got all night."

Tess looked at him, her eyes brimming with new enthusiasm. "I can't wait for everyone to meet you," she said. "You'll *love* Miss Ackerbee and Rebecca. And Wilf—"

"Hold your horses," Thomas interrupted. "Everyone is going to meet *me*?"

Tess's optimism popped like a pierced bubble. "Well, yes," she said, her smile dying. "When you come with me. You are coming, aren't you?" Moose scampered up Thomas's sleeve, perching on his shoulder to peer at Tess. "You and Moose both, I mean?"

Thomas looked at the floor. "I— Well, is that a good idea?" He didn't give Tess time to answer. "I mean, we don't know if there's power enough to bring *you* back, let alone me too. And this fella." He lifted a hand to Moose, who clambered on, then looked up at Tess with sad eyes. "We don't know whether the Star-spinner can bring more than one person even when it's working at full capacity and it's not worth the risk of trying. You should go alone, I think."

Tess's mouth fell open. "But I don't want to leave you," she finally managed to reply, her words swallowed by the sudden surge of sadness that swept up through her chest.

"Yes, well, I was pretty fond of you and all," Thomas said, looking away. "But let's not dwell on it, shall we? Needs must and all that."

"But I came here to find my family," Tess said, the ache inside growing more painful with every breath. She paused, chewing hard on the inside of her mouth. "I can't leave you behind."

Thomas looked back at her. The shine on his glasses from the starlight outside made it hard to see his eyes, but Tess recognized his forced grin. "It's not really your choice to make, though, is it? It's mine." His smile flattened. "I won't be going anywhere. And you'll always know where I am. Come and visit when you can."

"But you can't stay here," Tess said, looking around the observatory. "You don't even have a *house*."

Thomas's reply was upbeat. "I've got everything I need," he said. "I have Moose. And you've seen my cushy setup here. We'll be fine." The mouse sat on top of his head, sniffing contentedly at the air, and Thomas smiled, though his eyes stayed sad. "I want you to go, Tess. I—I mean, I don't *want* you to go but you'd better. While you still can."

"Well then, I'll stay," Tess said, her voice strained with desperation. "I'll stay and we can figure things out together. We can find a way to get the Star-spinner working again and we can test it and find out what it can do, how many people it can take at once and—"

"Look, it's just been me and Moose here for a long time," Thomas said, his voice low. "It's sort of how I want things, you know? We know what we're about, Moose and me." He cleared his throat and shot her an apologetic look. "I don't want anyone else, Tess."

Tess stared at him. She searched his face but he refused to

look at her properly. "I—I can't believe this," she said after a painful minute, squeezing her fingers hard around the Star-spinner. She suddenly found it difficult to breathe, like something was sitting on her chest. "Well, if that's how it is, then that's how it is. I'll miss you, even if you won't miss me. It's harder to live without your family once you know you've got one." She stared down into the Star-spinner's heart and let her mind fill up with thoughts of Violet, picturing her sitting on the rim of the void, ready for her next adventure. Tess felt something in her heart lifting, like a tether being released.

Then she looked up at Thomas, their dark brown eyes mirror copies of one another, and just as the last anchor to his reality lifted away and the Star-spinner sucked her back to her own world, Tess made a decision. She reached out and grabbed his hand.

The sky above Roedeer Lodge righted itself so suddenly that for a moment it felt like the stars were going to rain down from it like hail. Some people greeted the closure of the rift with joy; others cried out in terror or disappointment. Mr. Cleat watched from the ground, his hand clutched to his wound and his eyes burning with rage, as all around him the members of his Society started to shout questions and accusations and call for his arrest.

Wilf wasn't looking at the sky but instead at the place where her friend had vanished. "Where's Tess?" she said, but nobody knew how to answer her, not even the spider on her shoulder, who was trembling with shock and fear. Wilf held up a finger and Violet clung to it. *If you survived,* Wilf thought, glancing at her, *so can she.*

Prossy chanced a look up, and the second her eyes left Mrs. Thistleton's face, the woman pounced. She knocked Hortense to one side, bashing Prossy on the kneecap with the stick, and ran straight for Eunice, who'd happened to take the dagger from Prissy a few moments before. Eunice squeaked in fright and brandished the dagger, but Mrs. Thistleton soon disarmed her. The girl fell to the ground with a gash across her palm as Mrs. Thistleton took to her heels, tucking the dagger back into her coat as she ran.

"Stop her!" Prissy yelled, but in a moment she was gone, vanished into the darkness of the park.

"Dratted *woman!*" Prossy shouted, nursing her injured leg. Prissy ran to her side and helped her friend to her feet and Millie grabbed some napkins from a nearby table to come to Eunice's aid.

Wilf strode across the grass to Mr. Cleat and dropped to her knees beside him. "Where is she?" Wilf asked, her voice quivering with rage and grief. "Tell me!"

Mr. Cleat laughed quietly, staring at Wilf with bloodshot eyes. "You'll never see her again. That's all I can tell you."

He grimaced, trying to move. Wilf offered no help, boring through him with a glare instead. "At least you've got her *vermin* to keep you company," he said. "I should think you'll hardly be able to tell the difference."

Wilf drew breath to shout a retort, but the words were stolen out of her mouth by the sound of something that all the Ackerbee's girls recognized instantly—a sharp whistle, louder than a foghorn and clearer than a bell. Prossy and Prissy turned toward it, their faces twin pictures of hope, and Eunice started to laugh. Mr. Cleat simply frowned.

Wilf looked down at him, a satisfied look on her face. "If you think I'm angry, just wait until Miss Ackerbee gets here."

38

TESS AND THOMAS LANDED HEAVILY ON THE FLOOR OF THE DE-serted chapel, their breath painfully knocked out of their chests. Tess recovered first, sitting up to nurse a bashed elbow as she stared down at Thomas's wide-eyed, gasping face. He was focused on the ceiling above their heads, and Tess looked up. The hole in the rotten floorboards was gaping down at them—they must have fallen through. Despite everything, Tess felt a smile bubble up from inside her. *We made it. We're back!* Underneath that was the realization she'd been right. *And my theory,* she thought. *It's proven.* The next heartbeat brought a judder of terror as she thought about what it meant, but she tried to ignore it.

Thomas groaned as he started to push himself up on one

elbow. He straightened his glasses and looked around. "What happened? Did a bomb hit?"

"No. This is just how the chapel looks here," Tess said quietly. It took a moment for him to register what she meant.

"Hang on a minute," Thomas said, turning to her with a frown. "You don't mean to tell me you brought me back with you? Despite what I said?"

Tess chewed her lip nervously for a second and then found the courage to answer him. "It was an experiment of mine," she began. "I was testing a hypothesis."

Thomas looked exasperated. "What?" he said, shaking his head. "What experiment?"

"Remember when we first met?" she prompted him. "In the chapel back on your earth. And we wondered whether we were related. Do you remember that?"

"Of course," Thomas said, rubbing at his head. "Ow," he added.

"Well, it's like this. I don't think you're my brother. Not even my twin. I—I think you're *me*." Tess trembled as she said this, wondering how Thomas would take the idea. "Another version of me, I mean. Like an alternate self. I'm you and you're me."

Thomas blinked. He stared at her. His mouth fell open. "I—er," he managed.

"Think about it," Tess urged. "We look like one another. We live in the same place. We're each our parents' only child.

So many things about us are the same, only we live in different realities. Or, well, we *lived* in different realities." She gulped, suddenly feeling nervous. "Don't you think it's possible that we're, you know, copies of one another?"

"Versions of the same person, existing in different realities," Thomas said, straightening his glasses. "It makes sense."

"So when I held your hand, the Star-spinner brought you back too because you and me—we're the same," Tess said. Moose popped his head out of Thomas's top pocket, taking the air. His tiny dark eyes regarded his surroundings with great solemnity. "It brought all three of us back, I should say," Tess corrected herself, reaching out to stroke him between the ears.

"And you didn't know this would happen? Me coming with you, I mean?"

"No," Tess admitted, dropping her hand from Moose's head. "But I hoped it would."

Thomas slumped, reaching up into his jumper and pulling something out, and Tess gazed at it in surprise. It was one of his mother's notebooks. "Everything I need I've got right here," he said, and Tess wasn't sure if he meant her, or the book, or both.

Tess's stomach clenched into a knot. "I didn't want to leave you," she said, feeling bruised inside with guilt. "I hope you don't hate me."

"I didn't want to leave you, either, you clod," Thomas

replied, looking up at her with wet eyes and a fond grin. "I wanted you to come back here so you'd be safe. That's all. I didn't want you taking risks for me. But you did it anyway." He flicked the notebook at her, making her laugh. "And I could never hate you."

"I think we'll be safest together from now on," Tess said. "And I have friends here. A place to live that's safe and lovely and not mostly burned down. Miss Ackerbee and Rebecca will look after you, too, I'm sure of it. And we can figure out what to do next once we've had a chance to think." She put her hand into her pocket to feel the Star-spinner there, the weight she had grown so accustomed to. "But if it's really what you want, I can try to bring you home again."

Thomas's smile faded as he looked at his mother's handwriting on the cover of her book. "I don't know what I want," he answered.

Before Tess could respond, a faint whistle pierced the night. Thomas's face blanched and he cast about for somewhere to hide. Just as he was about to throw himself beneath a half-rotted pew, Tess grabbed his sleeve.

"It's all right!" she said. "It's not a bomb. I know that noise. I've heard it often enough during fire drills. I would recognize it anywhere." She laughed, turning to the half-open chapel door and peering into the night beyond. Distantly she thought she could make out the huge faradic lights that had illuminated Mr. Cleat's planes still shining into the night. Then the whistle sounded again, louder this time, and Tess's heart lifted. *Miss Ackerbee,* she thought. *She's come for me.*

"What is it?" Thomas asked, hauling himself off the floor. He straightened his glasses again.

"Come on. You'll see." Tess made for the door, crashing through the undergrowth outside. She waited for him and they ran hand in hand through the long grass, helped one another over the old garden gate and crunched down the gravel path to the front of Roedeer Lodge.

It was Mr. Cleat who saw her first. He greeted Tess's arrival by spitting on the ground, which made Wilf turn to see what he was staring at with such hatred—and she could hardly believe her eyes when Tess came through the gate with a boy in tow.

Tess slipped her hand from Thomas's and ran to her friend. They collided in a jumble, and when they broke apart, Wilf took Violet gently down from the top of her head, holding her out for Tess to take.

"She made it," Tess said, blinking back tears.

"Of course she did," Wilf said. "She's an Ackerbee's girl."

Tess laughed as the others crowded around and Thomas found himself swallowed by a cloud of excited, joyful explanations. Introductions were made and Thomas instantly forgot everyone's name but nobody seemed to mind.

Then the knot of girls opened and Tess made her way toward Mr. Cleat. He struggled to push himself up on one elbow and Tess knelt to peer down at him. His eyes had lost their manic intensity and were now just watery blobs, exhausted and red.

"I fixed it," she told him. "The mess you made. And it will never happen again."

Mr. Cleat snorted. "I wouldn't be so sure. And in any case, you wanted it as much as I did," he told her in a low twisted hiss. "You couldn't have done it otherwise. I'd be willing to bet you'll find a way to make that thing work again. Mark my words."

Tess recoiled. "I never wanted a single piece of anything you did," she said.

Mr. Cleat laughed, his teeth stained with blood. "That's a lie, girl. You can keep telling yourself that as long as you want but it will never be true." He spat on the ground again, right by Tess's hand, but she refused to flinch. "You're just like your dear old dad, always looking out for number one. You're no better than me! If you thought it would turn you a profit, you'd have that thing back up and running in no time."

Tess braced herself and thrust her arm beneath Mr. Cleat's, yanking him to his feet. He cried out in pain, but Tess forced him toward a nearby chair. "You think you're so special," he growled into her ear as she dropped him into the seat.

"You're not special. You were just lucky. All those years with the key to the universe in your hand and you never even *knew* it!" He paused to draw breath. "I could have chosen any one of you de Sousas, on any one of half a dozen worlds. This is all *your* fault!"

Tess met his eye. "I just wanted you to know," she said, holding his gaze, "that all the theories you worked so hard on are wrong. You can tell your Society that, from me." At these words Mr. Cleat finally slumped, making no reply.

A strong hand clamped down on his shoulder and Tess looked up to see Cornelius Henderson, the journalist, standing over Mr. Cleat. He tried to shrug off Mr. Henderson's grip, but it held. Mr. Henderson and Tess shared a nod. Then she gave Mr. Cleat one last cold stare and turned to walk away.

As she did so, her gaze fell on Miss Ackerbee's anxious face, her dark eyes behind her spectacles worried and filled with love. Tess began to run and her housemistress did too, tucking her fire whistle into its pocket at her waist. They met in the middle with a hug so tight that Tess didn't care if she never breathed again. Seconds later they were joined by Rebecca, who wrapped her long arms round the two of them.

"I heard your whistle," Tess said when they released one another. "I think I could have heard it from another world."

"It's designed to wake a houseful of sleeping girls, after all," Miss Ackerbee replied with a smile. "It *needs* to be loud."

Tess gazed into Miss Ackerbee's tearstained face and Re-becca's joyful one and felt Violet dancing on top of her head. *This is home,* she thought.

Then she looked up and saw Thomas standing a little apart from the group.

"Miss Ackerbee, I'd like for you to meet someone impor-tant," Tess said, the words making her chest fill. She beck-oned to Thomas, who stepped forward.

"Thomas Martin de Sousa, ma'am," he said, holding out his hand. Miss Ackerbee shook it. "A pleasure to meet you."

"The pleasure is mine, Master de Sousa," Miss Ackerbee said. Then she looked back at Tess, her eyes shining. "I as-sume we're going to tell everyone he's your brother? I suspect the truth would be rather alarming to most people." She kept her voice low; the only ones to hear her were Thomas, Tess and Rebecca.

Tess and Thomas shared a look. "How did you—" Tess started to say, but the words faded in her mouth. *She just does,* Tess told herself. *Because she's Miss Ackerbee.*

"There's a spare room in the attic," Miss Ackerbee said, twinkling at him. "It hasn't been used in years, but I'm sure we can get it shipshape." Moose popped over his shoulder and Miss Ackerbee blinked. A second later, her warm smile was back. "And we could always use another house mascot."

"And I'm certain there's room for another bed in Tess's

dorm for Millie," Rebecca added. "That is," she said, turning to the blushing girl, "if you'd like it?"

"I'm not the sort for education, ma'am," Millie said. "My place is in service and I don't think—"

Miss Ackerbee turned to her. "There will always be room for bright, brave and loyal children at Ackerbee's, Millie. You would be made most welcome."

Millie reddened deeper. "I don't know what to say," she muttered, her eyes sparkling with joy.

"Just say you'll come home," Miss Ackerbee replied, looking around at them all as the clanging bell of the police van sounded behind her, making her wince. "And the sooner the better."

39

"Right. Wilf? Third setting, please," Tess said, adjusting the angle of the light over her desk. On it lay the Star-spinner, displayed on a piece of white card that showed all the details of its workings. Tess held a sharpened pencil like a weapon and focused intently on the page before her as Wilf adjusted the device.

"You're sure this isn't going to tear some sort of hole in reality?" Wilf said as the Star-spinner clicked into place. She held it carefully by its edges as though afraid it would burn her.

Tess shrugged. "Shouldn't," she said. "But I guess you can never be *completely* certain."

"Tess," Wilf said, her voice tight.

"I'm joking, I'm joking," Tess replied, looking up at her

friend. "The starglass is shattered, so it shouldn't do anything while you're holding it. And as long as I'm not touching it, or thinking about other worlds, we should be fine." She cleared her throat. "Theoretically."

Wilf tutted. "You'd better share all the awards you're going to win with me," she muttered. "I want half of everything."

Tess sucked in her cheeks to avoid laughing and said nothing as she started to draw. *What I wouldn't give to have that magnifier back,* she thought, focusing intently on the pattern around the Star-spinner's marker stone in this particular orientation. *The detail I could get . . .*

"Remind me what we're doing here, again?" Wilf said after Tess had been drawing for several minutes.

Tess straightened her back as she sat up and used the pause as an opportunity to sharpen her pencil. "The theory is that each of these markings is a map to another reality," she said, cranking the pencil round in its sharpener. She gestured toward the drawing with her eyes. "So every time you put the Star-spinner into *this* position, for instance, you'll be brought to the same place." She pulled the pencil out and blew on its fearsomely sharp nib, grinning.

"And you reckon that's why it kept bringing you back to the same world, all the time you used it?" Wilf said, trying to understand.

Tess nodded. "I always did the same thing, so it makes sense that I turned up in the same place every time."

Wilf raised her eyebrows thoughtfully. "I wonder if it remembers?" she asked.

Tess frowned. "Remembers what?"

"The places it's been to," Wilf said. "The settings it's been placed in. You know, like leaving a record behind, every time it's used."

Something about these words struck Tess. "A record of the places it brought my dad," she said, staring at the splayed Star-spinner.

"We can retrace the steps he took when he brought you here," Wilf finished Tess's thought in hushed tones. She blinked and stared at the Star-spinner fearfully. "We can *really* do that?"

"Theoretically," Tess replied, grinning.

"You like that word a bit too much," Wilf said, returning the grin.

Violet scratched at Tess's hairline and automatically she looked toward the door. Violet always seemed to know when someone was coming, and these days that someone was almost always Thomas.

A second later he burst through the door, clattering into the laboratory like an overeager puppy.

"You won't believe it," he said, hurrying toward Tess with a newspaper in his hand. "Look at this!"

"Good morning," Tess said mildly, fixing him with a look. "Oh yes, we're having a fine time, thanks—and how are you?"

Thomas tsked. "Never mind about that." He tossed the newspaper across Tess's desk and pointed at an article on the front page. "Read this!"

Wilf craned her neck to see as Tess took in the article Thomas was so interested in. Tess missed a breath when she saw the sketch of Mr. Cleat that accompanied it—his angry expression seemed to leap right off the page and into her heart.

"Prison suits him," Wilf murmured, and Tess felt like she'd been shaken out of a dream. *He can't get you,* she told herself. *He's locked away and you're safe here with Miss Ackerbee. Back home. With your family.* She looked at Wilf and Thomas, their eyes kind and filled with understanding, and she smiled at them both.

She cleared her throat and began to read aloud. "The latest twist in the Roedeer Lodge saga unfolded last night with the discovery of what appears to be the wreckage of an airship in the trees of Fairwater Park," she began. "The shattered craft—of unknown make or origin—was found not far from the site of the as-yet-unexplained happenings of the small hours of May thirty-first last. No identifying documents were found in the craft's cabin, but a notebook inscribed with the name *Helena Molyneaux*—" At this Tess stopped short and looked at Thomas, her eyes wide with shock. "Helena Molyneaux!"

"I know," Thomas said, nodding.

Wilf frowned. "Who?"

"I'll explain in a minute," Tess said. She bent over the newspaper once more and continued to read. "A notebook inscribed with the name *Helena Molyneaux* was found wedged beneath one of the seats. A search has begun to trace Miss Molyneaux, who it is hoped can shed some light on the mystery."

"They won't find her," Thomas said, his eyes glittering with something Tess couldn't quite name. "But what does it tell you?"

"It must have been Mackintosh," Tess said as the pieces slotted together in her head. "He came through, the night of the rift. I *knew* I'd seen something moving on the roof of your house. I couldn't see it clearly, but I know now what it was: Mackintosh setting off in some sort of airship right before the roof collapsed."

"And he brought my parents' research notes," Thomas said. "The Oscillometer from Dad's observatory, too."

Wilf cleared her throat. Tess looked at her apologetically and began to explain. "Helena Molyneaux was Thomas's mother. She's . . ."

"Dead," Thomas said, his mouth a tight line. "And my dad. But they didn't exist here. So chances are this aircraft came from my world."

Wilf's eyes widened as she thought. "What do you reckon Mackintosh's doing here then? D'you think he'll be looking for our old pal Sharpthorn?"

"Mrs. Thistleton?" Tess's jaw dropped at the thought. "Maybe."

"I really wish we hadn't let her get away, and with that dagger, too," Wilf said mournfully.

"It can't be helped," Tess said, but in truth every time she thought about Mrs. Thistleton, it felt like someone clamping hard on her windpipe. She'd never forget the crazed fervor in Mrs. Thistleton's face the night everything had happened— Tess knew nothing would deter her and that if Mrs. Thistleton could try again she would. She imagined worlds falling like dominoes before Mrs. Thistleton's efforts to find the edges of the universe . . .

"What we really need to do is keep the Star-spinner safe," Thomas said. "Hidden away where she'll never find it."

"No," Tess said, meeting his eye. "We need to do more than that."

"What are you talking about?" Wilf said.

"Do you think there's more starglass out there?" Tess asked, looking from one to the other. "This world has a Tunguska site too. Right? All these connected worlds do. So it stands to reason there's more out there."

"And if there is," Thomas said, finishing Tess's thought, "Mrs. Thistleton might go after it. Maybe she'll even find a way to use it. And then perhaps she'll come for us."

"Right," Tess replied. "I think what we need to do is find some more starglass ourselves, and then"—she paused, licking her lips—"then we go and find my father. He made the Star-spinner to help people escape from a dying world—I'm sure of it. He'll help us, I know he will." *He's not what Mr. Cleat says he is.*

A sudden knock at the door made them all jump. Millie poked her head into the room. "Tess!" she called. "Miss Ackerbee wants to see you and Thomas."

Tess frowned at her. "Shouldn't you be in French?"

"Miss Ackerbee let me out of class to fetch you," she said with a grin. Gone was Millie's starched uniform and tightly bound hair, replaced with the slightly threadbare clothes of an Ackerbee's girl. She'd never looked happier.

"Come on then," Tess said. She shoved the paper underneath her notebook and put the Star-spinner in her pocket out of habit, and they all trooped out of the room.

"Good luck," whispered Wilf with a squeeze of Tess's hand when they reached Miss Ackerbee's door. Millie threw Tess and Thomas a wink and she and Wilf vanished down the corridor.

Tess stood up straight and raised her hand to knock—only for Rebecca to open it from the inside before she had the chance. She gave them a knowing grin. "Ah, yes. The de Sousas. Come on in, won't you?" She stood aside to let them enter. Miss Ackerbee was sitting on her sofa, some papers spread out before her on a low table. "Hello, you two," she said, putting down her teacup. "Will you take a seat?"

Tess and Thomas perched on a pair of chairs, and Miss Ackerbee smiled at their worried expressions. "Don't worry," she assured them. "You're not in trouble."

"That's what Rebecca said last time," Tess reminded her. "And look what happened then."

Miss Ackerbee laughed and bent forward to pick up a sheet of paper. "I've had a letter from a firm of solicitors," she told them. "They're responsible for the estate of the late Heriberto de Sousa, who once owned Roedeer Lodge—and who was not any relation, even a distant one, of Mr. Cleat. It seems, then, that Mr. Cleat's acquisition of the house wasn't quite within the law, which is one of the reasons he's enjoying some relaxation time at His Majesty's pleasure." She placed the letter before them. "So I made some inquiries about the possibility of you both being named as heirs and— well, it seems they've agreed."

Thomas's mouth dropped open. "What?" he asked before hurriedly gathering his wits and his manners. "I mean, I'm sorry. Pardon?"

"You're de Sousas," Miss Ackerbee said. "And even though you're not *technically* Heriberto's sole heirs, I think the lawyers would rather say you are instead of dealing with the truth—which is of course rather harder to understand. It seems easier to assume you're a long-lost grandniece and grandnephew of the deceased than a pair of children from different worlds who share the same name."

"You're saying—you're saying we own Roedeer Lodge?" Tess said, staring at the letter.

"If you want it," Miss Ackerbee said softly. "Yes."

Tess and Thomas looked at one another. Their identical eyes held identical expressions, and they knew that they were thinking the same thing.

"Haven't you always thought Ackerbee's could do with a new building?" Thomas said, looking at Miss Ackerbee. "I mean, there's nothing *wrong* with the house here—"

"Besides damp, and windows that stick, and a leaking roof," Tess interjected in an undertone.

Thomas nodded. "Besides *that,* but—well, how about we move?"

Tess and Thomas looked at Miss Ackerbee eagerly and Rebecca sank onto the sofa. Miss Ackerbee took her hand as they gazed at the children.

"Before you ask us—yes, we're sure." Tess smiled.

"Well, I don't know what to say," Miss Ackerbee replied, her eyes shining.

"Just say you'll come," Tess said. "It's a real home. A *family* home. We can make it into a happy place again."

Miss Ackerbee and Rebecca shared a glance. "In that case,

what other choice do we have?" Miss Ackerbee said, looking back at the children. "Thank you, Tess. Thank you, Thomas. Let's hope the future of Roedeer Lodge is happier than its recent past has been."

"I think we should set the bar a bit higher than that," Rebecca said, raising her eyebrows.

Miss Ackerbee laughed again and turned back to the children. "Now, you two, run along and join the others. I have a telephone call to make and then—well. Then we have a lot of work to do."

As they got to their feet, Tess hugged Miss Ackerbee, who bent to place a kiss on the crown of her head. "You remarkable girl," she murmured. "How proud of you I am. How proud we *both* are." Tess looked up into her house-mistress's face, which was shining with love. "Go on now, before I lose my composure," Miss Ackerbee said, wiping at her eyes. Tess looked at Rebecca, who'd come to stand beside Miss Ackerbee, her eyes soft, and they exchanged a wink and a grin.

Tess and Thomas left the room, pulling the door softly closed, and wandered toward the courtyard in a daze. Tess ran her fingers over the Star-spinner absently as she walked. From his perch in Thomas's top pocket, Moose sniffed at the air. Violet watched him fondly from Tess's shoulder.

"If we go back to Roedeer, what about Mrs. Thistleton?"

Tess said as they stepped out into the sunshine. "It's the first place she'll come looking."

Thomas nodded. "I know." Then he met her gaze. "But we both know it's where we need to be."

Tess took the Star-spinner out of her pocket and touched the inert starglass window. "It's the best place to get this working again," she said. "The house, I mean. In all the worlds, it's where we're strongest." She looked back at Thomas.

"Well then"—Thomas glanced away to wave at Prissy, who was beckoning them over to the corner of the courtyard—"if Mrs. Thistleton comes calling, we'll be ready for her."

They shared a conspiratorial grin as Tess slid the Star-spinner back into her pocket. Then they took one another's hands and ran into the sunshine to join their friends, their steps—as always—perfectly in tune.

EPILOGUE

"MR. MACKINTOSH?" THE LANDLADY KNOCKED AGAIN AND THEN unlocked the door to the attic room with her master key. "Sir? Are you in?"

She looked inside but the room was deserted. Mrs. Jones strode into the middle of the floor and tutted at the state of the place. She owned this house, including the room Mr. Mackintosh was renting, and she wasn't accustomed to such *uncleanliness*. It was disconcerting, to say the least. The bed was unmade, the curtains were closed, and there were papers strewn on all the surfaces she could see: open notebooks, correspondence and a notice board that was pinned with scribbled-on scraps.

"And now I'm adding to it," she sighed, looking at the

letter in her hand. It had come for Mr. Mackintosh that morning. *Whatever it is you're waiting on,* she thought, *I hope this is it.* She knew he'd been placing notifications in all the newspapers; she'd often had to run his errands for him, which she'd decided had given her permission to look at the message he kept trying to send. It was always the same: *Sharpthorn. I have come through.* Mrs. Jones had no idea what it meant.

Sighing deeply, she propped the letter in front of Mr. Mackintosh's radio set (though what he needed one of his own for, when there was a perfectly adequate wireless in the living room, she couldn't imagine) and turned to leave. Mrs. Jones began reciting a list of requests in her head for the next time she saw her tenant, which included telling him to open the windows and do his washing a bit more frequently. She was so preoccupied that she didn't hear the Oscillometer— which she'd taken for a radio set—crackle to life.

Mrs. Jones left the room and locked the door behind her. The air settled, dust motes trickling to earth through a random sunbeam. Everything was still.

And the Oscillometer hissed its unheard message out into an empty room, over and over again, before finally falling silent.

AUTHOR'S NOTE

Ireland's official neutrality during the Second World War (1939–45) was a complex thing, partly born of its then-fraught relationship with Great Britain and partly born of its desire to assert independence as a country, among many other reasons. My own grandmother often spoke to me of her experiences during what was called the Emergency, mentioning things like rationing and shortages, and the constant fear of invasion.

Despite Ireland's neutral position, it did offer unofficial aid to the Allies. Richard Hayes was a prominent Irish code-breaker who worked alongside MI5 during the war, for instance, and back-channel communications were always present between Ireland and Britain. Also, many thousands of Irishmen served with the British army in both world wars, often at great personal cost; coming home from battle sometimes meant being branded a traitor for the rest of your life.

In 1941, Ireland was under the leadership of Taoiseach (Prime Minister) Éamon de Valera and President Douglas Hyde. The president lived in Phoenix Park, close to Thomas's fictional home, and his official residence (Áras an Uachtaráin) suffered bomb damage on the night described at the end of the book. So, while Ireland didn't suffer the privations of countries like Britain during this dark time in history, it's not beyond possibility that children like Thomas did lie awake at night, wondering whether the next bomb to fall would land on their city.

The bombing at the end of the book was a real event, though I have taken some liberties with how it happened for the sake of my story. Early in the morning of May 31, 1941, the Luftwaffe (German air force) dropped four bombs on Dublin city. Three did minimal damage; the fourth landed in the North Strand area, killing twenty-eight people, injuring ninety, and making more than four hundred homeless. It was the worst single attack on Irish soil during the war.

Not mentioned in *The Starspun Web* are the efforts by the Irish army to shine spotlights on the attacking planes and to shoot them down; these efforts, carried out with badly maintained equipment, proved futile. It's still not completely clear why the attack was carried out on Dublin—perhaps the planes were lost and needed to drop ballast in order to make it back to German lines; perhaps it was a revenge attack, as Dublin had recently come to Belfast's aid when that city was hit in the Blitz. It may have been an attempt on Hitler's part to force neutral Ireland into the war, as Ireland was strategically useful to both sides. Perhaps the reason will never be known.

And in such gaps, stories grow . . .

This book is, in part, my humble memorial to the men and women of the North Strand, including my husband's grandmother, who luckily survived the attack. It is my attempt to pay homage to all who lived through the Emergency and the war, and particularly to those who lost their lives fighting the terrible evil of Nazism. *Ní bheidh a leithéidí arís ann*—"their like will never be seen again."

ACKNOWLEDGMENTS

I wrote (and rewrote, and *rewrote*) The Starspun Web mostly while standing at my kitchen counter, fitting in fifty or a hundred words here and there around my daughter's frenetic, colorful, enthusiastic little-girl life. So, it is to her that I owe the greatest thanks and the sincerest apology—the thanks for her patience with "busy Mammy" and the apology for all those times when "I'll be with you in a minute, love!" turned into much longer than that. Thank you, little star. I hope, one day, you'll be as proud of me as I am of you.

My husband, as has become his habit, made every possible effort and sacrifice to help this book along, and all without complaint. Thank you, Bucket. I'm so glad to have you in my fan club.

Working with editors as astute as Katie Jennings, Melanie Nolan and Karen Greenberg is a privilege. To them, I offer my most heartfelt thanks for helping me to hew this book out of the word sludge that was my original submission, and for reminding me of what I do best at exactly the right moment. Thanks also to the marketing, publicity and design team at Stripes Publishing, especially the wondrous Leilah Skelton and Lauren Ace, and to Susila Baybars for her detailed copyedit.

The immensely talented Sara Mulvanny and Sophie Bransby created a cover for this book that has gone beyond my hopes. Thank you both for the care and time you took to give this story such a beautiful wrapping, and particularly over the depiction of Ackerbee's (which, if you're ever in Dublin, is based on the real-life Lafayette Building on the corner of O'Connell Bridge).

Since my first book, *The Eye of the North,* was published, I have had the great joy of befriending and getting to know hundreds of teachers, bloggers, librarians, other authors and—most importantly—*readers.* I couldn't possibly name them all, but there are a few individuals I must mention. To Scott Evans, curator of the #PrimarySchoolBookClub, I owe a huge debt of gratitude; it was a singular honor to be named the club's first Book of the Month for March 2018. Thank you, Mr. E, for all you do! Thanks, too, to every teacher, TA and librarian I've chatted or interacted with on Twitter, email or my blog—your efforts to promote reading for pleasure among your pupils are hugely appreciated by me, and by all of us who try our best to create stories worthy of our readers.

Thanks to Lucy Fidler, of Layton Primary School in Blackpool. I am proud to be the Patron of Reading for this wonderful school, and I owe that honor to Miss Fidler. I'm also proud to have been in touch with Kinross Primary School as their Author Pen Pal over the past school year—thank you all! Remember: Always Be Curious, and never stop reading.

For their invaluable support and general cheerleading, I also wish to thank: Steph Ellis (@eenalol), Steph Warren (@book shineblog), Amy (@GoldenBooksGirl), Jessikah (@Jessikah Hope), Faye (@daydreamin_star), Victoria Dilly and the Book Activist (@bookactivist1), Aimee (@aimee_louise_l), Jo at My Attic Library (@myatticlibrary), Jo Clarke (@bookloverJo), Gordon Askew (@GordonAskew), Library Girl and Book Boy (@BookSuperhero2), Laura and Faith (@272BookFaith), Ashley Booth (@MrBoothY6) and everyone at Children's Books Ireland (if you're not already a member, do consider joining—childrensbooksireland.ie—and tell them I sent you!).

One of the best parts of becoming an author is getting to know other authors. Only they really know the challenges, frustrations and tiny triumphs involved in this strange old life, and among the people I've been most pleased to befriend over the past year or so are my old muckers Vashti Hardy, Juliette Forrest, H. S. Norup and Elizabeth and Katharine Corr (respectively, the authors of *Brightstorm, Twister, The Missing Barbegazi* and the Witch's Kiss trilogy). Everyone I've ever met in the world of children's publishing has been a person of the very highest caliber, and it's a wonderful feeling to be a small part of that amazing bookish family. Thank you all.

A huge thank-you to every child I've had the joy of meeting over the past year, and to the teachers and librarians who facilitated our workshops. Nothing gives me greater joy than to see a group of story finders with their heads bent over their worksheets, drawing or writing something that has been sparked by a suggestion from me. It's a privilege to be welcomed into your imaginations, and I'm grateful for it.

To my family and my family-in-law, I send my love and gratitude, particularly to my wonderful parents, Tom and Doreen. This book was partly dreamed up while listening to my mother-in-law and her sister talk about their mother's experiences during the North Strand bombing, and so to them I owe a massive thank-you. I hope this story would have done Mary proud. My extended family has been a stalwart source of support and encouragement right from the start— thank you all. My friends, who turned up in droves for the launch of *The Eye of the North* and who have always believed in me—I don't have words to tell you how much you mean to me.

Darlin' Hugo: thanks for being you.

To Polly Nolan, agent beyond compare: *go raibh míle maith agat*—"you're some woman for one woman."

And final thanks, as always, go to you, the reader, who has stuck with me through two whole books (so far). Getting to know you has been the greatest joy of all.